I0817781

Southern Belle

A MAX PORTER PARANORMAL-MYSTERY

Stuart Jaffe

SOUTHERN BELLE

Cover art by Duncan Long

ISBN 13: 978-1-7337308-5-3

First Edition: August, 2013
First Hardcover Edition: January, 2024

For Judith and Lloyd

Also by Stuart Jaffe

Max Porter Paranormal Mysteries

Southern Bound
Southern Charm
Southern Belle
Southern Gothic
Southern Haunts
Southern Curses
Southern Rites
Southern Craft
Southern Spirit
Southern Flames
Southern Fury
Southern Souls
Southern Blood
Southern Graves
Southern Dead
Southern Hexes
Southern Hart

Nathan K Thrillers

Immortal Killers
Killing Machine
The Cardinal
Yukon Massacre
The First Battle
Immortal Darkness
A Spy for Eternity
Prisoner
Desert Takedown
Lone Star Standoff
The Puppeteer
Blowback
Prime

The Ridnight Mysteries

The Water Blade
The Waters of Taladoro
Waterfire

The Parallel Society

The Infinity Caverns
Book on the Isle
Rift Angel
Lost Time
Pages of Glass
The Bold Warrior
City of Infinity

The Malja Chronicles

The Way of the Black Beast
The Way of the Sword and Gun
The Way of the Brother Gods
The Way of the Blade
The Way of the Power
The Way of the Soul

Gillian Boone novels

A Glimpse of Her Soul
Pathway to Spirit

Stand Alone Novels

After The Crash
Real Magic
Founders

Short Story Collection

10 Bits of My Brain
10 More Bits of My Brain
The Bluesman
The Marshall Drummond Case Files: Cabinet 1
The Marshall Drummond Case Files: Cabinet 2
The Marshall Drummond Case Files: Cabinet 3

Non-Fiction

How to Write Magical Words: A Writer's Companion
For more information, please visit ***www.stuartjaffe.com***

Acknowledgements

It never ceases to amaze me how many people get involved in helping me bring a story from my head to the page. This time around, my thanks go out to Joel Goldman, Mike Lowndes and the fine people at PML Media, Duncan Long for his amazing artwork, Amy Ball for proofreading and friendship, fellow writers Ed Schubert and John Hartness, and as always, my dearest and closest, Glory and Gabe.

Of course, my biggest thank you is reserved for you, my reader. Without you, none of this amounts to anything more than a guy making up stories for himself (which probably gets one locked up in some states).

Southern Belle

Chapter 1

THOUGH NEVER OFFICIALLY TRAINED to be a detective, Max Porter knew that the man in the black suit had been following him. Early that Spring morning, he had seen the man standing near the old YMCA building across from the office. The building had been converted into apartments, yet Black Suit never went in, never buzzed for anyone, never even peeked through the doorway. He only stood there, occasionally sneezing from the heavy pollen that covered the cars and sidewalk with a yellow hue.

Later, when Max left for lunch, he noticed a plain brown sedan trailing him all the way from downtown Winston-Salem, across Business 40, onto 421, off the Jonestown Road exit, and down Country Club Road, past the psychic and the auto repair, until he parked at Little Richard's. The old joint had the reputation of serving some of the best Lexington Barbecue in all of Winston-Salem, but Max thought it too much of a coincidence that Black Suit shared the same craving on the same day at the same time as he did.

A year ago, Max would have been shivering at the prospect of a strange man following him all day, but he had been through enough serious trouble — ghosts, witches, curses, spells — that Black Suit did little more than annoy him. At least, for the moment. Later he might get worried, but no way would he let anyone spoil a trip to Little Richard's.

When Max and his wife (and business partner), Sandra, first moved to North Carolina, they had no appreciation for the artistry of Lexington Barbecue. They had Michigan sensibilities. They understood beef and venison. But after his first taste of Southern-style barbecue, he became a true believer. Pulled pork in a vinegar-based barbecue sauce, piled atop a bun, and covered with coleslaw — the mere thought of it caused his mouth to water. While he had no doubt that the barbecue joints down in Lexington would blow his taste buds away, Little Richard's served the folk of Winston-Salem more than amply.

He had to admit that he was surprised Black Suit followed him into the place. From the outside, Little Richard's looked like a large restaurant — a family-style exterior with a big, neon sign that danced a happy pig across the front. Inside, however, patrons were met with an L-shaped, 50s décor dining room — one side a counter for to-go orders and paying the bill, the other a long, narrow path of tables filled with people. Little Richard's always seemed packed. Not a lot of places for Black Suit to hide.

While he waited to order, he took a seat in the back corner where he could watch everybody who entered — one of many trade secrets he learned from his other partner, Marshall Drummond. Drummond was a strong-willed, smart-mouthed sort of guy with the peculiar characteristic of being dead. He had been a detective in the 1940s when he wound up on the wrong end of a witch's curse. After Max moved in, discovered Drummond, and broke the curse, they'd been together ever since. Watching Black Suit settle into the corner furthest away, Max thought he should thank Drummond for all the advice.

Better not. It'd go to Drummond's head.

A young gal, perky and pleasant took his order — chopped on a big bun. Fans whirred non-stop and the wonderful, tangy smell of barbeque blew through the air. Before Max could identify which Muddy Waters song played through the speakers, the young gal returned with his food. Fast and delicious.

Max lifted the sloppy sandwich to his mouth only to find that he had been focused on the wrong man the whole time. An elderly man — snowy hair, bent body, walking with a rubber-tipped wooden cane — wove his way through the crowd until he reached Max's table. He plopped down, smiled wide enough to reveal a few missing teeth, and took one of Max's fries.

"Hey, that's mine."

"Oh, you can spare one." The old man sounded stronger than Max had expected, but he continually looked around and fiddled with the seams of his pants. A deep scar traced his jawline, and the lobe of his left ear had been cut off long ago.

"Do you want something?"

Pushing his thick glasses up his crooked nose, the man nodded. "I want to hire you."

"This is my lunch. I'll be back in my office in about —"

"I can't go there. I won't."

Max set down his sandwich and picked up a napkin. "You won't go to my office?"

"And we can't talk here. Not in detail. It's too dangerous."

"You're really not enticing me here, Mister, um?"

"Joshua Leed. Sorry. I should have told you my name from the start." He leaned on his elbow but kept his wrinkled face positioned to observe the crowd. "All I ask is that you come out to my house and meet me, hear my case, and that's it. You don't have to help me after that, if you don't want."

"I don't do house calls. It's not really a smart practice in my line of work."

"Of course, of course. Paranormal investigations can be location sensitive, but I assure you —"

"Paranormal? What is it you think —"

"Please, Mr. Porter, no need for that. I sought you out specifically because of your unique talents. After all, not everyone can see ghosts."

"Lower your voice." Max leaned in now, close enough to smell Joshua's heavy scent — some odd combination of herbs and spices as if he were a chef. "I only see ghost — as in singular, as in one."

"That may be, but your wife sees the rest."

"What the hell do you want?"

"Come to my house. That's all I ask. The longer I spend out in the open, the more at risk I am — we all are. Please. My house is in Thomasville — thirty, forty minutes from here. It's the only place that's safe. I'll explain everything else there."

Max shook his head. "Whatever you heard about me is old news. I'm not your man."

"People with gifts like yours don't suddenly lose them. It doesn't work that way. Or were you referring to the stories about how desperate you are for work? That is old news. I suppose all your money troubles have vanished now that you're on the leash of the Hull family."

So much for an enjoyable, peaceful meal. "I think you better leave."

"I'm sorry. I meant no offense. But it's no big secret. There are only three prominent families in this city — Hanes, Reynolds, and Hull. Not much dealing with them can be kept quiet for long. And while underwear and tobacco can be dangerous businesses, they're nothing compared to a family willing to deal with the supernatural. Since that's the same subject I deal with, it shouldn't be so odd that I would learn about you and your unique relationship with the Hull family."

Calling his relationship *unique* was like calling Jeffrey Dahmer's victims *dinner guests*. In fact, if not for a copy of the Hull family journal that would be made public should anything happen to him or Sandra, Max knew the Hulls would have disposed of him long ago. That leverage weakened considerably when the Hulls covered up a series of deaths that surrounded a recent case. Terrance Hull, the supposed family head, made it quite clear that Max, Sandra, and Drummond had no choice but to work for the Hulls. To refuse meant the police would take a sudden interest in those deaths, and Max had no doubt they would find "evidence" that linked him to murders he never committed.

On the positive side, Hull paid Max a hefty sum as a retainer which enabled him to be far more picky about what jobs he agreed to take on. "Mr. Leed, your information is wrong. I'm not interested in going to your house, and I'm not interested in your case."

The old man covered his mouth with his fist. "You've got to," he muttered. "If you don't, she's going to kill me."

"If someone's trying to kill you, you should be talking with the police."

"I doubt the police would take seriously an old man claiming that a ghost was going to kill him."

Rubbing the back of his neck to ward off a headache, Max said, "I'm sorry I can't help you. Perhaps you can —"

"Drummond."

"What?"

"Marshall Drummond was a friend of mine."

"And you didn't think it worth mentioning this before?"

"I don't want him to know about any of this. He can't know we've spoken, he can't visit my house, and if you agree to help me, he cannot, absolutely cannot, know that I've hired you."

Max hated to admit it but mentioning his partner had intrigued him. He knew so little about the ghost he worked with. To find someone who actually knew him, a friend no less and alive, that seemed like too much of an opportunity to turn away.

"Okay, Mr. Leed. I'll meet you at your house."

"Tonight. Meet me tonight, eight o'clock."

"Fine. Give me your address and I'll be there."

"And no Drummond. Whatever you do, do not bring Drummond."

"You have my word."

Leed stared into Max's eyes, searched his face, and finally nodded. "Thank you, Mr. Porter. I promise you won't regret this."

"I'd like to get back to my lunch now."

"Of course." He handed over a business card with a handwritten address on the back. Stealing one more fry, the old man shuffled his creaky body out of the restaurant.

Max watched him leave, and as he passed the far corner, Max caught sight of Black Suit. Of all the people in the packed room, Black Suit's eyes followed Joshua Leed out the door. Once Leed had left, Black Suit tapped away on a smartphone.

Max reached for his sandwich but put it back down. He had lost his appetite. Could this old man truly have known Drummond? The age looked about right. If Leed had been around twenty years old in 1940, then he'd be near his mid-nineties now. He certainly looked spry for ninety-something, but that didn't mean he was lying. Besides, if he were knowledgeable about ghosts and such, then being a youthful ninety wasn't absurd. Max had once met a man in his two hundreds, so he knew magic could be powerful enough to back Leed's story.

He glanced at the card in his hand. It read:

PARANORMAL INVESTIGATIONS
AND REMOVAL
JOSHUA LEED

Max sighed. "I'm going to regret this."

Chapter 2

MAX DIDN'T KNOW WHAT to make of Joshua Leed, but he decided to play along regarding Drummond until he had more information. Experience, however, had taught Max the dangers of going into a situation alone. So he called Sandra and asked her to meet him at his favorite haunt on Wake Forest University's campus — the Z. Smith Reynolds library. Not only did he love the library as a researcher, his true profession, but he loved it because he knew Drummond wouldn't follow Sandra there. That ghost hated libraries and research and books in general.

"Sure I've read some good stories," Drummond had said once. "Zane Gray and the like, but my real life was filled with enough adventure, and frankly, my post-life has had a good share of excitement, too. I don't need a book for thrills. I got memories for that."

When Sandra entered the library's lobby, Max's mind flooded with memories of his own. He remembered a summer afternoon picnic in a park when he first kissed her. He saw them on their first vacation as a couple when they barely left the hotel room. Then he recalled their first vacation as a married couple when they also barely left the hotel room. But mostly, he saw how beautiful Sandra was. They were getting older now, gray hairs had started to sprout, and the beginnings of wrinkles had formed, and yet, Sandra's beauty had grown too. Her dark hair and curvy body still drove him crazy, but that craziness had matured. When he looked at her in the past, he saw a vibrant, sexy young woman. As she walked toward him in the library, he saw a vibrant, sexy angel — a woman who held more than his heart in her hands. She had his very soul.

"You okay?" she asked as she approached.

"Just admiring the view."

She smiled, and he wanted nothing more than to kiss that gorgeous mouth. So he did.

"As much as I like your attention," she said, wrapping her arms around his neck, "I know you didn't ask me to come all the way out here for a kiss."

"Sadly, no. I've got to meet a potential client, and I don't want to go in alone."

Sandra cocked her head to the side. "You don't want Drummond?"

"I was specifically instructed not to bring him along."

Sandra's eyes widened. "That's odd."

"I know. We've got some time before we need to head out, so I thought this would be a good place to fill you in."

"No way Drummond'll come here."

Max laced his fingers between hers, loving the fact that she understood him so well, and he led her to a quiet table. As he told her the story of Joshua Leed and ignored her jibes at him sneaking off to Little Richard's, he never mentioned the man in the black suit. He didn't withhold the information consciously — not at first — but when he noticed the absence of this detail, he decided to trust his instincts and keep quiet about the man. What could he really say? He'd tell Sandra that Black Suit had followed him all morning, and she would bombard him with questions he couldn't answer. He had the same questions — anyone would — so what good would come of worrying her over something so unknown? Better to wait until he had something concrete to say. Besides, it was possible that it had all been coincidence.

With several hours to kill before they could head out, Max and Sandra drove to Hanes Mall and picked up a few things they had been needing for their house. Well, Max didn't think they *needed* any of it, but Sandra insisted that the throw pillows, organizational baskets, and new bedsheets were essential to fixing up their home. Though Max rolled his eyes, he never put up much of a fight. They had spent so many years struggling simply to put food on the table that part of him enjoyed seeing her splurge a little. After a bit more shopping, dodging an early evening rainstorm, and a quick dinner, they drove off for Thomasville.

It turned out there was no direct way to get from Winston-Salem to Thomasville. The major highways, 40 and 85, never reached close enough to be convenient. Looking online at a map, Max saw that with a direct road, the drive should have taken fifteen minutes, but the circuitous route required an additional twenty. Add in being stuck behind an old lady driving an even older Cadillac and the trip took three quarters of an hour.

Thomasville was a true small town. Formerly full of vigor, still clinging to the old glory days. It had only one claim to fame — furniture. Though the town produced far less handcrafted furniture than it had in its lucrative past, it still operated as a main destination for furniture buyers both corporate and individual. Where most towns would garner their main drag with a statue of some important local figure, Thomasville built an enormous chair — something Paul Bunyan would find comfortable.

Further from downtown, Thomasville became a series of large and small farms dotted with the occasional housing development. Joshua Leed lived in a small house on a wide fifteen acres. Other than the half-acre mowed around the farmhouse and a dilapidated barn, the rest of Leed's property grew wild.

A two-story farmhouse, squarish with a wraparound porch, looked rather new — built in the last five years or so — unless it was an old house that had been refurbished on the outside. Max didn't know enough about houses to tell. All he could say was the place looked comfortable, charming even. That was until he saw the inside.

Before they had a chance to turn the car engine off, Joshua Leed flicked on the porch lights and beckoned them in. Max and Sandra hurried, and both of them gasped at the sight. Leed converted what appeared to have been a lovely interior with old-style wallpaper and carefully chosen window treatments into a demented man's sanctuary.

Archaic symbols lined the walls like an insane graffiti artist had been let loose. Pages from equally archaic books outlined the windows. In the corners of each room, thick white candles burned, giving off the unpleasant odor of ripe fish. Salt lined every possible entrance into the house.

"Careful," Leed said so Max would step over the salt and not disturb it.

Max put a hand on his wife's shoulder. "This is my wife —"

"Sandra. Yes, I know. Pleasure to meet you."

Sandra shook Leed's hand as she continued to look around.

Leed followed her gaze. "Do you see any ghosts in here? I've tried my best to keep them out."

"Looks like you've done a good job."

He smiled — but his lips still trembled. "Can I get you anything to drink? Are you hungry?"

"Let's just get right into it," Max said.

"Of course, of course. Please, come in the living room and have a seat. You didn't bring Drummond along, did you?"

"He's not here. And even if he was, I'm guessing he couldn't get inside."

Leed scanned over the wards and spells he had written on the walls before double-checking the lines of salt. "Okay." He led them into the living room, a sparse area with a gray couch and a wooden rocking chair. Lowering into the chair, his joints popped like a string of firecrackers. He closed his eyes. "I can still see Drummond the day I met him."

"When was that?" Sandra asked.

"September 1938. Had I known that in a year Hitler would launch World War II and a few years after that I'd be turning into a human popsicle while fighting off the Bulge, well, I may not have risked so much earlier." He glanced at Max. "We both know that's not true. Risk or no risk, once the veil of the world has been pulled away, you can never truly go back. You sure you don't want a snack?"

"We're sure," Max said. "Please, tell us what's going on."

"Yes, yes. Let's see ... when I was fifteen, my family lived on a farm up in Virginia. I went to school during the day and helped with chores through the mornings and evenings. One day, I came home from school, ready to go milk the cows and whatnot, when I smelled something had died. It's a distinct, foul odor, and once you've experienced it, you'll never forget. Well, I followed the scent into the house and there they were. My mother and father, on the floor, covered in blood."

Sandra leaned over and placed a hand on Leed's knee. "I'm so sorry."

"It's not something you really ever get over. I was a wreck for a long time. But eventually I began to breathe again, to attempt to live, and when I was around seventeen, I met Dr. Matthew Ernest — a man who changed my life forever. He called himself a witch hunter, and he told me that my parents had been slain as part of a terrible coven ritual. Black magic. That sort of thing. It may sound silly, but for a distraught seventeen-year-old, these words held sway. Dr. Ernest gave me reasons for what had always been meaningless. He made sense to me. And more importantly, he gave me a target for revenge."

Leed's formed a fist with one hand. "I'm not proud that this was my motivation for joining Dr. Ernest, but I can't change things. I became his assistant, traveling, never staying the same place for long, helping him track down any witches we learned about. All the time, though, I kept my eyes and ears wide open, hoping to find a clue that would lead me to the coven that killed my parents.

"And then, one day, without expectations for the day to be different in any way, we found a young lady who wanted to escape her coven — the same coven that I had sought. She needed our help. Dr. Ernest tried to prepare me, tried to see that I would have the proper priorities. Well, you can imagine. It didn't go well. We captured two of the witches, but the rest got away." Leed grew silent, his eyes looking far away, his fingers absently rubbing the nicked part of his earlobe. "Ugly things happened, but I don't believe those details are important to recall for you. Suffice it to say that I had my revenge. Only as in most cases of vengeance, little relief came. I couldn't bring my parents back no matter how much pain I inflicted on those responsible, and I ended up losing part of myself every time I hurt my prisoners."

Max settled deeper into the couch. "I'm guessing the coven witches that escaped found their way down to Winston-Salem."

"Patience. I'll get there."

"Forgive my husband," Sandra said, still patting Leed's knee. "He can get a bit enthusiastic."

"Good. We'll need that kind of passion. But I'm an old man, so I don't move as fast — even in my storytelling. Seems backwards, doesn't it? Seems that with so little time left to live, I should be doing everything faster. Try to get as much crammed in as I can. But that's the way of it."

"Mr. Leed? The coven?"

"Right, right. Now, Dr. Ernest and I spent months tracking the coven. We picked off a few more members during our search but eventually we discovered the majority had slipped into North Carolina. See, we had developed a contact in the warehouse at the Sears & Roebuck Company. He carried a list of supplies that Dr. Ernest devised. It contained the kinds of practical things a coven required but wouldn't want to order in bulk locally in case it aroused suspicions — candles, salt, that kind of thing. If that list was ever ordered together and in large quantities, our man would call and give us the address. I don't think he ever knew why that list was important. And that call eventually happened, leading us to Winston-Salem."

"How did you end up meeting Drummond?" Max asked.

Sandra backhanded his chest. "Let the man speak."

"You have to understand," Leed continued, "Back at that time there weren't many witch hunters around. In fact, most people thought we were nuts. So word spread fast about new people who fought against these evil beasts — at least it spread fast amongst us. It didn't take long to learn of Drummond.

"That day we walked into his office, I knew we had found a man who could really help. So many times, we met crazies who thought cultists were raising Satan in their backyards or scientists who wanted to capture witches for study or overly prepared but intellectually under-qualified warriors. Drummond, on the other hand, stood out as a capable man of action. The kind of man who thought through an immediate problem without causing the mess to fall back on his men. One who understood the necessity of destroying these abominations without falling prey to sympathies because of the enemy's human appearance."

Sandra frowned. "You don't think witches are human?"

"What kind of human would do the things they did to my mother and father? No, I think they gave up that right when they started meddling in magic."

Max saw the strained tendons in Sandra's neck. She teetered on the edge of letting Leed know how wrong he was, but Max's simple touch on her shoulder brought her back. She glanced at Max with an embarrassed grin and settled into the couch, nestling closer to him as they listened to the rest.

"Drummond didn't want anything to do with us. He thought we were the very kind of crackpots we had avoided from the start. But we gave him two names and what information we had, and we left. Before dinner that same day, he contacted us. As we knew he would, he checked out our story and now he believed there was something worth looking into. And boy did he ever.

"I don't know how he pulled it off, but in less than a week, he identified where the witches were staying, what false names they were using, what jobs they held, everything. From there we learned the names of the other coveners, and we were set to curse them, to destroy the whole coven in one night."

"Curse them?" Sandra said. "Is that part of your vengeance? I mean, wouldn't it be easier to simply kill them?"

"True witch covens are extremely powerful. They bind and accentuate the energies of all the witches within the coven. Killing one only turns it into a ghost which can continue to feed the coven with its energy. But we knew of a curse that if done properly would break the power of the coven and lock the witches in their dead bodies, preventing them from roaming around as ghosts. It was a difficult spell to cast and required all six key witches in the coven to be killed on the same night.

"In order to protect ourselves and to insure that the coven did not reform or break the curse, we divide the killings amongst the three of us. Each man took two names from a hat. We agreed on the night that the curse would take place and made sure we each understood what was required. Finally, and most important, none of us would know where the others buried their witches. This way, should something go wrong, we were protected from each other. The planned night arrived, and we did what had to be done. And I truly thought it was all over."

"I don't think I'm going to like this next part," Max said.

Leed licked his lips and arched his head back. "It's been quiet all these years, yet something inside me always niggled at the idea that it might not be done. Then yesterday morning I saw this." With his cane, Leed pointed to a newspaper on the coffee table.

Max picked it up and saw a circled article headlined: PROFESSOR OF CULTS MURDERED. "This is Dr. Ernest?"

"Oh, yes. You can take that with you. Read it in detail. For now, believe me when I say that all the signs are there — this murder was an act of rage and revenge and the first step into freeing the full power of the coven. If you look close, read between the lines, you'll see that Dr. Ernest was murdered by a ghost, and the only ghosts in Winston-Salem that would want to harm him belong to the coven."

"But you said the curse prevented —"

"Obviously, somebody found a way to break our curse, didn't they?"

"And with Dr. Ernest's coven ghosts released, you think they murdered him."

"They'll be coming for me soon enough."

"To kill you for revenge?"

"Eventually. But first they'll torture me to find out where I buried their sisters. And if a ghost can kill another ghost, they'll go after Drummond, too."

"Then why all the secrecy from Drummond? If he was the one who helped you down here to begin with, shouldn't we warn him, maybe even elicit his help?"

Leed turned an incredulous eye toward Sandra. "Have you not taught him anything about ghosts?"

"What now?"

Sandra faced her husband. "I think he's referring to the idea that some ghosts can turn."

"Turn?"

With a frustrated huff, Leed said, "Just because Drummond resembles a human being, he's not. He's a ghost. And ghosts have their own set of rules. Supposedly, if you put them in highly stressful situations, ones that make them face their ghostly existence, and keep that pressure on long enough, they can turn into nasty, evil spirits."

"And this could happen to Drummond?"

"It can happen to any ghost. So, we can't trust him."

Max nodded — not because he agreed with Leed but rather because he could tell they had reached the crux of the whole story. "What exactly is it you want us to do?"

Wagging his index finger as if Max were an astute scholar, Leed said, "The witches are in an unusual state at the moment. They are not resting in their graves like most dead people nor are they wandering like most ghosts. They've neither moved on nor stayed behind. They are no longer cursed yet they are not free of the curse either. Since at least one of Dr. Ernest's graves has been disturbed, the only thing left for us to do is release the other corpses with a spell that should move them on to the next world while preventing them from rejoining their coven."

"Why didn't you use that spell to begin with?"

"I didn't know it back then. And by the time I learned, I had no way of using it. Dr. Ernest might have been able to be convinced to divulge his burial locations, but Marshall Drummond had been killed. Where he buried his witches is something I still don't know."

"Ah," Max said, getting to his feet. "You want us to find out Drummond's burial locations."

"Exactly. Find the burial locations and perform the spell. Otherwise, we'll have unleashed a powerful coven that will haunt Winston-Salem for centuries to come."

"Mr. Leed, I've done as you've asked. I've heard you out."

"And you'll take this case?"

"I'll look into it. See what I can find to back up your story."

Deflated, Leed put out his hand. "Of course. I shouldn't have expected more." As Max shook his hand, Leed gripped tight and yanked him close. "Just remember — under no circumstances can Drummond know what we're doing. I've dealt with evil spirits before. A ghost like Drummond becoming such a thing, losing all sense of right and wrong, would be catastrophic."

"Don't worry. We won't tell him." Max freed his hand from the old man, grabbed the newspaper, and headed to the door.

Chapter 3

THE FOLLOWING MORNING, when Max thumped downstairs and shambled into the kitchen, a fragrant pot of coffee greeted him. He had slept little that night, his mind replaying the odd meeting with Leed hour after hour, which resulted in becoming intimately familiar with the textural variations along his ceiling. Sandra sat at their table eating over-easy eggs as she read over the newspaper article they had acquired from Leed.

With a piece of toast in her hand, she gestured to the coffee pot. "Not even a half-hour old."

"It could be ice cold, and I'd drink it."

"I didn't think you slept well. Leed get to you?"

Max nodded and poured the coffee into a mug that declared him to be a *#1 Husband!* "The thing that bothers me the most is that I don't doubt him at all. I'll check up on his story, but I have a feeling that Drummond was involved with him and this whole witch coven thing. And it all got me thinking how little we really know about Drummond."

"Don't do that. I know that look."

"What?"

"You're thinking about researching Drummond."

"So?"

"Honey, you do not want to go researching friends. It'll only lead to trouble. You know better. Real friendship is built on trust, and Drummond is a man —"

"Ghost."

"Fine, Drummond is a ghost that you need to trust. Think about the things we've faced with him already. We would never have survived half of it if we couldn't have trusted him."

Max sipped his coffee, wincing as he burned his tongue. "Okay, okay. I'll stick to Joshua Leed. But if I look into him,

I'm going to find out things about Drummond by default. He's part of this."

"That's different. That's pursuing a case. Just don't go checking up on a friend."

Bending over the kitchen table, Max kissed his wife's forehead. "My guiding light to what is right. I'll stick to the case."

"Good." She turned her head up and puckered until Max kissed her lips. "How do you want to go about this?"

"I think I'll start with a shower."

"Good idea. You stink."

Max grinned. "Thank you."

"What's a wife for, if not to save you from embarrassing yourself in public?"

"My fragile ego and I are grateful. So, I'm going to clean up and go to the library at Wake. Find out what I can on this witch coven, see if it supports Leed's story. I think it will, but I've got to be sure."

"What can I do?"

Max rubbed Sandra's shoulders and cringed inwardly at what he planned to say. "I need you to spend the day watching Drummond."

"You want me to babysit the ghost?"

"I haven't been in the office since yesterday morning. That in itself shouldn't be too strange, but you know he still gets gut feelings, even if doesn't have a gut anymore. He might grow suspicious. If he breaks habit and risks going to a library to check up on me, I need you to call me, warn me."

"Is that why I'm getting a shoulder massage this morning?"

"I never said I was above bribery."

Sandra stood and faced Max with a devilish twinkle in her eye. "If you want me to spend my whole day with a ghost who loves hitting on me while reminiscing about his glory days, you'll have to do a lot better than that."

"What did you have in mind?"

She kissed Max hard. "Meet me upstairs. And remember, this one's all for me."

"All for you, my dear. All for you."

Not surprisingly, Max had no trouble finding information about witches. Between the Internet and the library, he had more sources than he could possibly consume in a lifetime. But as he narrowed his search, first to North American witches, then to North Carolina witches, then to North Carolina witch covens, he found what he needed.

Like vampires, some form of witch existed in nearly every culture going back well before written history. In the modern world though, witches appeared to break down into two major groups.

The first focused on witchcraft as a religion of nature. Wicca was the major label, and they bore little resemblance to the witches of yore. These were kind, peaceful groups that aligned more with the Native American sensibility of the natural world as a living, breathing godly spirit than they did with spellcasters attempting to manipulate the world around them in some pact with evil.

The second group consisted of those who relished in the tales of old. Those that believed they could control others and tap into mystical powers. They were attracted to the darker elements of the lore and put on a pedestal people like Isobel Gowdie, a Scottish woman who, in 1662, confessed to being a witch and detailed out the practices of witches, first coining the term coven. Gowdie claimed to be able to metamorphose into various animals and gave specific instructions on how she accomplished this. Most modern non-believers considered her confession little more than the ravings of an extreme psychosis, but many practicing witches praised Gowdie as a bold martyr.

While the details of Max's research found much in conflict (one group thought their power derived from the moon, another focused on the healing properties within the Earth, and some groups took a modern bent on the whole thing — such as a motorcycle gang in England replacing witches' brooms with 500cc bikes), there were a few consistent aspects to all witch covens. They held the number thirteen sacred, and many covens limited membership to thirteen people. Members commonly called themselves Coveners and the leader usually took the title High Priestess or High Priest. Most interestingly, all covens produced a book called the Grimoire which detailed that group's specific rules, members, and rituals.

"You're all forgetting one group," Max said to the books he read. This group of witches he knew too well — the real witches. The people who controlled true magical power. They could curse a ghost or raise a spirit. Relieve a pain or cause a heartache. They had tapped into the true powers of the universe and knew how to wield them. He had met one amateur, Melinda Corkille, and one bona-fide witch, Dr. Connor, but that had been enough.

He had no doubt that Dr. Ernest, Joshua Leed, and Drummond believed the six women they killed and cursed were the remaining members of a powerful witch coven. The question Max had — what kind of witchcraft did they belong to? If they were a true coven, they would have had a Grimoire. And if they were amongst that third, unspoken category, then that Grimoire would be a dangerous book to get hold of. But Dr. Ernest and Leed must have done just that — how else would they have managed to identify and track the six down to North Carolina? Max found the story of knowing a guy at Sears & Roebuck on the lookout for bulk candle orders a bit too much to swallow.

He pulled up the browser on his laptop and stared at the keyboard. He wanted to type in the names — Ernest, Leed, and Drummond — but he kept hearing Sandra in the back of his head. He closed the laptop and rubbed his face.

He would find another way. He jotted down a few reminders of things he wanted to ask Leed, particularly about the Grimoire and the names of the witches they had killed. If he could locate an article about a missing girl with the same name from the week after they cursed the coven, that alone would make him feel better about Leed. Yet even as he wrote his notes, he had to shake his head. Whether he had intended to or not, his mind already acted as if he had taken on the case.

"Of course I'm taking this on. Drummond's involved."

As he looked up from his notebook, he caught sight of man sitting at a cubicle in the back corner — his old friend, Black Suit. Too tired to play the cloak and dagger game any longer, Max got up and strode right to the corner. To Black Suit's credit, he didn't attempt to escape. He waited as Max approached, set his jaw and crossed his arms.

"What is it you want?" Max asked in a low, bored tone. He had learned this technique from Drummond — under the right circumstance, affecting a nonchalant manner threatened far more than a dangerous tone. He hoped this was the right circumstance.

"You're a very interesting man, Mr. Porter." Black Suit had a smooth, easy voice — nonchalant even. Max felt a chill across his skin.

"Okay, so you know my name. Do I get yours?"

Black Suit stood and reached into his jacket pocket. For an instant, Max thought he might pull a gun, but before Max could react, Black Suit produced a business card. Max glanced at it:

PETER STEVENSON
SPECIAL AGENT
FEDERAL BUREAU OF INVESTIGATIONS

Max curled his mouth. "I'm supposed to believe this from a business card?"

Stevenson glanced around as he pulled out a black leather ID holder. He flashed his official FBI identity badge. "Good enough?"

Max's gut twisted, and he thanked all things holy that he had declined breakfast that morning. "What does the FBI want with me?"

"Just to talk."

"Then why not come to my office, flash a badge, and talk? Why follow me around?"

"Had to make sure you were the right man to talk to."

"Well, you're still following me, so am I?"

"I think so. But others aren't so sure, and since I don't work in a small group like you, getting decisions made sometimes takes time."

"Am I going to be under arrest or something?" Max asked, the words choking in his throat.

"What for?"

"I don't know. You're the one following me."

Stevenson smirked, and Max wanted both to slap the man and run at the same time. "Relax, Mr. Porter. I told you we only want to talk."

"Fine. Talk."

"Not now. But I'll be in touch soon." Stevenson patted Max's shoulder as he walked away.

Max fell into the nearest chair and said nothing — breathing felt like enough of an accomplishment. He couldn't believe he had managed to say half of what came out of his mouth. It was one thing standing up to the Hulls or taking any of the gambles the world had placed before him, but to talk like he did to the FBI. Yet he did. An odd pride warmed his chest. He had used all he had learned recently in order to maintain his self-control and stand his ground.

"Max, you done okay," he said.

But patting himself on the back only went so far. It didn't change the fact that the FBI had taken an interest in him. He thought over all that had happened since he and Sandra first arrived in Winston-Salem. He had seen magic and ghosts, but unless Fox Mulder was based on a real man, he didn't think the FBI investigated such things. Max had witnessed real criminals and real crimes, though, and those the FBI might be quite interested in. Although his own involvement had been minimal, perhaps the FBI thought they could lean on him hard enough to turn him into a good snitch. Or a patsy. Whatever their interest, he had no doubt it would be bad for him.

His cellphone chirped, jolting him from his chair. His knee slammed into a desk and his heart hammered away in his chest. He glanced at the phone's screen — Sandra.

"Hi, hon."

"You sound funny," Sandra said.

"I just might never walk again thanks to your call."

"As long as it's nothing serious."

"Nah. Walking's overrated. What's up?"

"We just got a strange call that you're not going to like."

Max's stomach churned again. "Tell me."

"Mr. Modesto is on his way to the office. He wants to see you immediately."

Modesto. Terrance Hull's former right-hand man. The one who once handled all the distasteful work that spewed out of that family. Max didn't know Modesto's standing in the family anymore, but based on their last meeting, it had significantly improved. One thing was sure — this wasn't going to be a pleasant, social call.

With a sigh, Max said, "I'm on my way."

Chapter 4

Before Max had stepped foot in his office building, Drummond appeared next to him. Wearing the long overcoat and Fedora he had died in, Drummond always looked like a faded picture from the days of World War II. None of the pedestrians on the sidewalk noticed him.

"What in Sam Hill have you been researching all this time that you couldn't come back to the office for a little?" Though Drummond had a tough guy voice, he could whine with the best — spending five cursed decades stuck in one place can do that.

They walked by the empty storefront that once housed Decon Arts — an art gallery that had caused them plenty of trouble in the past. Max peeked in the window and noticed that the back door was ajar. He wondered if they would be having a new tenant soon.

"You see something in there?" Drummond asked, his icy presence freezing Max's shoulder.

I should've met Modesto at a restaurant. While any restaurant convenient to reach would be well within Drummond's range — a ghost could go pretty much anywhere within a wide radius around the point of death — the old ghost avoided certain locations because they reminded him of the things he could no longer indulge in. Drummond loved cigarettes, alcohol, and women. Possibly in that order. Food never ranked high on the indulgence list, but it still made the list. As a result, Max knew Drummond wouldn't bother him at a restaurant unless a dire situation arose. *Too late now.* Modesto might already be waiting.

As they entered the side stairwell that led above the store and to his office, Max said nothing. He didn't need the neighbors seeing him having an argument with empty space.

When they reached the third floor, an apartment door opened. No surprise. The crusty old lady living there seemed to camp out right by the door, waiting for any sound of life passing by. She took one look at Max, squinted her eyes at him and scowled.

Drummond snorted — well, he made a snorting sound. Max didn't know if a ghost could truly snort. "I ought to go in there and give that old bat a scare."

Max opened the door to his office and shook his head. "That's all we need. Police investigating a woman dying from fright."

After a kiss from Sandra, Max settled behind the huge oak desk that made up the centerpiece of his office. It had been Drummond's office first and contained all the original furnishing — big desk, built-in bookshelves, small tiled bathroom off to the side. They had put in another desk for Sandra and a small half-fridge for sodas, leftovers, and the occasional bagged lunch, but otherwise, it all remained the same.

"You still haven't told me what's going on. What's been so important that I've been sitting around with your wife all day?" Drummond floated over to Sandra and winked. "Not that I'm complaining. This gal is one of the best women I've ever had the pleasure —"

"You've never had the pleasure," Sandra said with a sly smile. "And you never will."

Max glanced at his watch — 10:30 am. "You called me right after Modesto called?"

"Yup. He should be here any minute."

Drummond perked up even as he shot a frown at Sandra. "You never tell me anything. So, Modesto called? What's he want?"

"That's what I'm here to find out," Max said.

"Oh, I see. If Modesto calls, Max drops everything and comes running."

"He's the face of the Hulls for us, and the Hulls are the ones paying our bills. Would you rather they throw us out of here and curse you again?"

"They wouldn't dare. Not with you holding that journal over them. Anything happens to any of us, and all their dirty secrets will be made public — it'd be the end of that family's power." Drummond poked his head through the outside wall. "Looks like he's here."

"Okay, you two," Max said. "Not a word. Just let Modesto say his piece and leave. I don't want him here any longer than necessary."

"Listen to you," Drummond said as he returned fully into the office. "I think I'm starting to have a positive influence on you."

Before Max could respond, they heard the steady thump of a heavy foot on the stairs. Modesto paused, perhaps considering whether or not to knock, and finally opened the door to enter. As usual, he wore a well-tailored suit and kept his appearance equally well-tailored. He was a tall man who looked rather bookish, but Max knew better. Modesto was the perfect man for his job — the kind of man who would do anything for his boss, no matter how distasteful, because he did the job for more than mere financial gain. He believed in his boss with a religious fervor, and that made him dangerous.

"Mr. Porter," he said in his clipped, exacting manner. "So good of you to be here as requested."

"Of course, I'd be here. I honor my commitments. I've got to say though that I was surprised by your call. Since hiring us on, the Hull family has yet to actually make use of us."

"Yes, well, your vacation comes to an end today. Our employer has a task that requires your unique talents. Or perhaps I should say the unique talents of your wife." Modesto glanced at the empty spaces around the office. "And others."

Drummond took a spin around Modesto's head. "I think he means me. Can I poke him a little? Give him a chill?"

Max could see Sandra biting back her laughter, and a smile crept on the edges of his own mouth. "Look," he said to Modesto, "I know you don't want to be here, so spit it out and let's get out of each other's hair."

"Eloquent as ever, Mr. Porter."

Drummond swiped his hand across Modesto's shoulder. "I hate this prick."

Modesto shivered and snatched a peek over his shoulder. "Our employer wants you to locate an object — a handbell — that is quite important to the Hull family."

"A handbell?" Max looked to Sandra, and she shrugged.

"An old family heirloom which was lost long ago. Mr. Hull has decided —"

"Which Mr. Hull? Is Terrance running the family business now or is it still William? Or didn't old William die?"

Modesto paused, his cheek twitching. "If our employer wants you to know the particulars of his family structure, than our employer will see that you receive such information."

"Must be Terrance, then. If William were still in charge, he'd want everyone to know it. Kind of a virility thing, I guess." Max propped his feet onto the desk.

"Regardless of what you think, Mr. William Hull is still quite active and fully cognizant despite his age."

"In other words, Terrance is in charge."

Drummond brought his hands together in one sharp clap. "O-ho, Max, you got him on the ropes now. He's already saying more than he likes to. Now, keep it up. Get him to reveal something more, anything at all."

"Is it Terrance, then, that wants this object — this handbell?"

"It doesn't matter who sent you this order. You are to fulfill your contractual obligation. The Hulls are spending a considerable amount of effort reclaiming the pieces of their heritage which have been lost over the years. You are on retainer for this very purpose. Find the bell and bring it to me. It's that simple."

"I doubt it's that simple."

"I don't really care what you think. I am only here because I have been ordered to do so. Your success or failure means nothing to me."

Max doubted that, too. Not because Modesto held any

regard for Max's well-being, but rather because Modesto would want anything the Hulls attempted to succeed. If dealing with Max was the burden for that success, then Modesto would do it gladly — even if he acted like it might kill him.

"Now that we know where you stand on this," Max said, "how about sharing some pertinent information?"

"What more do you want? I told you what you have to do."

With an exasperated huff, Sandra got to her feet and put both hands on her hips. "I swear, the two of you are children. Max, stop goading him. Just let him do his job. And you, Mr. Modesto, stop being a pain in our ass. You want us to find this bell, then you better start giving us what you know or I'll place a call to Terrance Hull myself and ask him why his errand boy is obstructing our progress."

Drummond turned to Max. "Why can't you be more like her? She's incredible."

Modesto blanched but quickly recomposed his controlled, cold demeanor. He circled the room once, his eyes roving over the furnishings as if he were an appraiser disappointed at what he saw. Finally, he turned on his heel and tapped his chin. "The bell is one of a baker's dozen — handcrafted, brass, and extremely rare. All the bells in the set are identical. The handle is painted white with a red stripe about halfway down. The outer rim of the bell has an ornate, geometric design carved along it and a rather flourished capital H marks the inside rim."

"How old are the bells?" Max asked.

"I don't know the exact age but they've been in the family for generations."

"When were they lost? How long ago?"

"At least a century."

Before Drummond could start yammering in Max's ear, Max sat up. "Why the sudden interest? Or has the family been looking for over a hundred years and still can't find this bell?"

"Honestly, I don't think anybody has bothered before to find it," Modesto said. Max never liked when people began a sentence with the word *Honestly*. It usually meant they were about to lie. "But Terrance Hull wants to restore his family to the great standing it held in the past. And having a complete set of these bells is a symbolic act in that direction. At least, that's how I interpret it. But neither you nor I need to have an opinion on these matters. You now have more than enough information to begin your search. I'll return soon for a full report."

Modesto gave one final look of distaste before turning to the door and walking out in his measured, clipped pace.

Drummond stuck his head outside the wall again. Once Modesto had left the building, he returned to the office. "That guy needs a stiff drink and a fine woman."

Sandra pulled a chair up to Max's desk and sat. "What do you think this is about?"

"Come on, Sugar," Drummond said, floating above the desk. "You heard the man. He let it slip — Terrance Hull has taken over the family, and he wants it to go back to its former glory. You know, the days when they took care of a pesky detective by bumping him off and cursing his ghost."

"You've got the *pesky* right."

Max said, "It's more than that. Remember what the witch Connor said to me the last time I saw her? She said the Hulls were trying to find three sacred objects in order to cast a spell that would resurrect Tucker Hull, their founding father. Tucker's journal, and Blackbeard's hair were the first two. This bell must be the third. That would explain why they want to find it all of the sudden."

"They've never been this close before."

As Drummond peered over the edge of the desk, his attention drawn to something on the floor, he muttered, "And bringing back Tucker would be the ultimate in restoring the family."

To Sandra, Max asked, "Can they really do this? Resurrect Tucker Hull?"

Sandra planted her elbows on the desk and her chin in her hands. "Beats me. Just because I can see ghosts doesn't mean I know everything about the supernatural."

"Then I need you to find that out. I'll start searching for this bell." Max raised a hand to stop Sandra from protesting. "You know how the Hulls operate. They'll be watching us. If I don't put on a show of at least attempting to find this bell, we'll have a lot more to worry about. Besides, searching for it and finding it are two very different things. And they've been after this for a hundred years or so. I don't think they'll be too shocked if it takes me awhile."

"Okay." Sandra rose and headed for the door. "I'll see what I can learn about resurrection spells."

Max caught her eye and jutted his chin toward Drummond. She shook her head but Max flashed his puppy dog look. She nodded.

"Hey, Drummond," she said. "You want to come with me? It'll be more fun than watching Max read about handbells."

But Drummond did not answer. Max followed the ghost's gaze to the newspaper Joshua Leed had given him. It lay open on the floor next to Max's laptop. The headline of Dr. Ernest's murder seemed to grow bolder every second. Drummond looked from Sandra to Max, his brow locked in confusion.

"What's wrong?" Max asked, hearing the tremor in his own voice.

Drummond pointed Sandra back to her chair. To Max, he gestured toward the bookcase. "You might want a swig."

Max didn't have to ask. He had been thinking the same thing. He walked over to the bookcase and pulled out one of several false books Drummond had always stored. Inside was a silver flask filled with well-aged whiskey.

After Max sat and had poured a shot for Sandra and one for himself, Drummond began to pace the room. He clasped his hands behind his back. He took another glance at the newspaper and said, "We've got to talk."

Chapter 5

MAX AND SANDRA WAITED as Drummond drifted around the room — his version of pacing. Questions stampeded through Max's mind, but he kept quiet. The fact that Drummond caught sight of the newspaper did not incriminate Max directly. After all, Max could have bought the paper that morning, and it just happened to flip open to the page detailing Dr. Ernest's murder. There was no undeniable link between Max and any knowledge of Dr. Ernest. Of course, if Drummond thought about it for more than a second, he'd wonder why Max had a newspaper in the first place when Max had been a digital guy for years.

Then I have to make sure he doesn't think anymore. "Are you going to talk or did you simply want us to watch your ability to float around the room?"

Drummond shot Max a warning frown. "Have a little patience. This goes back a long time. I want to make sure I have the details right."

The details. Drummond had taught Max that when a suspect starts concentrating on the details, chances are that lies will being coming out soon enough. Max exhaled as softly as he could manage. If Drummond picked up on his relief, the old ghost might get suspicious.

"My apologies. Take your time."

To Max's pride, Sandra picked up on the situation as well. "Should we order food? If this is going to run all day into dinner, we'll want to make sure we get something delivered."

"Good idea, dear. You want Chinese or Indian tonight?"

"Okay, okay," Drummond snapped. "I didn't know you were in such a hurry." He gazed at the office door, the frosted glass showing its age with cracks from the corners and stains on the edges, and his face relaxed as if he were sailing back in time, seeing it all happen before his dead eyes.

"That man in the paper, the one that died — his name was Dr. Matthew Ernest. He was a young man when I knew him, and though I only knew him a short time, I've always felt close to him. Sort of like how soldiers become brothers under fire." He pointed to the door. "The day he came through there, I had been working the oddball angle for quite a while. Ghosts, curses, witches — if it had a hint of the unexplained, people found their way to my door."

So far Drummond had stuck to the truth, but Max did not expect it to last. One of the first techniques Drummond taught him — if you have to lie, mix it in with as much truth as you can. It'll make the lie sound real and will be far easier to remember down the line.

Drummond turned back to Max and Sandra. He licked his cold lips and shook his head. "Doc came from up north. Virginia had been his last stop, but he'd been making stops in Pennsylvania, New York, and Ohio. Maybe elsewhere, too. I don't recall. See, Doc was a paranormal investigator. Not that such things officially existed back then — I suppose they barely do now — but back then he had no school behind him."

"So he just called himself Doctor?" Sandra asked.

"I think he had a doctorate in English or History. Something useless like that. Doesn't matter because when it came to the supernatural stuff he was the best. He knew everything. Taught me quite a bit. In fact, had I known he was alive all these years, I would have tried everything I could to contact him, get him to come help me when I was cursed."

"Why didn't he? If he was here all along." Max regretted the question as it left his mouth.

Drummond moved over to the bookcase and studied the titles, but Max caught the pained expression that crossed the detective's face. At length, Drummond rose a foot higher and turned back around. This time, he had complete control over every aspect of his countenance.

"Dr. Matthew Ernest was one of those people, like the two

of you, who learned that the world was filled with more than most would even believe. He saw ... well, when he was young, unpleasant things happened right before his eyes. From that point on, he studied all he could, prepared himself for when he was old enough to strike out on his own. When that day came, he waged war on all those creatures and those people who helped such creatures."

Sandra crossed her arms. "I've known those types. Some trauma sets them off, and they decide all things paranormal are cut the same, all things paranormal must be killed. You should be glad he never found out about you. He probably would have destroyed you before he ever considered freeing you from your curse."

"Probably." Drummond's far off gaze returned.

Max had to admit that if Drummond had been weaving lies into this narrative, he did so with extreme skill. Everything sounded authentic so far. But then Max reminded himself that the story had only begun.

"I don't know why I remember this but when Matt walked through the door, I was coming out of the bathroom. I think it's because of the look he gave me. He had this narrow face that somehow managed to widen when he saw the supernatural. I didn't know it at the time, but that was the look he was giving me. I've never been able to figure out if prognostication is real or just another myth that built up over the years, but now I wonder if maybe he knew — maybe he saw what would happen to me.

"Well, he told me he came down to North Carolina because of a possession case. Some nasty ghost had taken over this little boy, and he wanted to do something about it. At first I was going to kick him out of the office. When you're the only paranormal investigator in town, you end up seeing a lot of crackpots. You give it time. Once word gets out about us, we'll have the nutcases lining up. But something in the way he spoke, as if he were embarrassed to say the things he had to say, convinced me there might be something real going on."

"So, you helped him," Max said.

"I did. We got hold of a Catholic priest who didn't care too much for following Church protocol and had him perform an exorcism. That did the trick, boy was saved, and I thought that ended my time with Matt. But he knew of other cases in the South, and soon I was taking overnight trips to the coast, to South Carolina, Tennessee, Georgia, anywhere that I could get to within six hours or so. I don't know how he did it, but I got caught up in his urgency. I believed him when he said how we were doing more than just patching up the dam. That's how I saw myself. I was that kid with his finger in the dam, keeping the supernatural creatures from drowning the city, and here was this guy who said we could do more than plug up the hole. We could climb to the top and push the entire river back a few feet.

"It didn't work out that way. Ernest and I had a falling out, and he went elsewhere to continue his battle. And I continued mine. In my own way."

Max had to admit that he still had little idea what was a lie. Some of it was obvious — Drummond had not mentioned Joshua Leed or a witch coven, but perhaps that had not happened at first. It was conceivable that Dr. Ernest had met with Drummond years before he met Leed. He could have fought ghosts and witches and done exactly as Drummond had suggested. Later, Ernest teams up with Leed and when their coven goes to North Carolina, Ernest already knows the perfect contact to help them out. Of course, it could all be crap. Drummond could have made it all up to bury any information regarding Leed and the witch coven. Yet he seemed so genuinely saddened by the memory of Ernest. The only thing clear to Max — something bad had happened back then.

Sandra asked, "What caused you two to stop being partners?"

"It doesn't matter. The important thing to all of this, the reason I'm telling you anything, is that he was murdered."

"We can read the paper."

"Have you two learned nothing? Every article in the news is about more than the words tell. You have to read beyond the story."

Max glanced at the whiskey flask. So far he had no need for its contents. Something in Drummond's voice told him that was about to change. "Well, my first question then is why was he murdered?"

Sandra picked up the newspaper. "It says he was ninety-three. That's a strange age to be making enemies that want to kill you."

Drummond clapped his hands once and pointed at Sandra. "Unless your enemies are old, too."

"You think some pissed-off ghost killed him?"

Drummond hesitated. "The things that Matt faced, he destroyed. There wouldn't be any left to come after him."

"Then who?" Max asked.

Sandra rattled the pages in her hand. "It's all right here, hon." She winked at Drummond. "The article says that police were called to the scene when neighbors reported of loud screaming and gunfire."

"Ghosts don't use guns."

"Hurts too much," Drummond said.

Though Drummond could interact with the physical world, the longer and more complex the experience, the greater the pain. To load a gun, lift it, aim it, and depress the trigger would be a highly improbable task for a ghost. Besides which, Max reasoned, why go to all that trouble when ghosts had plenty of other means at their disposal. For a ghost willing to endure the sort of pain required to fire a gun, it might as well reach into its victim's chest and freeze his heart.

"So we're dealing with a person?"

"Maybe more than one." Drummond glanced at the newspaper. "Look at the photo. There are two bullet holes in the wall. One near the edge of the photo and one near the top — wild shots. This wasn't a planned murder. This was Matt being in the wrong place, wrong time."

"He was in his home."

"Wrong time then."

"You think this was a robbery gone wrong?"

Sandra shook her head. "Not if this photo is any indication

of the rest of his house. He doesn't have much."

Drummond drifted toward the window and gazed outside. "I don't think this was a botched robbery. Not the kind you're talking about. I think this was a robbery for a very specific item."

"Well?" Max flipped his hands outward. "You going to make us guess?"

"Matt's notes. All of his cases, all of the ghosts and witches he fought, everything he ever did would be in a set of well-hidden notebooks. To anybody who sought to know and understand and even attempt to control this other realm, those notes would be invaluable. Somebody, or perhaps a family of somebodies, would certainly find those notebooks worth killing for."

"Wait. You mean the Hulls?"

"You don't find it suspicious that you never hear from them, and then suddenly when this highly valuable notebook comes into play, up pops Modesto with a time-consuming errand to sideline you? Come on. You've been in this game long enough to know that a coincidence like that ain't no coincidence at all. And what's worse, we're just finding out about all this. The Hulls have a few days on us. We've got to get moving."

"At what? We don't have a client. We don't have a real case. We don't even have evidence."

"That's why you and I have to go to the crime scene before it gets turned loose." Before Max or Sandra could object, Drummond swooped in between them. "That notebook is somewhere in Matt's house. They had that much right when they robbed him. I may not have seen Matt in decades, but I guarantee he would keep something that important close by. And since stuck-up Modesto visited with this excuse for research, we can guess that they still don't have the notebooks and need you busy so they can find them. Which means the notebooks are still at Matt's house." Sandra opened her mouth, but Drummond raised his hand and barreled onward. "For the moment, that house is sealed off as a crime scene. That won't last forever. The moment it's turned loose, you can bet anything that Hull will have paid somebody to go squat there until they find the notebooks. Heck, he might even just buy the house and search at his leisure." Max tried to interrupt, but Drummond raised his other hand. "Now the house has been sealed off for a while already. We don't have a lot of time until its turned loose. We need to go tonight. Get in that house while Hull can't easily get in there. If he sends someone to break in like we're going to do, if they get caught, it'll blow back right on the Hulls and that means payoffs and cover-up and all sorts of headaches. Why go to all that trouble when there's really only one guy they have to worry about getting a whiff of this? Why not just send that guy on a senseless research project? This is it. We have to go sneak in there tonight."

Nobody said a word. Drummond stayed quiet, watching for their reaction. Max and Sandra simply waited to make sure he was done.

Sandra broke the silence first. "You can't do this. It's crazy."

"Why?" Drummond asked. "It's not like we haven't broken into places before."

"Those weren't crime scenes. The police already have their eye on this place."

"Lucky for you two, you have a ghost to help out."

Sandra turned her sharp eyes onto her husband. "You just going to sit there?"

Max had not been paying close attention. He tried to place how this notebook and the Hull family and Modesto's research project all fit together. Drummond made a strong case, and while breaking in would be dangerous, it would be far more dangerous to let Hull get his hands on vital supernatural information.

Except Drummond had lied — by omission at the very least. Perhaps there was no notebook. Perhaps this was all a ruse so that Drummond could learn if the witch coven had been involved. If that were the case, then Max should simply tell Drummond about Leed and save themselves the risk of breaking into a crime scene. It would also mean that Modesto's research project was authentic which led to other questions Max didn't want to consider at the moment. Questions of Tucker Hull.

Max glanced up to see Sandra and Drummond staring at him with narrowed, fed-up eyes. Sandra's eyes spoke of Leed and danger and how they needed to figure out fact from fiction before taking any rash actions. Drummond's said that they were partners and that's all that mattered, that he had good reason to lie, that Max needed to trust the ghost that had saved his life in the past.

"I think I'll have that drink," Max said and attacked the whiskey flask. As the fiery liquid warmed his belly, a simple idea popped into his brain. He only hoped he could word it right to satisfy everybody. "If we're going to do this, we need to do it smart. Drummond, I want you to go scout ahead. We've got plenty of time until it'll be dark enough to do this. Go now. Go find out the lay of the house, figure out how I'm getting in, every detail you can think of. We need to get the notebook and get out as fast and safe as possible. Sandra, I need you to stay here and do paperwork."

Sandra's face burned red. "If you think —"

Max raised a hand only to have it swatted away. "Listen to me. This is all about appearances. You do the paperwork while I go to the library to start Modesto's research. You know how Modesto and Hull are — they'll be watching us. If we don't start working as usual, they'll get suspicious."

"Listen to him, doll," Drummond said. "We can't afford to tip them off."

Locking eyes with Sandra, Max hoped she would calm enough to catch what he meant by appearances. It wasn't amazingly subtle, but Drummond seemed to have fallen for the whole thing.

With an ugly glare, she rolled her chair back to her desk and started working, slamming pieces of paper into one pile or another, then typing on her laptop hard enough to make Max cringe. He couldn't tell if she was acting or truly mad. His gut told him to bet on the latter.

Avoiding Sandra's gaze, Drummond shifted his hat down at an angle and headed out the wall. "Looks like I've got scouting to do."

Max exited as quickly if not as smoothly. He fumbled with the door and slipped on the stairs. Once he sat in his car, he texted a simple message to Sandra: *Meet me @ Wake Library.* Hopefully, this would make things clear enough that by the time she reached Wake, any real anger would have dissipated. Once more, his gut contradicted his thoughts.

"Okay," he said to the steering wheel, "let's get to the library and have a little time to relax."

Before he could turn the ignition, Max's cellphone rang. The screen read Unknown but the number looked familiar. He was about to press ignore when it hit him — the card in his pocket. Stevenson the FBI agent.

"Hello?" he said, unwilling to check the business card, holding on to the hope that it might be a wrong number or even a telemarketer.

"Max? It's Stevenson."

Max's heart dropped. "What do you want?"

"Things have changed. We need to talk. There's a ballgame at the Dash Stadium this afternoon. Meet me there when you can get away."

"I don't really follow minor league ball."

"If the game hits the seventh inning stretch and you don't show, I'll come find you, and I won't care who sees us together. You associated with anybody you think might not like seeing you talk with an FBI agent?"

Yeah. I can think of too many. "It's a bit crazy right now. Let's meet tomorrow. I can —"

"Mr. Porter, let me make this quite simple for you. Either you show up at that ballgame, or you'll end up in jail for murder."

Chapter 6

THE SANCTUARY OF THE LIBRARY could not ease Max's nerves. What he had hoped would be a quiet research session followed by an intelligent discussion with Sandra, one in which they found a logical and measured response to Drummond's behavior, had become a mass of confusing, pressure-filled worries. In less than twenty-four hours, his calm, pleasant life had cracked open onto a sizzling frying pan of lies, threats, and secrecy.

He sat at a library computer intending to search for some basic information on handbells, but he couldn't muster the willpower to type in his query. Clouds rolled in, darkening the main floor which took in a lot of light from outside, and soon the heavy hits of a Spring downpour followed. It would only last a few minutes, but it reminded Max of how fast things can change. He had mounting problems to juggle and not a single worthwhile lead, but if he didn't find some angle to follow, the situation would change without any control.

He felt fairly confident Drummond was lying. He suspected Leed was lying. He had no idea what angle Modesto and Hull were taking, or if their work truly had anything to do with this. Then there was FBI Agent Peter Stevenson — the most pressing question in his mind.

What could this man possibly have that would tie Max to a murder? Perhaps it was all a bluff to get Max out to the ballfield. If so, it would work. Max had to know how the FBI fit into this.

"Deep breath," Max said and inhaled. He rested his fingers on the keyboard. Sandra would wait at least fifteen or twenty minutes before heading out to the library — just to make appearances should anybody be watching. It would take at least another twenty minutes for her to drive out to Wake. That meant he had time before she would arrive, time in which he could scramble his senses worrying about things he had no control over, or he could at least attempt to get some research done.

Though his fears continued to nudge the back of his neck, he managed to get his fingers typing and quickly had a list of books and websites to check out. All of this information would be the basics on bells, their construction, their history, that kind of thing. He didn't care about the details, he only wanted to leaf through the books and websites to look at the pictures. He knew from Modesto that the handbell had a white handle with a red stripe, that the outer rim bore a geometric design, and the inner rim had a fancy H. Assuming these things were valuable to collectors, especially since Hull had collected them, Max hoped to find a picture of one used as an example for some aspect of bells.

Ten books and twenty-three websites later, Max had nothing. On a whim, he checked out eBay. While numerous bells were for sale, only two approximated the Hull bell, and neither matched the description close enough to be worth investigating further.

He never expected these avenues to be fruitful, but the basic approaches were always worth trying. Sometimes he got lucky. When it came to the Hull family, though, he knew well the difficulty in uncovering even the remotest reference. William Hull, Terrance's father, had worked hard to erase their mark on the history books.

"Maybe Modesto is telling the truth," Max said. Perhaps Terrance wanted to re-establish his family's presence in the world. Or perhaps he wanted to continue his father's efforts. Either approach would make his desire for the handbell somewhat logical. Unless this was really about Tucker. Best not to think about that — Max had enough troubles to consider.

An idea struck, and he began a new query. Most collector's items, especially ones that had been around for a long time, had some type of pricing authority. Comic books, baseball cards, samurai swords, anything that people wanted to buy and trade, somebody else cataloged it all.

From the handbell musicians association website he began a winding journey that ended with the a cluttered site called A Mostly Complete Handbell Buyer's Guide. Once there, he narrowed the search from a starting point of close to a million. Most handbells were not constructed in a baker's dozen, so that cut the list down into the thousands. Adding in the Winston-Salem, North Carolina area as a criteria brought up seven results. Four of those had been constructed in the last three decades — much too recent for it to be a cherished family heirloom when the Hulls reached back to the foundations of the city. Of the remaining three entries, only one set had been constructed in 1723 — a baker's dozen with white handles, red striped, ornate design on the outer rim, and another design on the inner rim. No mention of the letter H, but Max's gut knew this was his target.

While the listing did not bring him any closer to finding the lost bell, he now had a picture of one as well as confirmation that this wasn't a goose chase to keep him away from other matters. The bell was real, and the price tag of only one — $74,000. The complete set was worth far more than the sum of its parts. According to the buyer's guide, a price of two to three million dollars would be appropriate.

Two to three million dollars.

"I didn't need to know that," Max said, his nerves lighting up once again.

Hands covered his eyes, and Max yelped, jumping in his seat. Sandra's sweet voice giggled. "Sorry, hon. Didn't mean to scare you."

As Max hugged his wife, his heart continued to pound away. "Don't do that to me. Not with all that's going on."

"What is going on? Drummond's worrying me."

"Me, too. All of it is. Even this handbell thing. The timing of it is weird. But Drummond lying, or at least withholding the full truth, that's not like him."

"And this whole notebook thing — I didn't believe his story

at first, but now he wants to go break in to that house. There's got to be something worth going in there for."

Max scanned the room to make sure nobody paid extra attention to them. In a low whisper, he said, "I think most of his story was true. I think he had met Dr. Ernest and worked with him well before Joshua Leed came into the picture."

"I agree. But then why not tell the full story? Why stop before getting into the witch coven? Worse, he lied about that. He purposely made it sound like that part of the story never existed."

"That's why I agreed to this break in. We've got to keep playing along with him until we know more of what's going on."

"I don't like it. These late-night things never turn out well for us."

"If you've got a better idea, please tell me."

Sandra stuck out her tongue.

"It's those mature responses that make me love you more." Max kissed her tongue.

"Be careful."

"Of course."

"No, you need to be more careful than usual. Drummond is lying to us and he's lying about something that surrounds a murder. That's stressful and confusing. It means he's got pressure building inside him. I may not be able to help much when it comes to witches and curses, but I know ghosts. Pressure like that — the kind that comes from having to face the secrets of your past — that's the kind of thing that can turn a ghost."

"Turn? That doesn't sound good."

"Not all ghosts are sweet and friendly."

"I'd hardly call Drummond sweet or friendly."

"Good ghosts, kind ghosts, can lose themselves, lose whatever made them decent. They turn. Become evil."

"Like what? Haunted houses, poltergeists?"

"Or worse. A ghost like Drummond, one who knows us well, could cause us both serious harm. He would be like an insane psychotic that still remembers the key details of our lives but has no empathy, no morals, nothing that would stop him from abusing that knowledge."

"I get the picture. What do we do to stop this?"

"I don't know for sure. I've never been in a position to try stopping a ghost from turning before. But I know that the worse this pressure builds upon him, the more likely he is to turn."

"Well, you're full of great news." Max rubbed his face. Now he had to worry about Drummond going crazy. And Agent Stevenson expected him soon. He needed to get going.

Sandra dismissed it all with a wave of her hand, but her eyes didn't believe. "I'm probably being paranoid. Don't worry about it unless Drummond starts showing cracks."

"Cracks?"

"Just an expression, hon. Not literal cracks. At least, I don't think real cracks would form." She trembled out a grin and kissed him.

"I know it's boring but please go back to the office and wait for Drummond. If I haven't returned when he gets there, call me. I've got some more research to do."

"Yes, sir," Sandra said with a mock salute.

Once she left, Max gathered his things together and waited at the entrance. He watched her as long as he could, then waited another three minutes after she left his view. The idea that he hid from his wife wriggled under his skin, but until he knew what the FBI wanted, he wouldn't dare give voice to his concerns. They had enough to contend with. No need to get Sandra fired up with more worry, too.

As he walked to his car, he saw no sign of her. He drove off campus onto Silas Creek Parkway, a stretch of road that made a long arc around the city, until he hit Peters Creek Parkway. A left turn towards downtown brought him straight to the BB&T Ballpark.

He had no trouble finding a parking space — mid-week, afternoon, minor league baseball games never packed the seats. The park had been constructed less than ten years ago and still bore the feel of newness about it. Not really good for a ballpark. The seats were too new, the paint too clean. The place lacked the sense of history which was part of a baseball game experience.

Except I'm not here for a ball game.

Max strolled around toward the left field seating entrance. Partially to stall and partially out of need, he stepped into the men's room. While standing before a urinal he heard the crack of bat and heard muffled cheering. He couldn't go. Though the restroom was empty, he felt a dark presence hanging over his shoulder as if the entire FBI had him under surveillance.

He rinsed his face with cold water, dried off, and made sure not to look at his reflection. Seeing the fear in his own eyes might have been enough to send him running.

"For crying out loud, Max," he said. "You've faced down the Hull family. This is nothing more than an FBI agent with a threat." Hearing it so simply stated raised his confidence. After all, even if he did end up in jail for a crime he never committed, jail could never be as bad as burning alive — and that had nearly happened to him once.

When he finally walked into the seating area, the bright sun warmed his face. Shielding his eyes with one hand, he turned around and searched for Stevenson. It wasn't hard to find him. The FBI agent made no attempt to blend in. Still wearing his G-man black suit and shades, he raised a game program in the air to signal Max over.

Stevenson picked up a plastic cup of beer sitting between his feet on the cement floor. "You had me thinking you wouldn't show."

"Didn't seem as I had much choice." Max watched the game. Winston-Salem versus Wilmington. Fifth inning. 4-2. Two outs, no men on base.

"Sorry about that. I don't like threatening people but I didn't think you'd come otherwise."

"Probably wouldn't have. You don't exactly come off as the real deal." Max sat in the hard wood seat with metal trim. He had never been a big baseball fan, but once in awhile, he did enjoy going to a game, eating a hot dog, and sitting in these seats. It was as much a part of the game as the game itself.

"I am an FBI agent. But I don't handle the traditional cases."

"Does that mean I'm not really going to be charged with murder?"

Stevenson sipped his beer. "That part's real, I'm afraid. There are people I work for who think you are very involved in this thing."

"You want to tell me what this thing is? Who did I supposedly murder?"

"How long have you known Dr. Matthew Ernest?"

Max rolled his head back and looked heavenward. "You've got to be kidding."

"Oh, I don't think you murdered Dr. Ernest. At least, not directly. You didn't pull the trigger is what I'm saying. But the man led a strange life, and he had a way of making even his closest friends turn into vicious enemies."

"I've never even met the guy. Never heard of him until yesterday."

"Was that when you spoke with Joshua Leed at lunch, or was that when you met Leed at his home in Thomasville? How long have you known Mr. Leed?"

Max stared at Stevenson, not sure if he wanted to cry or scream. "I only just met him."

"Yesterday, right?"

"Yes. That's exactly right."

"Seems you just met a lot of people yesterday."

The player at bat cracked off a fly ball to center field for an easy catch, closing out the inning. Max wondered how many outs he played with. How many times would he deal with Hull and avoid losing? Maybe this was his final at bat. "Am I under arrest? Do I need a lawyer?"

Crossing his legs in an incongruously feminine manner, Stevenson said, "Relax. We're far from that sort of thing. Right now, I'm merely investigating Dr. Ernest. Well, and now his murder. Dr. Ernest was wanted for questioning in connection with a slew of murders stretching from here all the way up into Massachusetts, running over the course of the last five decades. Strange cases, too. Not a typical nutcase that wants to cut up pretty girls because Mommy kept him in a diaper too long. No, Dr. Ernest rode the whole magic bent. Killed girls in a ritualistic way. Gruesome stuff. But I don't have to tell you that, huh?"

Even without Drummond there to point it out, Max could hear the agent fishing for information. "I don't know anything about this."

"You ever read *Frankenstein?* I don't mean some bolts-in-the-neck version, but the real book. Mary Shelley."

"No."

"It's a good book. Very different from what you'd expect. Actually, all the classic horror stories are like that — *Dr. Jekyll and Mr. Hyde, Dracula* — and even modern tales like Carrie. People see the movies and think they know the whole story, but they're wrong."

Although the sun burned hot on the open field, Max found the warmth pleasant. He only wished the conversation were equally pleasant. "What does this have to do with —"

"In *Frankenstein,* you've got the monster, of course, and Dr. Frankenstein and his assistant. Since you haven't read the book, did you ever at least hear about the assistant's assistant?"

Max shook his head.

"Of course, you didn't. Nobody's ever heard of that character because the character doesn't exist. The book would've been a failure if there had been a third person in that group. See, when men do evil things they try to keep it from getting known. If they didn't, if they would only come out and proclaim their guilt, well then I'd have an easy job. Dr. Frankenstein, Igor — two people can keep a secret between them if the motivation is strong enough. But three people. That won't work. That always leads to someone being an odd man out. Sort of like you and Dr. Ernest and Joshua Leed. Now I'm not saying you were part of their group or that you encouraged Leed to get rid of Dr. Ernest, but I do know that the three of you are connected, and that whatever secrets you held are now held only by two people. Perhaps you and Leed got tired of taking orders from the good ol' Doctor and thought the time had come to strike out on your own."

"It's not like that at all."

"What is it then? Did Leed convince you that Dr. Ernest led a witch coven into Winston-Salem and you two tried to stop him from turning your beloved city into a haven for the dark arts? Or did he tell you that Dr. Ernest was a witch hunter? It's got to be one or the other."

"Witches? Who are you? Fox Mulder?"

Stevenson chuckled. "As far as I know, the FBI doesn't have a real X-Files division. But we do have people like me, specialists in some of the less traditional areas of investigation. You should be able to understand that. Your little research firm seems quite similar, focusing on lots of cases that are less traditional. Isn't that why you're researching witch covens?"

Max shifted, his seat no longer the familiar, comfortable bit of the game that brought with it pleasant memories. "I didn't kill anybody. And I don't know anything about Dr. Ernest. Leed didn't kill him either. In fact, Leed contacted me because he found out about the murder and he wanted to hire me to look into it. I'm guessing he didn't trust the police to handle it because he knew people like you were looking, too."

Stevenson formed a fist and hammered his chest until he let out a belch. "Why didn't you say so from the start? I could've saved my *Frankenstein* bit for another occasion. Unless, you're not telling me the whole story. Is that it, Max? Are you holding out?"

"Holding out about what?"

"Perhaps Leed wants more from you than you said. After all, he went around the country with Dr. Ernest for years. He's a person of interest as Dr. Ernest's accomplice. Maybe he's thinking of picking up where the doctor left off. Maybe he wants you to join him. Disciples can be like that, you know."

"Why me, then? I told you I've never met either of them before yesterday. It wouldn't make sense for him. Why rest all your illegal plans on somebody you've only met?"

"That's the same problematic thought I've been having." Stevenson patronizing grin scratched under Max's skin. "Unless what you're telling me is bullshit. If, in fact, you did know them, perhaps handled research for them at some point in the past, then it all adds up quite neatly."

"Your math is wrong."

"I hope so. Truly do. You and your wife seem like nice folks, and I'd hate to be the one breaking up a good marriage because I've got to arrest you."

"I didn't do whatever you think I did."

Max stood to go, but Stevenson grabbed his wrist. "You may be innocent of what I'm talking about, but you aren't innocent. So, let me give you this bit of advice — stay away. Everything, everyone connected with Matthew Ernest turns evil. You want to get my people off of you, then remember to stay away. Because pretty soon, I'll have to be interrogating you officially."

"I'll remember." Max yanked his arm free and stormed out of the ballpark. It felt good to stomp up the stairs, shoving out every bit of tension the conversation had created. By the time he reached his car, he was puffing and sweating. He slid into the driver's seat and glanced at his reflection in the rearview mirror. Stevenson told him to stay away and the first thing he'll be doing that night was breaking into Matthew Ernest's home. "Well, I said I'd remember — not that I'd listen."

Chapter 7

AS EVENING APPROACHED, Sandra and Max leaned back in their office chairs and bit into their slices of pizza from The Mellow Mushroom. The restaurant was only a few blocks away, yet Sandra preferred bringing the pizza in. "That place is always jam-packed and noisy."

Breaking the stringy cheese bridge between his mouth and the pizza slice, Max nodded. "That's because the pizza's delicious."

Drummond popped his head through the bookcase. "Are you two done yet? I've got to go over the plan."

"Then stop hiding in the walls and tell us."

Drummond soared out to the middle of the room, chest puffed out, arms crossed. "You know damn well that even though I can't eat any of that food, I can sure smell it. That's cruel. May even qualify as torture."

Max raised his arms. "What do you want from us? We're alive. We need food. I wasn't about to drive all the way home to eat just to turn around and come back here. Plus, we figured it would be worse for you to stretch all the way out to our house. You'd be complaining of a migraine long before we set foot in Ernest's house. This seemed like a fair compromise."

"Fine. Just finish up already." Drummond relaxed his posture and glanced at Sandra. "Sorry I swore. You're too refined a lady to have to put up with that."

Sandra smiled. "The fuck I am."

This tickled Drummond, and he barked out a series of laughs that nearly choked him.

Wiping his fingers clean on a paper napkin, Max wondered how long he could keep his cool. Drummond's lies, the FBI, Leed — it all swirled inside him like a ship caught in a squall.

He wished he could tell Sandra, his close confidante. But he had to protect her, too.

He took a sharp breath. He could do this. Stay focused and find the way through. They had survived past calamities that way, and they would survive this one the same.

"Okay, I'm done eating," Max said. "Tell us the plan."

With a longing gaze at the pizza box, Drummond settled in a chair opposite Max. He had no need for chairs, of course, but Max appreciated his effort to seem human. "Matt's home is on Ebert, south off of Silas Creek Parkway." Drummond's enthusiasm for detective work cleared his mood. "It's got crime scene tape around it but no cops anymore. They're probably done with it and waiting for the release order. No need to waste resources watching over it now."

"Then we're too late?"

"We're fine until it's released. After that, somebody will hire a cleaning crew to make it look like nobody ever died in there so whoever owns the house now can sell it. That's why —"

Sandra washed down the last of her dinner. "We know. It has to be tonight."

Pausing to look from Max to Sandra and back, Drummond screwed up his face but eventually shook it off. Fine by Max. He had no desire to explain marital relationships to a ghost.

"The way I figure it," Drummond went on, "I'll go in first and unlock the door. You walk in, get the notebook, and we leave. Should be easy."

Max coughed. "When is this stuff ever easy? Heck, we don't even know where in the house the notebook is."

"I'm pretty sure I know. Most of the house is normal and unimpressive. But there's a room I can't get into. The door has a ward on it. It's a symbol you draw so that —"

"We've seen them." Max recalled the bizarre symbols all over Joshua Leed's house. Then he saw Sandra's shocked face and realized his mistake.

Drummond raised an eyebrow. "When have you ever seen a ward symbol?"

The silent tension around them grew thicker. Max's brain

raced for a plausible answer as Drummond stared at him with that detective eye — the look of man who could spot a lie with minimal effort. Max opened his mouth, hoping to sound natural, when it hit him. He had seen a ward before. "Don't you remember the art forgery case?"

Sandra shuddered. Max knew she hated any reminder of being chained in the basement of the Corkille home while that crazy family attempted their awful spells. Still, she understood Max's angle. "That's right," she said. "That Corkille bitch drew all sorts of stuff on the floor, and you couldn't get in to stop her."

Drummond's face turned cold. "Well, we did find a way to stop her. And those symbols were not wards. She used blood to create that barrier."

"The concept's the same, though. Right?" Max asked. "Use some sort of magic to keep a ghost out of a certain area."

"I suppose. Anyway, Matt put a ward on one door in his house. I tried to go through the walls to get around it, but he must have wards on the inner walls of the room because I couldn't get in. Actually, that's not right. I could force my way in, but getting close to an active ward is like touching a hot stove. It burns hot and painful and that's what keeps you away. If I can handle the pain, I could go in."

"No need, though. You open the outside door, I'll go in to the warded room, find the notebook, and we get out of there."

"Like I said. Easy."

Sandra cleared her throat in a melodramatic manner to get their attention. One look at her face, and Max knew he had messed up again. "What's the matter, Hon?"

Sandra looked at the two men and shook her head. "You seem to have forgotten my part in all this."

Like walking through a minefield, Max slowly said, "Okay. What's your part?"

"That's my question to you. You didn't actually think I'd let you go running off tonight alone, did you? We're partners in this outfit. I'm not a secretary. If you think it's important to find this notebook, then I'm going with you."

He couldn't help but smile — her fierce eyes and determined jaw made her even more beautiful than usual. "I'm sorry, but you can't come this time."

"Excuse me?"

Inching back from the desk, Max said, "Honey, I'm going to be committing a burglary on Ebert Road. That's not really an empty road. There's houses all around."

"That's why you need my help."

"If you come with me and we get caught, who's going to bail us out? Our friend, the ghost?"

"You really think breaking into an empty house is somehow more dangerous than the other things we've faced?"

"Of course not." Max felt his pizza lurch in his stomach. "I just —"

"You just nothing. I told you when we decided to keep on working together that it had to be on equal terms. It's been easy to play at equality when nothing much has been challenging us, but this is your real moment of truth. This is the time when you prove you're worth your word. Are we equal or not?"

Max swallowed hard. He looked to Drummond, but the detective stared at Sandra so shocked, he didn't realize he had slipped halfway through his chair.

At length, Max tilted his head in a slight nod. "I said we'd be equal and we will."

Drummond lifted a bit in the air. "Sugar, I've always liked you, but I swear, you make me wish I'd find a way to be alive again."

With a flirting wink, Sandra said, "Now why would you want to do that? I'm a married woman."

"Don't bother me with details. That's the whole point of a fantasy."

"Hey, you two," Max said. "I'm right here."

Sandra giggled and picked up the pizza box. "I'll take this downstairs. Otherwise, the place'll stink by morning."

When she left, Max dropped his head. "Promise me, if something goes wrong, you won't let anything happen to her."

Drummond said, "You know I'll protect her."

"I know. Thank you."

"Don't be so worried. Like the lovely lady said, we've been in scrapes before and we've helped each other out. Frankly, it'll be good to have her along. Trust me here — a woman like that keeps you grounded, keeps you from doing stupid things, keeps you safe."

Max noticed an odd tincture to Drummond's voice. "You knew a woman like that once?"

"You don't want to hear about that."

Bolting upright, Max said, "Of course I do. I'm always happy to hear anything you want to share."

"Oh." Drummond looked genuinely confused as if he never expected such an enthusiastic response. "Um, what do you want to know?"

"Anything. Who was she? How did you meet? Did you love her? Come on."

Squirming in mid-air, Drummond said, "There's nothing to tell. It's boring. And you don't tell me anything either. I don't know much about you and Sandra."

"What do you want to know?"

"Nothing. That's your private business."

For a second, Max thought Drummond might disappear into the Other — a ghost realm that resided in another plane of existence. He stayed, however. He pressed himself into the back corner, but he stayed. Max walked over to him and in a soothing tone, he said, "Maybe this is one of those differences between the era you lived in and the one we're in now."

"Your whole generation wants to share way too much." Though still in the corner, Drummond had regained his sturdy posture.

"It's a good way to build trust. You know as well as I do that we need to trust each other."

"All that we've been through already hasn't proven enough?"

"I trust you. Otherwise, I wouldn't be going out on this job tonight. But you can't have too much trust, and the more we know about each other, the better it'll be for our success in whatever we investigate." Max backed away. "I'll make it easy for you. Let me tell you about one of the first dates I ever had with Sandra."

"Why does that matter?"

"Just listen."

Doing little to hide his perturbed attitude, Drummond gestured for Max to begin.

"Now this wasn't our first date. I think it might've been our third or fourth. We'd both been recently burned — I'd been dumped and she had been cheated on — so we were taking things really slow. I hadn't even kissed her yet."

"Even by 1940s standards, that's ridiculous."

"Point is we were both gun shy. These people we cared about had betrayed us. Maybe you never had that problem, but I'll tell you, it throws you for a loop."

"I'm sure it does." Drummond looked to the bookcase, his eyes lingering on the whiskey book.

"So we go out to dinner, catch a movie, nothing out of the ordinary. A plain old date. I take her to her apartment and at the door, I pick up her hand and kiss it softly. We smiled at each other, and I'll never forget this — she said to me, 'Y'know, I appreciate how you've been with all this.' I knew right away what she meant. I told her that I understood. She said, 'We're never going to get over it unless we deal with it.' I agreed but I didn't know how to deal with it. She said she knew. She grabbed my head and kissed me hard. The next morning, I'm lying in her bed with her beautiful head nestled on my chest and I never had to worry again."

Drummond pointed right at Max's face. "If you think I'm sleeping with you to strengthen our trust, you're out of your mind."

They both laughed harder than necessary.

"You boys ready?" Sandra asked from the doorway.

They took one look at her and burst into genuine, raucous laughter.

Chapter 8

EBERT ROAD RAN NORTH and south starting below the city near Baptist Hospital and heading far down into Davidson County. The properties along this long stretch encompassed quaint starter homes and durable rentals, beat up double-wides and rundown farmhouses, as well as lovely middle-class homes and showy McMansions. Only the destitute and the ultra-wealthy went unrepresented. Dr. Matthew Ernest lived in a single floor, two bedroom starter with a swatch of grass meant to be considered a yard.

Max parked a few houses back and watched the street. Normally, Ebert Road had a steady stream of traffic — a fast way to cut up to Silas Creek Parkway while avoiding the more heavily traveled roads, one of those back routes only the locals knew about. At two in the morning, however, the buzz of an amber streetlight and the clicking of the car's cooling engine were the only activity around.

Clasping Sandra's hand, Max kissed her. "You come in with me, take a look around, tell me if there's anything besides Drummond there. Once we're sure the place is clear, I want you to come back here and start the car. Watch for me and be ready to go fast."

"No problem."

They slipped out of the car and crossed the street. Walking on the grass, they avoided the sound of shoes against concrete. Though the night air had cooled considerably, Max still found it surprising that he smelled burning wood in the air. Who would need a fire going? But he allowed himself a few seconds to indulge in the pleasant aroma before focusing on Dr. Ernest's house.

From the outside, the house appeared to be one of several

small properties that received the same lack of care. Tall grass and weeds grew in some yards and a few bore the leftovers of kids at play — plastic bat and balls, rusting bicycle, a baseball cap, a Frisbee, and a discarded t-shirt. The houses across the street were of the same size, yet those owners made a greater effort at upkeep. Max envisioned a Hatfield/McCoy feud developing between the two sides of the street.

Together, Max and Sandra headed around the back of Dr. Ernest's house. They tried to be quiet but Max kept stepping on hidden dead branches and Sandra tripped in the tangles of Bermuda grass, falling flat in the yard. Each time they froze and listened. If anybody had heard, they didn't take notice.

Max took out a penknife and held it against the first bit of yellow crime scene tape that crisscrossed the door. Most days did not bring him to the point of committing a jail-worthy offense, so he had no experience with what he would feel. His hand did not shake. That was good. But his mind kept flashing images of home, safe and comfortable.

He rapped his knuckles on the rotting wood frame. "Drummond?" he whispered.

The lock clicked, and Max slowly turned the knob. He pushed the door open with care as if handling a newborn. Despite his efforts, the hinges whined in protest.

Drummond popped his head through the door. "Are you two trying to get caught?" They entered a narrow kitchen that led into a wide living room. Once Sandra entered, she closed the door, making less noise than Max, and Drummond gestured toward her silent work. "Next time put her on door duty."

Max flicked on his flashlight and checked out the house. "Holy crap." A raging storm had blown through. Most of the picture frames lay shattered on the floor and those remaining on the wall hung askew. The walls themselves bore jagged cracks from floor to ceiling. Furniture had been toppled over and cut open, foam stuffing strewn about. Hardcover books had been ripped apart. Dishes and glasses covered the kitchen with sharp shards. Even the pillows and blankets littered the floor in strips.

Though Max had seen many bizarre things, this was his first crime scene. He could only wonder at the intense anger required to cause this much damage. On the living room carpet, the dark splotch near the head of a corpse's tape outline reminded Max that the anger went far beyond ransacking a house. This was murder.

"Is the place clear?" he asked Sandra.

Her eyes roamed about the room, her lips trembling. Finally, she nodded. "Drummond's the only ghost here."

"Go back to the car."

Sandra stepped closer to him and brushed her cheek against his. Before Max could say anything, she pressed her mouth against his ear. "Keep Drummond calm. Don't let him turn."

As she walked back to the door, Max watched her face. She stared at the destruction in the room and shuddered. Max looked over it all again, except this time he imagined a turned ghost, an evil ghost, causing this damage.

Drummond appeared at his side. "Ready?"

Max started, hoped Drummond didn't notice, and stepped further into the house. "So where's the room?"

"First thing's first." Drummond moved about the living room with a thoughtful look on his face. He stopped at one wall, traced the cracks with a finger, and grimaced. Max hadn't noticed it before, but the particular series of cracks Drummond paid most attention to bore a striking resemblance to claw marks.

Drummond then lowered into the floor until he had a close up view of the where Dr. Ernest had died. Max marveled at the sight. He was getting a firsthand view of the way an old detective investigated a crime scene. Not exactly, considering Drummond's current position, but close enough.

"You find anything?" Max asked.

Shooting back up into the room, Drummond said, "Not yet. Come on. Let's get the notebook."

Another lie. Max knew it, could feel the lie as cold as Drummond's skin. That ghost had noticed something about those cracks in the wall.

Off to the side of the living room was a short hallway with three doors at the end. The left went into a compact bathroom. The right entered a bedroom that Dr. Ernest had set up as an office. The door on the end was closed and a series of symbols lined vertically had been carved into the wood.

Drummond floated a few feet away. "That's the one."

"I gathered that." Max rested his hand on the door.

"There isn't a fire on the other side."

"You want to come here and do this?"

"I do, but you know I can't."

"Then shush already."

Max opened the door and poked his flashlight in the room. It looked like a boring bedroom ripped to shreds. Single bed, white sheets, plump pillow, gray blanket, little table with a lamp and a cracked Kindle, chest of drawers and a mirror. Nothing special. Except for the fact that all of it had been struck by the same tornado as the rest of the house.

With trepidation, Max walked into the room. More archaic symbols lined the walls, written in a shaky hand. Of course, at ninety-something, Dr. Ernest's hand might shake from age, but Max suspected fear had more to do with it. Regardless of the reason, the result chilled his skin.

"This wasn't in the paper," Max said.

"What?"

"The newspaper article. It never mentioned this room. Why would they not write up something as sensational as this? It's a bizarre story with this room."

"The photo in the newspaper came from the police. They don't want the public knowing about a possible cult thing in the backyard until they have an idea of who's responsible. That's why they haven't released the crime scene yet. Once they do, the reporters will swarm in and get their sensational story."

As Max searched for the notebook, he thought about Joshua Leed and the angry cursed ghosts of witches, the turned ghosts, that had done this. Sandra was right. They had to make sure this didn't happen to Drummond — or the police would be wrapping yellow tape across their office door, and all that would remain of Max and Sandra would have been shredded into confetti.

"You find it?"

Over his shoulder, Max whispered back, "No. Any idea where I should look?"

"Sheesh, do I have to do everything? Check drawers, check under the mattress, if you need to, pull up the carpet or floorboards."

Since the drawers were already ripped out and strewn across the floor, Max started with the mattress. Underneath, he found plenty of dust bunnies and a forgotten plate. From the floor, it appeared that the drawers had contained mostly clothing, though a few papers, too. Max checked them — correspondences with Wake Forest University and UCLA. Dr. Ernest had begged for funding support, dismissed accusations leveled against him for improperly representing himself, and argued that his research held both valid and valuable purpose. Both universities offered terse replies in the nature of *Don't contact us ever again.*

Max dropped the letters and cruised his flashlight for another turn around the room. About to give up and call for Drummond's advice, he stopped the light in one corner. The carpeting had an odd bulge as if someone had pulled up the edge and failed to put it back completely.

"Max? Anything?"

"Hold on." Max approached the corner, his mouth drying up, and poked at the carpet. He slipped one finger under the edge, felt the coarse weave, and gently pulled it back. The top of a manila envelope peeked out. Max's chest tightened. Ever since moving to the South, he had learned one clear thing — nothing good for him ever came in a manila envelope. "I got something."

"Was it where I said?"

"Nope. It's in a closet." Max had no desire to hear Drummond crow about his great investigative prowess. And even though it was a stupid thing to lie about, Max had to admit he always felt a little satisfaction when he could deny Drummond a chance at bragging.

Snatching up the envelope, Max hurried out of the room. Every second longer in that house meant another second to get caught. He rushed through the living room and out the kitchen, but as he closed the door behind him, he caught a glimpse of Drummond staring at the claw marks in the wall.

Crouching, Max scurried across the yard and up the sidewalk. Sandra had the engine running. She pulled into the street, Max jumped in, and they were off.

"I really hate doing that," Max said, exhaling a long breath. "No more breaking and entering."

As she drove, Sandra pointed to the manila envelope in Max's lap. "Is that it?"

Drummond appeared in the backseat. "Of course. I told you it was there, didn't I? Don't forget, if not for me, you couldn't have done this."

"I *wouldn't* have done this if not for you."

Sandra put them on a main road, and the more distance they traveled away from the house, the better Max felt. "So what's in it?" she asked.

Max slid his finger under the envelope's lip. He pulled out a stack of papers and inspected them. "Damn. Nothing's ever easy."

"What's wrong?"

"It's gibberish."

Drummond tried to grab the papers but his cold hand slipped through. "Let me see those."

"I don't mean it's gibberish like a raving madman, I mean it's just letters and numbers. It's a code."

"That sounds like Matt. He was always a bit more paranoid than necessary."

Sandra peeked at the papers. "Tomorrow I'll get to work on that."

Both Max and Drummond gaped at her. Max said, "Since when did you become a code cracker?"

"Back when we used to get newspapers I always liked the

puzzle pages. Crosswords, jumbles, ciphers."

"I know that, but you haven't done that stuff in a long time."

Sandra smirked. "You don't really think I spend all my computer time at work focused on business? I'll have you know that my Daily Sudoku, Daily Cipher Break, Mad Ciphers, and Cipher-Squad skills are also quite adept — in case we get attacked by mutant cipher-bearing zombies. Besides, who else do you know that can help out? Let me take a shot at it."

Max shrugged. "Okay."

"Okay?" Drummond said. "This is serious stuff. Not a fun, little game."

"Like she said, I don't know anybody to turn to for this, and I certainly can't do it. You?"

"No," Drummond mumbled.

"Then it's settled." Max started to stuff the notes back in the envelope when he saw a thicker page inside. He pulled out a torn black and white photograph of a young woman with striking eyes and full lips sitting in a summer dress under a tree with a weird branch like a burnt finger. It looked like a frame taken out of a movie. Mostly open fields around her and the blurry edge of a building in the distance. The setting made him think of the old-time romances with sweeping violins and passionate kisses that faded to black. But her hollow, lost, hopeless face told another story — one of tragedy and horror.

Max heard Drummond's breath catch. Turning around, he saw the ghost's focus locked on the photograph, dread covering his head like the stylish hat he wore.

"You know who this is?" Max asked.

"Looks like some girl." Drummond's tone had lost all emotion. His face colder, deader than normal.

"Who is this? Why does Dr. Ernest have her picture?"

Under his breath, Drummond said, "Son of a bitch." Then he vanished from the car.

Chapter 9

MAX SLEPT LITTLE THAT NIGHT. The high of pulling off a successful job, of knowing he had escaped jail, kept him up at first. But then his mind tumbled over black and white images of the woman in the photo. What had happened to her to cause those beautiful eyes to look so haunted? Why did Dr. Ernest include the picture in the coded file? And what about her spooked Drummond?

By the time Sandra woke, Max had already eaten a toasted bagel and granola cereal. She glanced at the cold pot of coffee and grunted.

"Sorry," he said, picking a raisin from his teeth. "The last thing I needed was caffeine. I'm still wide awake."

She shuffled over to the counter and poured the dregs into a mug. "You'll crash this afternoon." Placing the mug into the microwave, she added, "Are you excited about the case or are you thinking about that picture?"

"*Excited* is not the right word."

"Confused, then?"

"How about *terrified?*"

The microwave beeped and Sandra sat with her head over the steaming mug of day-old coffee. "That seems a bit much. We've handled stranger cases than this."

"Never one that involved Drummond lying like this or one in which he sees a photo and runs off."

"Maybe we should confront him. Ask him directly."

"How much more direct could I have been last night?"

Sandra placed a hand on her forehead. "Not so loud, hon. Coffee hasn't kicked in yet."

"When it does," he said, softer but no less urgent, "I need you to figure out that code."

"Last night, you guys doubted me completely, and now you think I can just figure it out instantly. Unbelievable."

"I'm not expecting miracles. That's the point. I need you to get started because it's going to take time, and something tells me we don't have a lot of that left."

"You're getting hunches now?"

Max shared a smile with her and kissed the top of her head. "Watch out or pretty soon I'll be a full-fledged detective. Hunches and everything."

"Don't worry. I'll put all my effort into that code."

"You'll do great. Do you want to work at the office, or are you going to stay home?"

She lifted her coffee cup. "No decisions, yet."

"Well, when you're fully caffeinated, let me know. I'm going to take a shower."

Within minutes, hot water cascaded down Max's body, soothing not only his weary muscles but also his weary mind. He knew better than to attempt to solve everything at once. One step at a time and all that. And the first step, after his shower, would be to question Drummond.

"Sorry about taking off last night," Drummond said.

Shouting, Max slipped and crashed to the bottom of the shower. The jolt on his rear sent painful vibrations straight up his spine. "Really? You can't wait until I'm out of the shower and dressed?"

He heard Sandra race up the stairs. "You okay in there?"

"Fine," Max called back. "Drummond surprised me, that's all."

"Drummond's in there?"

"I am, my dear," Drummond said, a hint of amusement in his voice.

After a short pause, Sandra went downstairs without another word. Max grabbed a towel, dried off, and stepped from the shower. He looked at Drummond and shook his head. The ghost hovered above the toilet, hunched over either in thought or with the urgent need to use the facilities.

"You know there's a toilet in the office?"

Drummond raised an eyebrow. "Cute. Now can we focus on the case? Has your better half cracked the code yet?"

"Of course not. She's only waking up, and it's going to take some time."

"Can't be that hard."

As Max dressed, he shot Drummond an incredulous smirk. "I dare you to say that to her face." He sat on the edge of the bed. He felt like a mountain climber pausing long enough to see the steep path ahead but knowing that if he stopped for too long, it would be twice as hard to get going again. "Tell me about the woman in the photo. Who is she? Why is she important?"

"She's not. Never was."

"Then you admit to knowing her."

Drummond's face tightened. He loomed over Max, his head brushing the ceiling, and a misty darkness flowed off his shoulders like fog made of shadows. "You listen to me," he said, his voice deepening to the point of vibrating Max's bones. "We're not going to pursue her. She's got nothing to do with this case. Do you understand? Nothing."

"Calm down. Don't get so excited." Sandra's warnings about evil-turning ghosts reverberated in Max's mind. "I understand. I do. Whoever the woman is, she's not important to our investigation."

"That's right." The dark mist drifted into the bathroom looking like more steam from the shower. "Let's stay focused on Dr. Ernest and the Hulls. Forget about the photograph."

"Good idea." Max watched as Drummond returned to his normal, ghostly self.

"Huh?" Drummond blinked fast as he looked around. "Sorry, pal. I think I dozed off. Didn't know I could still do that. I guess you're so boring that my old instincts kicked in. So, what's a good idea?"

It took Max a few seconds before he believed that Drummond had forgotten the last moments, but once he did, he decided to take advantage of that fact. "You, um, had the idea of going into the Other and seeing if you could find Dr.

Ernest. After all, he died quite recently. He might be lost and looking for some explanation."

"Yeah. I suppose so."

"It's a good idea. You go to the Other, find him, and tell him all about us. He'll be able to help discover his own murderer."

Drummond smacked his hands together. "That is a good idea. Glad I thought of it. Okay, I'm off for the Other."

"Good luck," Max said. Though he didn't expect Drummond to find anything useful — probably stumble upon some smalltime hood that picked the wrong day to go haunting houses — Max did hope Drummond's excursion would eat up most of his day. In the meantime, he hoped to give Sandra all the quiet she needed to work on the code. He would go back to the office, and —

His phone rang.

As Max picked it up, Drummond waved good-bye and disappeared. "Hello?" Max said.

"Please. Get here quick."

"Who is this?"

"She's coming for me. You've got to help."

"I think you've got the wrong number."

"Mr. Porter, please. This is Joshua Leed. If you don't get here soon, I think I'll be murdered like Dr. Ernest."

Chapter 10

MAX PUT ON HIS COAT and grabbed his keys. He avoided Sandra's glare. Hoping to sound reasonable, he said, "I need you working on that code."

She folded her arms and jutted out her chin. "You cannot go into this situation alone, and Drummond's out of the question for now."

"I won't be alone. Leed is there."

She raised an eyebrow which dismissed that entire argument. They went back and forth for five minutes until Max finally said he couldn't waste more time and rushed to the car. Sandra had a tough, stubborn streak in her, but Max knew she wouldn't jump in the car unclean and in her pajamas — not for this. But he also knew he'd pay for his actions later.

He wished he could have told her the truth. He wanted her to know that the FBI had been pressing on him, that Joshua Leed might be connected with a mess larger than they realized, that Drummond's secrecy might cause them more harm than he wanted to think about — but to tell her would be to bring her closer to the trouble he wanted to avoid. A part of him dug into his conscience, reminding him that they had learned to be open and honest with each other, that they had past experiences which proved hiding things never helped. But they had never dealt with the FBI before, never had to worry about charges and going to federal prison.

The drive to Leed's place did little to ease his mind. Often a drive would be a cleansing experience for his problems, but as he neared Thomasville, his focus shifted away from Sandra and on to Leed. He feared when he arrived that he would only find a body.

When his cell phone rang, he swerved onto the shoulder, the

rumble strips shivering the car until he got back in his lane. He glanced at the phone — his mother. He considered letting it go to voicemail, but he had been avoiding her calls too often lately. Another thing Drummond had taught him well — a detective can't put all of his life aside for a case. Do that, and he never has time to live.

"Hi, Mom."

"Maxwell. It's so good to hear your voice. You're a hard man to reach."

"Sorry about that. It's been kind of crazy lately."

"Oh? Is business good, then?"

"We're doing fine. Busy but fine."

"Well, you shouldn't be too busy for your family. That's important. When you forget family, you forget what makes you the person you are, and then where would you be? You listen to me. I may be old, but I'm not an idiot."

"I never said —"

"You kids think I'm a fool but I know what I'm talking about. The ones we love are the most important part of our lives, and you shouldn't take that for granted."

Max thought of Sandra. "I agree."

"You should. So, I want you to come visit me. You're always welcome and I haven't seen you in too long."

"I'll see when Sandra and I can work in a vacation."

"Oh, yes, you can bring Sandra along, too."

Max finished the call, a gentle smile finding its way onto his lips. He could already hear Sandra's reaction to both his mother's lack of including her and the idea of a "vacation" visiting his mother. She would laugh hard before spewing a rapid tirade caused by years of such slights. Then she'd laugh some more.

Before Max could put the cell phone down, it went off again. He glanced at its face and read: *Modesto.* "Damn," he said and answered the call.

Modesto sounded more impatient than usual. "I expected a report by now."

For a moment, Max forgot what he had been assigned to do

for the Hulls — Drummond, Leed, and a witch coven seemed more pressing. "Right, the handbell."

"You seem to be very relaxed regarding this research. Do I need to remind you of your current situation? Our employer is not fond of sluggards."

"I've done some preliminary research."

"We had hoped for more by now."

"You haven't given me much to go on."

Modesto could not hide the oozing triumph in his voice. "Why, I assumed a man as brilliant as you would have needed far less to start with. I'll inform our employer that you're the wrong man for our research needs."

Clenching the phone, Max said, "You go ahead and do that. Of course, you better be ready to explain why you failed to give me the necessary information to assist me. I mean, after all, that's part of your job, right? To assist me? And don't think for a second I won't contact Mr. Hull directly and let him know what a swell job you're doing. You do remember what happened the last time you screwed up for Mr. Hull, don't you?"

A long silence ensued. Finally, he heard Modesto's throat clear. "Finish your research soon. I'll expect a full report by —"

"Sounds good. Bye now." Max cut the call. Despite everything, he had to smile. "Sometimes it's the little victories that matter." He only hoped he would reach Leed in time for another victory.

Though he had seen Leed's house before, driving up to it in the daytime made it scarier. Like Norman Bates's home on the hill. Max kept expecting the silhouette of a strange woman to appear in one of the upper-windows.

As he stepped from the car, Joshua Leed opened the front door and waved Max in as if he were a soldier being urged to sprint across an open field. "Hurry!" Leed attempted to crouch low, but with his bad leg, he simply ducked his head and leaned heavier on his cane as he moved to the edge of the porch.

"Come on. I can't leave the door open."

Max jogged up to the porch, crouching a bit despite how silly he felt, and entered the house. Leed slammed the door shut, locked the deadbolt, and poured salt across the entranceway. When he faced Max, his sunken eyes and sweating cheeks shivered.

"Thank you for coming," Leed said. "I knew I could trust you. You didn't tell Drummond, did you? Not a word, right?"

"I didn't tell him anything."

"Thank goodness." With trembling hands, Leed limped to the kitchen. He looked thinner than before, frail and unkempt. "I need your help."

Max followed him. "Are you okay? You seem a bit —"

"You'd look the same if you were being hunted down by the dead."

"You mean the witch coven?"

"After I met you and your wife, I set out to destroy the witches I had cursed. I went to each site and I did what I had to. Something went wrong, though. I was never as good as Dr. Ernest at all this stuff. I don't know what I screwed up but things have only gotten worse. One's after me. She won't stop, either. Not until we're all dead."

"You didn't destroy both of them?"

"I did. That's the problem. I did exactly as Dr. Ernest prescribed, but still they come." He tried to pour a cup of coffee but spilled it on the counter.

"When was the last time you slept?"

Leed shook his head. "I won't sleep again. Not until we finish this."

"We?"

"I can't do this alone. I'm too old now. Besides, you and your wife are the only ones around here that know, that understand, what's going on. You've got to find out where Drummond's witches are buried. You've got to do this, but you can't let on that you know anything. Drummond's a ghost and this is personal to him. That's a highly emotional combination — all the ingredients for an evil conversion. But you get that information from him and we'll put a stop to this coven. Then, maybe I'll sleep."

Max sat at a little breakfast nook and scratched his head. "Look, I understand you're scared, and I believe that you and Dr. Ernest and Drummond all dealt with this witch coven way back when. But something doesn't quite fit. Drummond's behavior lately, for one. Something else, though. If you give me a little time to look into this more, then —"

A loud pounding erupted on the walls as if giants threw each other around the house. Max could see the drywall vibrate with each thud and dust sprinkled from the ceiling. A hundred horror movies flashed through his mind.

Leed cowered at the sound, gripping the edge of the sink to keep from falling over. He locked eyes with Max. With each successive thud against the walls, his face shifted to worse levels of terror.

"They killed Dr. Ernest. They're coming for me next. Oh, it's all our fault, all of it. We didn't know, didn't understand. You think you're doing right, fighting evil forces, saving the world around you, but it's never so simple."

Max put out his hand and noticed the tremor in his fingers. "Come. Let's get out of here."

"My soul is damned. I've used the same magic that they used. I did so against them, to save us, but I used it nonetheless. I'm damned."

Glass shattered upstairs and the pounding on the walls intensified. Max's heart pounded in time. He grabbed Leed's wrist but the frightened man found the strength to yank himself free.

"Whatever's doing this," Max said, "it doesn't have to take you. Come with me. We can solve this. Trust me."

Leed straightened and his face shifted from horror to acceptance. He shook his head slowly. "It's over for me. I'm too old, too tired."

The pounding ceased.

Max stood motionless, his skin still jangling with nerves. Leed opened a drawer and pulled out a photograph. He stared at it, and a tear fell down cheek. "I should've known all along that this was more than just a witch coven. Dr. Ernest always held back from telling me the truth. But I was young and foolish. And I wanted the adventure." He held out the photo to Max. "Here. Take this and —"

A screech like an animal being slaughtered erupted around them. An unseen hand flung Leed up against the wall. Pots clattered to the floor. Max winced at the sharp odor of sulfur.

He stepped forward to help but something jerked him backward. He tried to move again and was slammed against the breakfast nook wall. An enormous weight pressed into him as if a huge man leaned back against his chest.

Across the kitchen, he watched as the attack shoved Leed higher up the wall until his head touched the ceiling. Leed tried to speak, but his throat only made a clamped, gurgling sound. His face darkened and his eyes bulged.

Max strained to raise his arm, move his leg, anything, but he had been made immobile by this force. He found enough breath to scream out. "Leave him alone!"

Leed's face opened in surprise. "You did it," he said, staring at the emptiness in front of him. "You killed my parents."

Moaning laughter twisted around the screeching sounds. Max heard a sharp crack, and Leed's head lolled to one side. The weight holding Max lifted, and as he discovered he could move freely, Leed's body dropped to the floor.

Max rushed across the kitchen and checked Leed's body. No pulse. No breath.

Clenched in the man's hand, Max noticed the photograph he had pulled from the drawer. With his sweat soaking his shirt and his mouth bone dry, Max reached for the photograph. Not one to enjoy touching a dead body, especially a freshly dead body, Max tried to pull the photo free without making contact. It slipped out with ease. Maybe fresh dead had its advantages — no rigor mortis, for one.

The photo turned out to be a page torn from a book. The picture was black and white and depicted a large building ablaze, smoke pouring high into the air. A group of onlookers stood by and watched as if it were a grand show.

Max stuffed the picture in his pocket and hurried out of the house. As he drove away, his heart hammering blood into his head, he thought of that picture. What could have been so important about it? He saw Leed's head crack to the side and remembered the feel of the ghostly weight against his chest.

After a few minutes, Max pulled over. He rushed from his car and took a few steps towards the trees lining the road. He threw up.

Max took Exit 103 off Route 85 and parked at Denny's. About thirty minutes later, Sandra arrived, and they shared a booth built for six. Despite the booth's size and the lack of a crowd, Max felt closed in.

When he finished telling Sandra about what had happened, he whipped his head around the room. "She's not here is she?"

Sandra took a quick look. "Not a single ghost here."

"We've been through a lot, but this ... I've never been more scared in my life. I couldn't move. And even though I didn't see anything, I could feel it, smell it — her. Leed said it was one of the witches come to take revenge on him. He said we had to stop it. I think he's right."

"Calm down, honey."

"But she'll come after us. She can't go after Drummond, he's already dead. But if she wants to hurt him, she could come after us. He'd have to watch us die knowing it was his fault."

"This is the reason I should've been there."

Max pulled back. "You're going to give me an 'I told you so'? Really?"

"What I'm saying is that had I been there, I would have seen this ghost. We would know exactly who we're dealing with. I know you want to protect me, but surely we're far beyond that now. You know you need me. So stop holding back and let me be of use."

"Holding back?" Max tried to look surprised but she could always read him.

"I don't know what the big secret is, but you've been as bad as Drummond."

"It's not like that."

"It's exactly like that." She smiled to show him she wasn't angry, that she worried about him and wanted to help. "You know better than this. If we don't trust each other, then the whole thing falls apart."

Max sighed. He pulled out the photograph of the fire and slid it across the table. Sandra looked it over. "Well?" he said. "Leed died clutching that picture, it's got to mean something."

"There aren't any ghosts around it, if that's what you're looking for. And sometimes an object that gets handled by ghosts a lot will have a glow to it. This has nothing like that. It's just a picture."

Max looked over the picture again — massive mansion-sized house, smoke and fire obscuring most of the building, lots of people sitting far afield watching. They were dressed well. Very proper. Could be any time from the 1940s or before. Max never doubted that the picture held an important clue, but why did it have to be so difficult to find? If Joshua Leed wanted to show him something, why not draw a circle around it? Or write it down? Or for-crying-out-loud, just say it? Why wait until the evil spirit of a witch is killing you? Would it have been so difficult to trust a little before everything went to crap? And Drummond was no better. If he continued to hide the truth, the consequences might be as severe, if not worse, than what happened to Leed.

Sandra reached across the table and rubbed the wrinkled lines on Max's forehead. "You've got a frowny-thing going on there. What are you thinking about?"

"I'm sick of not having answers."

"Then go get some. How many times will I have to remind you that you have a skill beyond seeing a detective's ghost? You're an excellent researcher. Go do some research. Find some answers."

Chapter 11

THAT EVENING WHILE SANDRA SLEPT, Max sat at the kitchen table with a notebook, his laptop, and a lot of questions. He decided to focus on Dr. Ernest and Joshua Leed first. By following their path, he hoped to figure out where the other witches had been buried without resorting to a confrontation with Drummond — an unpleasant thing under normal conditions, but now one that might transform the ghost detective into an evil spirit.

Within a short period of time, Max had begun to build a solid picture of this duo. They had done little to cover their tracks (hence the FBI's interest), and Max's research skills had improved over the last few years. One thing became abundantly clear — Leed had lied about a lot.

For starters, Dr. Matthew Ernest never taught at any university. In fact, he never earned anything beyond a Bachelor's Degree. The "Doctor" in his name was a complete fabrication. That he and Joshua Leed became witch hunters appeared to be true. They spent a lot of time in online forums arguing the reality of witches and ghosts, trying to persuade any who would listen that a war existed just beneath the surface of our daily lives. If not for the fact that Max knew they were right — at least about the existence of these things — he would have dismissed their rantings as lunacy.

Unfortunately, the rest of their world view was at best misinformed and at worst, downright deadly. They were convinced that a grand war continually took place between mankind and the supernatural. Max agreed that the two didn't necessarily mix all that well, but a war? No. They thought communing with benevolent ghosts through physical contact would be advantageous. Max had suffered through the intense pain of that experience — not something he would call advantageous. They suggested that all ghosts wanted to move on to a better afterlife, and that their job was to help facilitate the journey. Sounded nice, but Max knew of at least one dead detective that had no interest in moving on anywhere.

By searching old newspaper articles, Max learned that Ernest and Leed spent as much time evading the police as they did hunting witches. Their names popped up in everything from big newspapers, like the Philadelphia Inquirer, to small county newspapers, like The Davidson Reporter. They were sought for questioning in at least a dozen missing person cases and several homicides. Max surmised that most of these interrogations went nowhere since the public police logs lacked arrests following the sessions.

In the 1950s, however, on three occasions, both Ernest and Leed were charged — once with kidnapping, twice with murder. In the case of the murders, whatever evidence the police had went up in flames, destroyed in a bizarre fire. With the kidnapping, the police had the girl in protective custody. She claimed that they lifted her from a grocery store parking lot, told her they knew she was a witch and that they planned to kill her. At some point during her captivity, they decided they had made a mistake and let her go, making her swear to never tell a soul. She swore as instructed, and then headed straight for the police.

"This is where you changed," Max said to the laptop screen.

He could picture them having a difficult conversation. Ernest insisted they use their skills with the dark arts to silence this girl. Leed objected — after all, why did they let her go in the first place if they would only kill her in the end? But Ernest pressed on, pointing out that they had made a mistake, a tragic mistake, that he didn't want to hurt this girl, but that she jeopardized all they had worked for, that if she were allowed to testify, they would go to jail for a long time, and then who would be looking out for mankind? Who would fight the witches?

Max could hear Leed's arguments weaken as well as his

resolve. He may have despised the decision, but Leed eventually agreed. They put a curse on the girl, and within a day, she had died from unknown causes.

While a lot of this story was supposition on Max's part, he had done this sort of thing enough to know when his imagination had struck close to the truth. This felt true. The newspaper articles, public police logs, and filed lawsuits that he could find supported his conclusion. And even if he missed the mark a little, it didn't change much.

The facts remained that Ernest and Leed had deluded themselves into attacking women, some of whom were actually witches. No doubt, the ones they tracked down to North Carolina were real. Drummond might have been a bit gullible at the time, but he wouldn't kill random people just on the word of these guys. Since Drummond participated in the curse, Max had to assume the story of a North Carolina coven held merit.

Unfortunately, while Max managed to put together a grim picture of Ernest and Leed — essentially two unintentional serial killers — he found little to link them up with the coven. Their history died when they reached Winston-Salem. Considering Leed's paranoia, Max guessed they purposely hid after dispatching the coven in order to protect themselves from retaliation.

Max thought about different avenues to research — more basics on witch covens, searching for acknowledged witches in Winston-Salem, looking up some of the symbols Ernest and Leed had drawn on their walls. As his bouncing ball screen saver kicked in, he realized none of this would help him much. He already knew most of the witch basics from his previous research and his own unfortunate experiences with Dr. Connor, the Hull's witch on retainer. Finding current witches in Winston-Salem might be interesting, but the coven in question had been destroyed decades ago. The best he could find would be a relative of one of the witches, and he doubted any relative would be very forthcoming in the matter. As for the symbols, he needed to look them up but his mind didn't want to focus on that at the moment. In fact, there was only one thing he kept thinking about — Marshall Drummond.

Max rested his fingers on the keyboard. "Okay, Drummond. You've got more answers than I do, and if you won't tell us, if all you're going to do is lie, then I'm not going to feel guilty about looking into you a little deeper."

He typed Drummond's name into the search field but hesitated. He craned his neck to peek toward the stairs. Listening for any sound of Sandra, he held still.

"Don't feel guilty," he finally said and tapped the Enter key.

After a few hours, he had to admit that much of Drummond's life remained an undigitized mystery. He found several newspaper reports of cases Drummond had worked on as well as records of his private investigator's license and such. Nothing too telling, though. Until he found reference to a book called *The Driving Darkness: One Psychiatrist's Look into the Roots of Mental Illness.*

The book made sure to change all the names of the patients as well as identifying features — sex, weight, hair color, eye color, etc. However, Max noticed that the author, Dr. Paul Clarkson, had worked at the West Carolina Insane Asylum at the time when he wrote the book. A while back, Drummond had confided that he once entered the care of that facility under his own volition.

Drummond had been a beat cop when he encountered a ghost who needed his help getting hidden money to a niece. Talking of the supernatural experience led to his removal from the police force and the start of his career as a private investigator. It also led to a mental breakdown.

An hour into reading the book, Max thought for sure he had found Drummond's case. The book had changed Drummond into a young, pretty girl named Daisy, but only that case matched the tone of Drummond's experience. Max, of course, knew he could be wrong, that he might be finding the outcome he wanted to find, but the other cases in the book either bore no sign of reality or bore signs of too much reality. They were people disturbed by abusive, tortuous childhoods or mystic delusions. Only the case of Daisy spoke of the reality Max had come to know. She had to be Drummond's case.

According to the book, Drummond's therapy session uncovered that the ghost he had encountered was not, in fact, his first touch with the supernatural. His mother, Eunice Drummond, had suffered periodic seizures her entire life. Her parents had taken her to several doctors, but no cause could be determined. When she left home, she stopped seeking out doctors. As she once told her son, "I had no need for them. I've always known what causes my seizures."

She then explained that she believed angels and demons would possess her body while she slept. Even if she nodded off for a quick nap, her soul opened to them. She had no way to prove it. Nothing beyond the seizures happened. But she promised her son that she knew this to be the case — because while in that state, she saw what they saw, she knew what they knew.

She refused to tell little Marshall Drummond the specifics. "If I told you half of it, you'd never sleep again."

Churches became prominent in their lives. She would take Marshall to a new church for weeks on end until she decided whether to move on to another church or to speak with the reverend or priest or whatever title that church used. When she spoke with the man, and it always was a man, he either thought she was evil or crazy. Then Marshall would be taken to a new church as Eunice kept searching for one that believed her.

"But don't think ill of them or their church," she told him on numerous occasions. "A church, the actual building, is like a living being itself. So, you respect those who worship there and you respect the building itself. Otherwise, bad things'll happen."

When Marshall was nine, they joined yet another church but something went wrong. Eunice thought they might have finally found people who understood her, and she excitedly went off late one night to meet the pastor at his home. She came back, bruised and disheveled, spewing hatred towards them and threatening to burn down their church. Marshall tried to remind her that churches were alive, and she struck him across the cheek.

Two months later, at Marshall's tenth birthday party, she suffered a seizure that would not stop. His father and the other adults did all they could, but she died. An autopsy showed that she had a massive tumor in her brain, one that had been growing for years. Marshall then understood that his mother had been imagining the possessions, that she could have been saved if she had seen the right doctor, and that all the stories she had told him concerning the supernatural world were nothing more than the hallucinations of a damaged brain.

But then he saw a ghost.

He learned such things were real.

Guilt plagued him.

The book went on to discuss how these events shaped "Daisy's" life, and as far as Max could tell, Dr. Clarkson was criminally incompetent. After only two months with "Daisy", he concluded that the patient would be served best by a heavy drug regiment and surgery on the brain. Thankfully for Drummond, Dr. Clarkson's consistently draconian prescriptions led to his dismissal from the asylum. Not surprising since Drummond had picked this particular institution for its forward-thinking attitudes towards its patients, an attitude Dr. Clarkson clearly did not share.

Max's cell phone vibrated on the table. He looked at the phone's face to see that somehow it had become seven in the morning and that his unwelcome friend, FBI Agent Stevenson, wanted to talk. "Hello?" he said, his voice scratchy and low.

"Open your front door," Stevenson said.

"Huh?"

"And bring a cup of coffee with you."

Max walked toward the front door. He saw the silhouette of a man standing outside. "For crying out loud," he muttered as he opened the door.

"No coffee?" Stevenson said.

Squinting at the morning light, Max leaned on the door frame. "What do you want?"

"Somebody broke into Matthew Ernest's home."

"Really?"

"Yup. Broke in, walked around, and left. Doesn't look like the person took anything. Guess they only wanted to have a look."

"You came here at seven in the morning to tell me this?"

"Thought you might be interested. Oh, and Joshua Leed was murdered last night." Stevenson paused, and Max could feel the man's eyes probing around, observing Max's reaction, comparing it to the reactions of guilty people. "You don't seem too surprised."

"Leed hired me because Ernest had been killed. He was convinced somebody wanted him dead, too. I've barely started looking into any of this and now he's dead. Looks like he was right."

"That's one possibility. But I don't find that possibility matches my facts too well. Of course, there's the other possibility."

Though Max really didn't want to hear the answer, he had to ask. "What's the other?"

"The other possibility is that you killed Joshua Leed, much like you killed Matthew Ernest."

Max hung his head. "I told you I never met Ernest. And Leed only just hired me."

"But you're the only one who can confirm that story. I'm telling you, Max, it's looking worse and worse. Especially because I don't like being lied to. People do it all the time to me. They lie about their alibis, lie about their involvement in crimes, lie about their guilt and their remorse. It's disheartening after a while. I'm going to tell you something that's not a lie, though. Federal prison — it ain't for you. I've seen plenty of guys go off to do time, and believe me, you won't be able to handle it."

"I won't have to, since I didn't do anything."

"Can I tell you a little secret? Some of us in the FBI, guys like me, we actually prefer the serial killers. Those guys, once their caught, they want to tell you everything. Much more pleasant way to do the job. Guys like you, with all the denials and the lies, it makes my day drag on and on."

"I did not kill anybody."

Stevenson clicked his tongue. "If you say so. I sure hope you're telling me the truth, though. Because when I find out I've been chasing my tail due to your lies, that will piss me off. That's when you'll find out how tough an FBI Agent can be." He lifted his head to see past Max's shoulder and smiled. "Good morning, Mrs. Porter. I hope I didn't wake you. Just having a friendly chat with your husband about federal prison. You have a nice day, now." With that, he walked back to his car and drove off.

Sandra waited until the car had gone. Her face had paled as she put together the bits of information she had. At length, she asked, "Is he serious?"

"The FBI thinks I killed both Dr. Ernest and Leed."

"The FBI? The real FBI?" She closed her eyes and covered her mouth. Unsure what her reaction meant, Max's skin prickled. He warmed when she looked up, determined and strong. "You are not going to jail for a ghost witch's crimes." She gave Max a tight hug. "What do you want to do?"

"I want you to figure out that code."

"I will."

"But first, I hope you know how to stop a ghost from turning because we're done being nice to Drummond."

There were numerous reasons Max loved Sandra. That she knew the perfect balance between when to challenge him and when to support him had to be near the top of that list. As they drove in to the office, she didn't pepper him with questions or doubts. Maybe she wanted to hear Drummond's answers as much as he did. Even so, her strength only propped him up higher.

When Max threw open the office door, he found Drummond waiting near the bookshelf. "You've been lying to us, and it's got to stop right now."

Drummond thrust his hands in his coat and shook his head. "Good morning to you, too."

"Don't even start with the sarcasm. Things are going out of

control real fast."

"What are you even talking about?" To Sandra, Drummond said, "Did you guys have a fight or something? Forget to give him his morning coffee?"

"Joshua Leed contacted me and told me all about the coven you guys destroyed way back when. I don't know why you've been lying about it, but the FBI thinks I'm the one who killed Leed and —"

"Leed's dead?"

"That's not the point."

"How? How did he die?" Drummond's eyes flared as he closed in on Max.

"I think it was the same way Dr. Ernest died, and I think you know more about it than I do. So, please, tell me what's going on before this evil ghost comes after me."

"Nothing will come after you. You weren't part of this."

"Didn't feel that way when I was pressed against a wall watching Leed be torn apart."

Drummond turned away and hid his face beneath his hand. "I'm sorry that happened to you. Believe me, I never thought you were in any danger. I never even thought you knew about Leed."

"Obviously."

Drummond rushed over to Sandra. "Have you been hurt in all this?"

"No," she said. "But if anything happens to Max, it'd be worse than if it happened to me. Worse for me, worse for you, and worse for every ghost I can get a hold of."

Drummond recoiled at the venom in her tone. His eye took on an odd, half-lidded look, and Max wondered if he had witnessed a ghost turning evil. But Sandra did not appear concerned, so Max decided to push on. He pulled out the photo of the girl under the tree and slammed it on the table.

"Time to start talking."

Drummond looked at the photograph and bowed his head. He traced the girl with his pale finger and opened his mouth to speak. That's when they heard a knock and the door opened.

Mr. Modesto entered. "I'm here for your report. Make it quick. I dislike spending time around you."

Max looked back to Drummond, but the ghost detective had vanished. "Damn," Max said.

"I take it by your eloquent rebuttal that you have failed in your task and have nothing of significant value to report." Modesto strolled up to the desk and glanced at the photograph. "What does this have to do with the handbell? Anything? Or are you still taking on other cases?"

"You haven't given me —"

"You've been kept on retainer by the Hull family for this very purpose and now you are shirking your responsibilities. Finding this handbell should be your top priority. Any other matter must be delayed or dismissed. Should you fail to find the handbell, your usefulness to this family will be gone. Do you understand? You'll be cut off from our employers support."

"Try not to drool when you say that."

Modesto's nostrils flared as if smelling an unseemly odor. "I admit I would be elated to see your departure from this family, and quite frankly, from this city. If you could manage to screw up enough that you were forced to flee the state or country, that would be ideal. But as it stands, we still need you. Our other researchers have also failed to find the bell."

"Other researchers?"

"Don't be so naive. Do you really think a man like Hull would rest such an important task in just one individual? And *you* for that matter?"

"That's it." The morning alone had been enough to boil Max's tolerance, but adding in the past few days melted away any chance he had at maintain control. Sandra stepped towards him but she saw his red-eyed rage and backed off. "Get the fuck out of my office."

"Excuse me?"

"You want to come in here over and over and threaten me? No. I won't have it. I don't care how much money Hull's throwing at us, and I don't care who he's got on his payroll. The fact is that we still have a copy of the Hull family journal, and while your employer has made it clear that there's a point where he won't care if we make his past public record, I don't think this little handbell comes anywhere close to that point."

Modesto's face turned cold as if a ghost had passed through him. "That would be a serious mistake to make."

"Oh, really? Because I've noticed that you've made a big show of pushing and pushing for this handbell yet you've done little in the way of actually helping us with information. You know how secretive the Hulls are, and yet you expect me to find this handbell on an old legend and nothing else. And now, you want to suggest that you've hired others to do the same. I don't believe any of it. In fact, part of me is wondering if Mr. Hull even knows you're doing this."

"Now you are being belligerent and, to a greater extent, plain stupid."

Max stepped straight at Modesto. "If I'm so wrong, then why are you still here? You've hated me for a long time. Surely I've said enough by now that you could go report this to Hull and have me sent the hell out of here."

Though a trickle of sweat slid down the side of Modesto's cheek, he never flinched. "I assure you, nothing would make me happier. Unfortunately, you have caught me in a bit of a lie."

"I knew it."

"There are no other researchers. That's it. The rest is true, and I have been ordered to tell you to make this the top priority. I suspect the only reason you're still here is because our employer feels no other researcher that could be acquired on short notice will accomplish what we expect of you."

Max did not expect that answer and it worried him. He thought he had pegged Modesto, but this looked to be more serious than he realized. What could be so important about a handbell that they couldn't hire somebody else?

Modesto walked to the door. "I do think I've been a tad unfair with you, however. I could have given you more information but purposely withheld in hopes that you would fail. Your outburst, however unprofessional and distasteful, impressed upon me that by trying to sabotage your efforts, I was inadvertently hurting our employer's efforts."

"I liked you better when Hull had fired you. Since you got re-hired, you talk like a bigger prick than ever."

The corner of Modesto's mouth rose. "The set of handbells were named the Bells of the Damned." With that said, Modesto made a slight bow toward Sandra and exited.

Max looked to Sandra, his mouth agape, his eyes wide. She laughed. "Guess you have some more research to do now."

Chapter 12

MAX STAKED OUT A TABLE at the Z. Smith Reynolds Library that allowed him a good view of those coming and going. The long hall that had an exit at the far end opened to a section with stairs on one side and the checkout desk on the other. All within Max's view. Though he knew he would have his face buried in books and his laptop, he wanted to be able to glance up from time to time and make sure neither the FBI nor a Hull representative watched him. Paranoid, yes, but he knew better than to doubt the value of a little paranoia.

As he set up his workspace, he thought about the best research approach. He already had all the basic information he needed. Normally, if he wanted to find out serious information regarding things that once were part of the Hull family, he would plan to sift through the numerous diaries, legal papers, and letters located in the special collections section. He would still have to do that laborious work, but first, he thought he should try his luck with another Internet search because this time, he had a name.

Searching The Bells of the Damned brought up thousands of hits — bad horror novels, forgotten metal songs, forgotten metal bands, and such. He followed links to several sites that claimed to have pictures or information for the Bells, but they depicted the wrong ones. However, all the sites he visited began their descriptions the same way — *These famously cursed bells ...*

This gave Max a glimmer of hope. A bell with a true curse on it would leave a trail. Of course, most "famously cursed" items were no more than superstitious tales, but considering the source of these bells — the Hull family — Max thought the likelihood that these bells bore a true curse rose significantly.

He checked out a few sites that specialized in hauntings, unexplained occurrences, and strange American legends. Though all of the stories lacked the name Hull, Max pieced together a possibly authentic version by picking out the references to North Carolina, the Moravians, and other bits of Winston-Salem history he knew. He then spent several hours verifying his guesses with primary source material from the special collections.

As best as he could figure out, the Bells first surfaced long before the merge of Winston and Salem, back when Tucker Hull had broken with the Moravians. His dabbling in magic had caused an irreparable rift that sent him away, but his obstinacy had kept him from leaving the city. Like any predator, Tucker lived on the edges of the herd, watching for any Moravians who felt marginalized, alone, and ignored. He would pick them up in a warm embrace and create servants to his beliefs.

"He started a cult," Max said to his laptop as he typed out his notes.

As numbers in his group increased, his explorations of magic deepened. He would task individuals with learning witchcraft while others spent days in meditation, attempting to open the mind into accepting, and thus seeing, ghosts. No form of the supernatural went untouched. He even had a few members look into some of the ancient Eastern religions, which to his mind seemed to embrace magic.

Living so close to the Moravians guaranteed trouble. The Aufseher Collegium, the section of the Moravian government set up to handle secular matters, forbade any members of their group to associate with Tucker Hull's "new" religion. But they were too late.

Max found a partial letter in the special collections dated 1832 from an unidentified woman to her lover T. It read:

> *I pray these reports will aid you in all your efforts. They must, otherwise I could not stand being kept apart from you. I cannot stop seeing you everywhere I look. My breath catches thinking of you and even as I write these*

> *words, my heart leaps to my breast. My dearest T, how much longer must I continue this charade. Father suspects I have a secret lover but he is too proud to confront me. As much as he is angry, he is too afraid to have it confirmed. And I would, too. If he asked, I would not lie. I would let the Elder's Council throw me out, exile me from all my family and friendships, for then I could be with you always. I want nothing more than to rest by your side, to be yours in every way you desire, to bear your children. My passions for you burn hotter every passing day. How much longer will you make me wait? Let me leave this lie and become yours. Let me study with you. I understand what the others do not. Let me write your Grimoire. Let me be your High Priestess.*

Like a twisted Romeo and Juliet, Tucker Hull had seduced a young Moravian woman and kept her amongst the Brotherhood for as long as he could manage. She was his spy.

Max shook his head. "No way could this end well."

Most of the other sources Max uncovered were not so direct, but diaries that on the surface appeared innocuous, actually held enough clues for Max to identify as members of Hulls growing cult. One in particular, the diary of Peter Cottonwall, mentioned a beautiful set of thirteen handbells which his leader, the beloved T, found joy in having his lady play. Apparently Tucker's Juliet played quite well and charmed many the few times she slipped away from the Brotherhood.

Tucker might have been planning to use his spy for many years, but she had other expectations. In another partial letter with the same handwriting, one that the library did not recognize belonged to the same author (but then, most libraries were so poorly funded that they may not have yet gotten to the letter for classification), she wrote:

> *Please do not be cross. To have both you and Father forsake me would be more than I dare consider. If not*

> *for Mother, I suspect I would be thrown from the house this very night. As it is, though, I have been given a fortnight and no more to make arrangements for my removal from the house and the Brotherhood.*

Whether this naive girl's father discovered the truth or she outright told him in a fit of defiance, Max could not tell. Regardless, the end result remained the same. She left her home and went to her lover's arms.

Except according to Cottonwall's diary, her arrival brought only trouble. She appeared unexpectedly (as far as Cottonwall knew) during a group meditation session, and Tucker would not embrace her. She had failed him, and he ordered her to leave. The scene that occurred involved plenty of crying, pleading, and begging but in the end, Tucker refused even to look at her. Cottonwall wrote:

> *The strangest sight of it all occurred next. For as I attempted to shut out this annoyance, per T's instructions, I could not but help myself and I snatched a glimpse of this once-prized witch who had now fallen from T's graces. T had his back to her and though she continued to say the words of begging for forgiveness, her eyes told a uniquely alternative story. She looked upon T with a fire that bespoke of the demons of old. An ancient, horrifying glare that has caused me no amount of a good night's rest since I laid eyes upon it. I fear what she has planned for T. I fear for all of us.*

The next few years progressed without incident, but Max felt confident that during that night of betrayal, this brokenhearted witch cursed the thing that Tucker loved about her most — the handbells. The name, the Bells of the Damned, cropped up later, once the bodies began to fall. And a lot of them fell.

On March 29, 1858, the body of a slave named Eli was discovered in a pond in Bethania, North Carolina. Suspicions fast turned to Eli's wife, Lucy Hine, a freewoman, and a slave named Frank. While searching Lucy's home, authorities discovered the floor still wet from being washed yet traces of blood were visible. Once the floor dried, a blood trail clearly led from the house to the pond. More blood was found on Frank's clothing. The two were convicted of the murder and, by 1859, executed.

But nobody ever could figure out the motive. Lucy and Frank denied being lovers. And Eli was not known for being abusive or in any manner cruel to his wife.

"Why he even bought her a beautiful set of handbells," one woman was quoted in a newspaper article.

In November 1873, according to a report in the *People's Press,* Sarah Tilkey attended her regular music class at Salem Female Academy. The Academy for girls had been founded by the Moravians in 1772, a unique step in the South, and had built a solid reputation for excellence. In fact, girls from all over the country sought a position at the school.

While practicing her music, young Sarah sat close to one of the stoves. It had been a particularly cold winter, so she may have sat closer than normal. That was when an ember popped and landed on her dress.

As she dashed through the school screaming, flames engulfed her body. Physicians rushed to the school, but the burns were too extensive. After a few prayers were read for her, she passed away.

While Max could not learn what instrument she played, he did know that the Bells had been donated to the school two years earlier by the family of Thomas Lash — owner of the murdered slave, Eli.

There were other cases that might have been attributable to the Bells, but Max could not find the primary sources to confirm. For his own purposes, he considered them valid cases because it let him continue to follow the trail of bodies. This included a few suspicious deaths at the Salem Hotel, a double murder, and a lynching.

Then came the case of Ellen Smith. There was a relatively

enormous amount of information available about the case since it made headlines in almost every local and surrounding paper. Even the *Union Republican,* one of the larger presses, wrote numerous articles throughout the years following the case.

In the early 1890s, Ellen Smith had been employed as a maid. She was a poor, portly girl who worked diligently but was considered to be "an idiot" — a term which Max knew back then meant she had some form of mental disability. Most people liked her and thought of her as a good worker. She was fifteen.

Then she met Peter DeGraff, a good-looking ladies' man, slim and fit, smooth tongued, and a bit unpredictable. He met Ellen in January 1890 and began courting her soon after. He was twenty-one.

DeGraff showered Ellen with trips to buy clothes, visits to the local barrooms, and plenty of food. The money, the handsome man, and the attention stole her heart. She became madly in love with him. She also became pregnant.

Unmarried and expecting, she was sent to live and work for a man named Captain Stagg. Max could not find any more about this man, but he did discover another Union Republican article (this one from 1894 looking back at the case) in which the reporter stated that though Ellen Smith delivered her child, it was either stillborn or died within days of birth. Shortly after, Ellen returned to Winston and looked up her lover, Peter. But DeGraff wanted nothing to do with her.

Ellen began stalking DeGraff, and his refusals intensified. On several occasions, people overheard him threatening to kill her. But then suddenly, he behaved nicely to her and sent her a note. The note professed his love for her and asked that she meet him on an upcoming evening by the spring at the new Zinzendorf Hotel.

Built in Winston's West End, the Hotel had been the brainchild of R. J. Reynolds and other community leaders. It was an enormous structure, reminding Max of a Disney castle made of wood. As a gift to the Hotel, an anonymous source donated a beautiful set of thirteen handbells — white with a red stripe and curious markings on the inside lip. They were prominently displayed in the lobby entrance. It was hoped this resort hotel would help make Winston a business and vacation center for the region.

That night in 1892, however, the hopes were in Ellen's heart. She wore a dark calico skirt and a light-colored blouse, and she bought a new, yellow handkerchief, perhaps as a gift. She then headed off to the Hotel.

The following morning, a hotel employee came upon a gruesome scene. As reported in the *Union Republican*: "A white apron was found hanging upon a bush near the body, which was that of Ellen Smith, which was lying face downward, bloody, and the body swollen and disfigured and a prey to flies."

"The old journalists sure could paint a picture," Max said.

What followed went beyond the scope of Max's research but in the end, after much drama and several years, Peter DeGraff was convicted of the murder and hanged. This unfortunate and ghastly murder became one of the biggest stories and trials in all of Winston-Salem history. For Max, however, the most astonishing aspect to the tale came when he learned of the ill-fated hotel.

On Thanksgiving Day 1892, the same year as the Smith murder, a fire broke out in the wooden hotel. It spread fast, and in no time became uncontrollable. Guests and staff rushed to safety in the distance, bringing with them whatever possessions they could manage. A photographer took advantage of the tragedy and made a picture of the event.

Max's heart stopped as he stared at the familiar photo. The massive building awash in flames and smoke while a crowd of onlookers gawked from their chairs and boxes. It was the same photograph Joshua Leed had died trying to give him.

Max picked up the picture and stared at it. There had to be something more to see than just the fact that the hotel had a connection to the Bells of the Damned. Leed could have told him that much. Instead, the man risked and lost his life for the photo.

"What am I supposed to see?"

Using the magnifier on his smartphone, Max searched the image starting in the top left corner and working his way methodically across and down. There were strange images within the thick smoke pouring out of the hotel, but Max thought that might only be his imagination seeing things much like recognizing objects in the shapes of clouds. Whatever Leed wanted him to see had to be more substantial than that.

When he reached the crowds, he found that most of the people had their backs to the camera. A young child stared at the camera, the body blurred a bit but the eyes glowing bright. Was this it? Max couldn't be sure. The figure had a definite supernatural feel to it, but calling it as such made Max feel like he had found Big Foot in a shadow on blurry film.

Then he saw it, and he knew right away Leed had wanted to show him this. He knew it from the way his hands tingled and the way he had to remember to breathe. Sitting behind the blurred figure, clear as the fire itself, Max spotted a young woman, her profile showing enough detail that he knew the face. Without a doubt, he looked upon the same woman as in the photo Dr. Ernest had saved. The same photo Drummond hid from. Strangest of all, the woman in Ernest's photo was no older than the woman at the Zinzendorf Hotel fire — but they were taken almost fifty years apart.

Chapter 13

WHEN MAX ENTERED HIS OFFICE, he found Sandra on her computer working on the code and Drummond floating around the ceiling humming the theme to the '80s television show Mike Hammer. The old ghost had tightened his face like a child throwing a tantrum. When he saw Max, he swooped down.

"It's not that great a life being a ghost, and your wife is making it worse."

Sandra ignored the commotion, so Max headed to his desk.

Drummond grabbed his hat and threw it on the ground, but it vanished and reappeared upon his head. "You know, you ought to be nicer to me. I do nothing but help you."

Max snapped his eyes upon Drummond, silencing the ghost. "Sandra." She didn't answer. Louder, Max called again. "Sandra!"

She jumped and whirled around, her eyes wide with fear. When she saw her husband, she relaxed and pulled her mp3 player's buds out of her ears. Despite his anger at Drummond, Max had to laugh.

"What's going on?" she asked.

Drummond wagged his finger at them both. "Some days, you two are in cahoots against me. It's not fair. I had to spend decades alone here and now that I've got some company, you guys keep trying to shut me out."

This brought Max right back to the problem. "You're the one shutting us out. You've been lying to us ever since you saw that article about Dr. Ernest's murder."

"You better watch it with the accusations."

Max opened his notebook and slapped down the photograph of the Zinzendorf Hotel fire.

"You're getting good at that," Drummond said.

"I'm not in a joking mood."

"Fine, fine. What's the big deal. It's a photo of the big Zinzendorf fire. Pretty famous photo, locally. Not exactly that big of a find."

Max pulled out his smartphone and brought up the snapshot he took of the magnified portion. "Look familiar?"

Drummond's sarcastic expression dropped away. His chin quivered a moment before he locked up his jaw in a tight clench. Narrowing his eyes, he flew to the back corner of the office.

"Come on," Max said. "I'm not an idiot. You've lied to us repeatedly, afraid we would find out about this woman. We've got murders and witch covens and these cursed handbells, and I know you have information for us."

"The handbells are cursed?"

"They're called the Bells of the Damned, and I'm pretty sure they had something to do with this fire as well as quite a lot of deaths for more than a century."

"They're cursed."

"That's right. I want to know how that's connected to your girl here."

With a bewildered gaze, Drummond looked across the room to Max. "And that's really her? Sitting there, watching the fire in 1892?"

"I think so."

"Then I was wrong." Drummond lowered his head and shuddered. Max swore Drummond sounded relieved. A moment later, the ghost returned to the desk, sniffling and dabbing at his eyes. "I'm truly sorry that I caused the two of you trouble and worry and all. I didn't know I was wrong all this time. I thought ..."

Mimicking her husband's usual behavior, Sandra leaned back in her chair and kicked her feet up to the desk. "Care to explain what you're rambling on about?"

Max tried to maintain a serious face, but he knew Sandra had the right idea. Something had changed, had eased, in the room. He sat at his desk. "Please. Tell us what's going on. Maybe we can help."

Drummond looked from Sandra to Max. "If anybody can help now, it'd be you two. Before I say anything, though, I ask one favor. Meet me out at Tanglewood Park. I'd rather not talk of this here where I've spent so many years cursed. I'd rather be where this all began."

"Of course," Sandra said. "It's the least we could do."

Tanglewood Park contained sprawling acres upon acres of wooded trails, a pool, homes from the 1700s, stables, tennis courts, an arboretum, and even an old locomotive engine. Families loved the place as did wedding and event planners. It also sat far west of the city which meant Max and Sandra had plenty of time in the car.

"Of course?" Max said. "Why would you agree to go all the way out here? We don't have time for this. You should be working on that code."

"Honey, sometimes you've got to give a ghost a little slack. Clearly there's something emotional involved with this woman. You could see how choked up he got. Letting him tell it his own way will make it easier on him."

"I don't care if it's easy for him. He lied to us."

"All the more reason to go to the place that is connected to this strong emotion. He'll be so consumed with the memory, he won't realize how much he's telling us."

"Wait, wait. This is going to be a *strong emotion* for him? Isn't that what we're trying to avoid? Y'know, so he doesn't go evil on us."

Sandra shrugged. "I made a tough call."

"Are you crazy?"

"We need to know what he knows. At this point, I think it's worth the risk. What else are we going to do? Sit around and wait to be murdered like Ernest and Leed?"

Max had nothing else to say. She was right, as usual, and he figured he would be better off planning ahead rather than arguing a moot point. Except that his brain had no plan in mind. He drove in a blank daze, trying to make sense of the numerous bits of information he juggled, but made no progress.

When they reached the park and paid the two dollar fee at the gatehouse, they headed slowly along the narrow drive until they passed the stables. A twelve-year-old girl rode her palomino inside a fenced paddock filled with jumps for her to practice on. Two women, Max guessed her mother and a trainer, watched with tense excitement. As they receded in the rearview mirror, Max marveled at how much he had learned to read off of people's body language.

"Over there," Sandra said, pointing to the open field on the left. They parked and walked over to where Drummond floated, staring at a tree.

"I think she knew," Drummond said as they approached. "I don't know how, but she had to have known that the witch hunters were coming and that they would contact me for local help."

"Who was she?" Max asked.

"Her name was Patricia Welling. I was out here for a friend's wedding, but you know me, I don't like that kind of thing. So, I went for a stroll and wound up around here. I looked over and saw this exquisite woman by this tree. She wore a blue gown and we shared a cigarette. I never asked her what she was doing out there. I assumed she was there for the wedding, too, since she dressed so fancy. Well, we talked and laughed and while I'm not one to share this kind of thing, you should know that we kissed, too. In fact, we began to see each other most every night."

Max looked at the tree so he didn't have to meet Drummond's eye. "When you say that you saw each other, do you mean ..."

"Okay, yes. We were like rabbits. You really don't believe in subtlety, do you?"

"Just trying to be clear."

"I know how this sounds, but the truth is that we had fallen in love. Even looking back at it all, knowing that she had arranged the relationship, I know she loved me. She probably had not intended to fall for me, but it happened."

Sandra laced her fingers between Max's. "Is that when Dr. Ernest showed up?"

"We had two incredible weeks together. The kind of time that changes a man, makes him think about packing it in, giving up a dangerous life, settling down, maybe even some kids. I even turned away cases so I could spend more time with her. For those two weeks, I swear I thought nothing could change. Then I walked into my office one morning and there's this professor from up North with his tales of witch covens and special rituals. He came with two names to follow up on. Jane Bitter and Patricia. I sent him and Leed after Bitter. I figured they'd come up with more information from her and I could avoid having to approach Patricia about any of it. Except right then, I don't know if I recognized it at the time but I know it now, that was the moment a darkness began to form inside me."

"You poor thing," Sandra said.

"Turned out Jane was the real deal. A full witch and part of the coven he and Leed had been hunting down. They destroyed her that night but not before getting her to confess a list of six more members. Right away I saw that Patricia was on the list. We each took two names, and since I had supposedly made contact with Patricia already, they let me have her name. We agreed on a night for the job to be done, and I had two days to figure out if she was really a witch or if Jane Bitter had lied."

As Drummond spoke, Max watched him carefully while trying not to be obvious. Sandra appeared to be lost in the romantic nature of the story which worried Max even more. As his resident ghost expert, he needed her to be looking for any sign that Drummond's story might be turning him.

"The evidence Matt had compiled in a file gave me little to help. In fact, the two days passed quickly, and I still had no idea what to believe." Drummond's fingers curled into fists.

Max said, "This is a painful memory. Why don't we take a

break, let us process everything you've said, and then we'll come back —"

"No." Drummond barked. "I've got to get this out."

Sandra looked to Max, lines of worry creasing her forehead.

"The night came and I had decided to deal with the other witch first. I guess I wanted to avoid the whole thing as long as possible, as if maybe some savior would come in and make that horrible night disappear. I went to the home of Joanna Lee. She lived in a small house on First Street, and I remember thinking that I'd have to be careful about the neighbors hearing anything."

With a sour chuckle, Drummond moved across the field toward the car. Max wanted to be hopeful that this meant Drummond had calmed down, but the ghosts stern expression left little room for such hopes.

"I walked in there, and she had been waiting. She attacked me with a carving knife. I don't like hurting women, but in this case, I had no choice. She would've sliced me up, if I had let her. So I fought back, and despite her yelling some foul things, her biting and random kicking, I managed to subdue her long enough to tie up her feet and get her hands behind her back. Then I had to do the cursing ritual.

"I drew a circle around her with salt and a pulled out an ivory knife that Matt had given me. With it, I had to carve three symbols into her back, deep enough to hit bone. She screamed as I did this, tears soaking the floor. She wanted to wriggle away but the cuts were so deep that movement only caused her more and more pain. And I suspect that she held on to the hope that whatever curse I inflicted on her did not involve her death. But she was wrong. When I finished the last symbol, I grabbed her hair and pulled back her head, and with that ivory knife, I slit her throat."

They had reached the car, and Max opened the back door for Drummond. "I'm sorry you had to go through that."

"It got worse. She didn't die. She bled and sputtered, but she didn't die. She wrenched her head around to see me, and I've never seen such a tormented face. Blood pouring out of her neck, down her chest, and her eyes blazing at me in pain and hatred. I didn't know why she was still alive, and I had no clue what to do. This was long before cellphones. I had no way to contact anybody quickly. At least, nobody I wanted to contact. With all the noise we had made and that she continued to make, I figured the police would be showing up any second." Drummond glanced at Max. "Close that damn door. I'm not a fragile little thing you need to escort around."

Max closed the door and tried not to show his fear.

"Sorry," Drummond said, but he maintained his intense expression. "Please, let me finish this." He looked back the way they had come. "Blood poured out of her, more than I ever thought a body could hold, but it pooled inside the circle. No matter how saturated the salt became, that curse kept all of her contained. And then I saw it. The middle symbol, the one that cut deepest into her spine, I had missed putting in two lines. I shoved her over and tried to correct the mistake, but she fought back hard. It was all that much harder because I had to make sure not to disturb the salt. I managed to get through it, though, and the second I finished the symbol, she dropped dead. I followed the rest of Matt's instructions, burying the body, covering it with salt, and a page with more symbols that Matt had written for me.

"I spent an hour walking the downtown area — drinking. I'd seen some strange things before that, but nothing so horrifying. I really didn't know if I could do it again, much less to Patricia. After awhile, I ended up at her doorstep. I don't recall what we said, but I think she knew why I had come. She also knew she could change my mind with a kiss. That kiss — that's when I knew without a doubt that she loved me.

"We spent the night together. The most passionate night of my life. Everything we had become together poured out of us, pooled around us, in a desperate, tragic embrace. But then the morning came, and I could only think one thing — the only reason she could possibly have known of the coming tragedy between us was if she had been a witch all along. Otherwise, she would be asking me why I was so intense. What was wrong? Anything like that. But she hadn't. She knew exactly what was wrong because her coven sisters had died that night.

"Knowing that she was a witch didn't make it any easier. But it did strengthen my resolve, because if I didn't finish the job, the otherworldly revenge would be ghastly. See, we weren't just killing them. That's what we should have done. But Matt and Leed convinced me that cursing them would be better. Maybe that's why the universe saw fit to curse me later." Drummond pointed to the car door. "Just because I'm a ghost doesn't mean you can't be polite. Open the door."

Max frowned but a warning look from Sandra kept him quiet. He opened the door for Drummond and then got behind the wheel. "Back to the office?"

"Not yet. I haven't finished the story."

"Then where?"

"Get on 40 East. Back into the city."

As Max drove, Drummond continued his tale. He spoke with such vivid detail, Max had no trouble picturing the scene. Drummond stayed in bed as the morning sun broke through the drab curtains. He listened to Patricia taking a shower as his thoughts tumbled over each other. There had to be a way out of this — some loophole that would both destroy the coven yet somehow let Patricia remain alive and his.

He slid out of bed and into his clothes. The ivory knife weighed heavy in his coat pocket. Magic. Why did people mess with it? In all his time spent dealing with the supernatural, he had yet to find anybody who had benefited from using magic. Then again, there was one way he could stay with Patricia — join her. Leave this world of violence and sadness and join the coven, learn the dark arts, become a husband far beyond anything she could have expected.

"I was seriously tempted," he said before pointing toward an exit. "Take Peters Creek Parkway up into the city. Stay on it for a bit."

Max followed the directions even as Drummond dropped back into the heart of his story. He had been standing in Patricia's bedroom, not moving, just thinking. He wanted nothing more than to throw off his clothes, rush into that shower with her, and forget the world. And why shouldn't he? Because he thought she might have been expecting him? Because she might be this witch? It didn't make sense. He had followed Ernest and Leed blindly and now he contemplated a torturous death for the woman he loved.

He reached up to his shirt and began unbuttoning. She deserved better from him than what he had given. That kiss had said it all.

The bathroom door opened. Patricia stood in the doorway wearing nothing at all, one arm stretched along the frame, the other behind her back.. She smiled at him and his heart skipped. From behind her back, she pulled out the ivory knife and her smile fell.

Drummond's hand reached into his coat pocket — a flashlight. She had switched them at some point. He looked up at her. "It's true, then?"

"Don't do this to me," she said, her voice soothing and at odds with the tension in her grip. "Whatever you think I am, I'm not."

"Then how do you know what I'm going to do?"

"Because I love you, and when you love someone, you take an interest in what they do. I know the kind of cases you specialize in. A weapon like this — it can't have any good purpose. You've been hiding it since last night. First time you ever refused to let me take your coat."

"You're only protecting yourself, then? Is that it?"

Her throat quivered as she stepped closer to him. Her beautiful body swayed like a snake hypnotizing its prey. He only had to tell her that he didn't care. Give over to her and he could live happily ever after. A fairy tale washed in dark magic.

But as she took her final step, she turned the blade towards him. Drummond reacted to the threat with muscle memory. He deflected her thrust, grabbed the wrist of the knife hand, and redirected the blade into her soft belly.

"A witch after all," he muttered.

She fell over, blood staining the ivory, her breathing the only sound. Though tears blurred his vision, Drummond hurried through the ceremony. His heart broke with each step. He circled her in salt, pulled out the blade, and carved the intricate symbols into her back. Her shock had shut down her reactions. Like an abused wife, she simply took the punishment. It was a small mercy to him, it let him finish the job without pause, but his heart wept with every cut. When he finished the last symbol, he thought he might be able to get through the whole thing. Until he pulled back her head to slit her throat.

Her eyes shot open, and she peered back at him. "Please, don't do this. I'm no witch. I'll forgive you for all of this. Please, don't kill me."

Sandra wiped the tears in her eyes. "What did you do?"

Drummond told Max to pull over. "I killed her. I hated myself for it, but I had to do it. I couldn't be sure what was true, and if I let her go, nothing good could happen. If she was a witch, she would go on and the failed curse would destroy us. If she wasn't, she would go to the police and we'd never have a chance to shut down the coven. Matt and Leed did their best to convince me we had done right. They even stayed around for two months to check up on every lead they could find, to make sure no other witches in the coven could be found. Their assurances plus the fact that no revenge was exacted upon us, led us to the conclusion that we had succeeded.

"But I didn't believe it. I couldn't have been so wrong about her. So, I've spent all these years since wondering, knowing, I had killed an innocent woman. Except when you showed me that picture of her at the fire — only a powerful witch with access to the magic a coven created could have pulled off the kind of spell that'd let you live so long."

Max reached over and patted through Drummond's hand. The act caused an icy chill to cover Max's body, but Drummond clearly appreciated the gesture. Then Max's eyes widened. "Wait a second. Since she really was a witch, we have to destroy her body like Leed said. Otherwise, we'll be attacked, too. Right?"

"About that." Drummond tilted his hat and sat back in the

car. "See, after I finished with — after I finished, I had a big problem. Since I had waited until morning to do it, I couldn't easily dispose of her body. Not in broad daylight. So, I wrapped her in the carpet and went back for my car. I stuffed her in the trunk and drove her to the office."

"Are you saying she's in the office?"

"She was. But then some people decided to renovate the Zinzendorf Hotel."

"You mean *rebuild*. Not much left to renovate."

"No, they rebuilt it shortly after the big fire. But in my lifetime, they decided to renovate it, and when the time came, I broke in one night and slipped the body into the walls."

Max clapped his hands once. "Great. Let's go get her."

"Here's our problem."

Max sighed, and Sandra shook her head. "You really thought it would be easy?"

"In 1970, I was a cursed ghost stuck to the office. A squatter had taken up residence — Hal. Real pain in the neck. He had a buddy, Dale, who would stop by to smoke pot from time to time. One day, I'm listening to them talk —"

"You little eavesdropper."

"You try being imprisoned to that office. I took whatever entertainment I could get. Anyway, these fellas are talking and Dale mentions that the Zinzendorf Hotel was going out of business. They were going to raze the whole thing. I had maybe a month before things went sour with the coven's curse. So, I started haunting Hal. He had moved enough furniture around, disrupting the full curse on me, that I could make my presence known. Luckily, Hal had a keen fear of the supernatural. I convinced him I was the ghost of Patricia and that he had to move my body or else I'd plague him forever."

"So where is she now?"

"He found her the night before they tore down her floor. He brought what was left back to the office. I then had him wait until they poured the foundation for the new building and then when the time was right, Hal put her in the mix." Drummond nodded out the window. "That building across the street is where the hotel used to be. She's in the foundation."

Max's hope deflated as he looked across the street. The Federal Building. Well, that's what the locals called it. Really, it was the US District Court — courtrooms and holding cells, bursars and chambers, lawyers and police. "You gotta be kidding me."

Chapter 14

MAX DROVE UP TO Fourth Street and headed for the office. Double parking in front of the building, he faced Sandra. "I need that code finished."

"I will. I'm close, I think. You're not really going to break into the Federal Building, are you?"

"I have no idea what I'm going to do."

She gritted her teeth into a ridiculous smile. "Well, at least you know where you stand."

Max couldn't help himself. He laughed hard as she walked toward the office. "I love you," he shouted after her. In response, she put an extra sway to her hips.

Once Max pulled back into traffic, Drummond slid through the car into the passenger seat. "So what are we going to do?"

"I really don't know overall. Right now, though, you and I are going back to Tanglewood Park. We've got some unfinished business out there."

Drummond tried to pry out a clue as to what Max had in mind, but Max focused on driving. He took it as a good sign when Drummond settled back, tipping his hat over his eyes. Max didn't think ghosts actually slept, but he couldn't be sure.

When they finally reached the park, Max drove out to the open field where Drummond had taken them earlier. He trudged out to the tree and stared at it.

"You came all the way out here to see this tree again?"

Max turned in a circle, his eyes searching all around. "You've taught me a lot about being a detective. I really appreciate that."

"What does that have to do with being here?"

"One thing that's really stuck with me is the importance of having a partner you can trust. Until this whole thing started, I believed I could trust you."

"You know you can trust me."

"Except I'm learning how little I know about you, and then there's the fact that you've been lying to us for quite awhile."

"You lied, too. Pretended not to know Leed or Matt."

"I was wrong to do that. That's why we're here. We need to make things right before we go any further. This whole thing is giving me that same feeling I've had before — that we're headed down a dark path. I don't think we can do that and survive, if we don't trust each other."

Drummond thrust his hands in his coat pocket and tucked his chin down. "I got that feeling, too."

"Wrong angle," Max muttered and walked several feet beyond the tree, turned around and nodded with satisfaction. "There."

"What?"

"From this angle, it's clear that this tree is the one in the picture. There's the weird branch and in the distance is the stables."

"What picture?"

"You know what picture. The gal under the tree. It was taken right here. Am I wrong to think that she was Patricia? And that you took the picture?"

Drummond chuckled. "You really are getting good at this."

"What I don't understand is why you buried her in that hotel when it made more sense for you to bring her out here. The way you brought us out, the way you look at that tree, the fact that you took the picture — if you felt so strongly about her, and I believe that you did, then why dump her in some anonymous way?"

"I didn't want to." Drummond stared at the tree as if he could see her still. "My original plan was to bring her here in the middle of the night. But time was against me. It was important for the curse that she die near the same time the others did. At least, I thought it was. I failed that by waiting until morning."

"And if you wanted to bury her by this tree, you'd have to

wait until late that next night."

"Exactly. I couldn't wait that long. No way would the curse be effective."

"Okay." Max headed back to the car. "I appreciate your honesty. Now, it's my turn. I have to tell you something, and it may be difficult to hear but you must stay calm."

Drummond floated next to Max. "I'll try. No promises, though."

"Do you know anything about ghosts turning?"

"What does that mean?"

Leaning against the car, Max explained what little he knew on the subject. "That's the main reason we lied to you. We didn't want to upset you."

Drummond pursed his lips. "But I've been upset plenty of times. Heck, every other day with you is upsetting."

"This isn't an everyday kind of case. This involves Patricia." Max gestured toward the tree. "You're already going into this with intense emotions. Add to that the things we've been encountering, that I fear we're going to encounter, and well —"

"You guys thought I'd pop."

"Something like that."

Rubbing his hands together, Drummond said, "Guess I've got to avoid getting too upset. Keep control of my emotions. Right? I can do that. I'm not saying I'll be perfect, but I can do it."

"Good. Because things aren't adding up right."

Drummond rubbed his hands faster. "Now we're talking. You're getting a gut feeling. What about? What's not right?"

"Well, Dr. Ernest and Leed left after that night cursing the witches, right?"

"Yeah."

"At some point, years later, they both come back. Presumably, they didn't bother looking you up because they already knew you were dead. Though, considering their interests, you'd think they would have found out you'd been cursed."

"Maybe they did know. Maybe that's why they came back."

"Then why didn't they ever try to help you? No, they didn't know about you. Which brings me to the question: Why did they come back? It wasn't to retire here. One of them settling down here, maybe I could believe it — retiring but still wanting to keep an eye on the coven that stuck with him. But both of them? No. They came down here with an agenda."

Drummond straightened as his face dropped in astonishment. "Patricia. This is about her."

"How so?"

"They both had pictures of her. The Zinzendorf fire and the one I took. But they already knew she was a witch, so why would the pictures matter?"

An uneasy shiver raced along Max's back. "That's a good question." The silence that settled between them broke only when Max's phone rang. He looked at the caller's name and knew right away what had happened. "Sandra's broken the code."

Chapter 15

"IT WASN'T THAT COMPLICATED, really. Just a substitution code but with a little math thrown in to find the right letter. I should've realized earlier but I started out looking for more difficult methods."

Max kissed Sandra. "I had no idea you were so good at this."

"Well, I had to do some research. It's not like I'm a code-breaking savant. I just like doing puzzles."

"That last part, I knew."

Drummond waved his hand over Dr. Ernest's papers. "Can we dispense with the back-slapping and get on to the actual meaning of all this?"

"Right." Sandra broke from Max's embrace. "Apparently, Dr. Ernest cursed one witch while you and Leed did two. But his was the High Priestess of the coven."

"Why did he lie to us about that?"

"The way he writes, I think he lied about most things. His name wasn't even Matthew Ernest. His real name — Tom Ratzenberg. He seems pretty paranoid in here, so perhaps the lies were an attempt to send witches off on a false trail."

"How do you know any of that's true then?"

"We don't. But he places the High Priestess in a church and that sounds like the kind of place one would bury a cursed witch. Don't you think?"

Max picked up his keys. "Only one way to find out. Thanks for all your hard work, hon. I'll call you the minute we find out anything."

"Ah, no." Sandra put her hands on her hips, and her mouth shrunk into a tight circle.

"What's wrong?"

"You are not leaving me behind. I'm not some fragile little girl you've got to sideline every time you have to go out."

Max attempted a warm smile, but he saw the way she grew angrier, so he cut it out. "I'm not trying to sideline you. I only meant —"

"I know exactly what you meant. And I'm telling you that I'm coming along. Besides, how many times have I been an essential help to you? With you only seeing Drummond, you never know when you'll need my talents."

"That's the problem. I don't like putting the woman I love in danger all the time."

"Well, when you stop playing hero and realize that I'm the one who knows the code and which church to go to, you'll realize that you're stuck with me."

Max paused, his brow crinkling and releasing along with a slew of emotions. Then he wrenched open the door. "Can we go?"

"Of course." Sandra walked out with a perky jaunt to her step.

Drummond followed behind and shared a commiserating look with Max. "All good women can be a pain in the ass sometimes."

"I heard that," Sandra called from the stairs.

In the back of his mind, Max knew Winston-Salem had a lot of churches. All the biggies — Baptist, Protestant, Catholic. Some of the more niche — Korean, Unitarian, Quaker. There was even one synagogue with a fantastic little bagel shop up the block. And, of course, there were the Moravian churches.

These tended to be smaller, less ostentatious affairs. In some of the rural areas surrounding the city, the churches were straight out of horror movie — a one-room building, low ceiling, peeling white paint on the wooden exterior.

"So what's the address?" Max said as he pulled the car into traffic.

Sandra typed away on her laptop. She frowned and typed

some more. "It's not showing up on the map. I've tried Google, Bing, Mapquest."

"What's the name of the place?" Drummond asked from the backseat.

"The Moravian Hope Church. You ever hear of it?"

Drummond's casual demeanor dropped. "Oh, yeah. I know that one."

"That doesn't sound good."

"It's not going to be on any map, but I'll get us there. Get on 40 West, like you're going back to Tanglewood, and I'll let you know where to get off."

The day had slipped away from Max, and as he drove, the sun blinded him. Squinting, he said, "How much longer?"

"Don't be in such a hurry. This isn't the kind of place you want to go to anyway. Even back in my day, this place had been an old wreck. It's off in the woods. People used it in the early 1800s. For all I know, Tucker Hull prayed there. But for whatever reason, they stopped attending it. Maybe they built a bigger place, maybe it went with Hull when he split, or maybe the rumors are true."

"Rumors?"

"It's said to be haunted. Back when I was alive, I didn't give much credence to the idea. The stories about it sounded more like tall tales rather than authentic ghost behavior. Until I met with Ernest and Leed. Then I believed the stories wholesale. But now — I'm not so sure. We best be extra careful."

"What stories?" Sandra asked.

Drummond exhaled slowly. "They said a witch coven would sneak in at night and perform their ceremonies. Of course the stories added sensational details — naked dancing, drinking of blood, baby sacrifices, that kind of thing. That's what made me doubt it all to start. But maybe something was going on back then. Maybe with the same coven we're after."

"With that kind of story, no wonder Ernest buried his witch out here."

Max followed Drummond's directions off the highway and deeper into the countryside. He turned off the paved roads and proceeded along gravel and then dirt until he reached a yellow, metal bar gate. "Guess we walk from here."

"It's not far," Drummond said as he passed through the car door.

Max retrieved two flashlights from the trunk of the car and handed one to Sandra. He then grabbed a shovel and headed out. Though the sun had not quite hit the horizon, under the canopy of trees, blue darkness prevailed. Max shivered. He had grown comfortable at seeing Drummond's pale visage, but watching the ghost float through the woods surrounded by the night and hearing the night's sounds proved eerier than he had expected.

Within five minutes, the church poked out of the darkness like another ghost. Max, Sandra, and Drummond all stood silent before the ruined building's front porch — two steps leading to a warped platform before a double door. Max moved forward, his flashlight drawing freakish shadows upon the building's old white walls.

"Hon." Sandra reached out as if to yank him back. "Maybe we should check around the area first. In case Dr. Ernest buried the witch out here."

Drummond clapped his hands, the noise echoing around them. "Excellent idea."

Max doubted the body had been buried outside the church, but like his companions, he needed more time to build his courage. "Let's stick together."

As a group, the three worked their way around the perimeter of the church. They saw no signs to indicate any sort of ritual burial nor did they see anything to suggest the ground had been disturbed in recent days. They startled a rat, but Max felt confident the rat had startled them worse.

When they came around to where they had begun, Max knew the time for stalling had ended. He marched straight to the front porch, and not wanting to give Sandra a chance to talk him into turning back, he opened the door. The ancient hinges creaked.

He pointed his flashlight through the door. The open space

had little in it anymore but graffiti and layers of dust. On the left side, a closed door had been painted with a crude pentagram. A handful of pews faced the back wall like tombstones. Stepping in, Max's footfalls filled the emptiness with a hollow sound.

While Sandra moved off to the right, Drummond remained in the doorway. "I'm glad I'm already dead."

"Gee, thanks for the confidence booster," Sandra said.

Max tried hard to ignore the feeling of an unseen weight pressing on him from all sides. He had never been the type to get claustrophobic, but he'd rather that be the explanation than anything else. He leaned the shovel against a pew and approached the door with the pentagram. Supernatural possibilities filled his head.

He put his hand against the door as if he might feel a fire burning on the other side. Of course, he only felt wood — rough and cold. Better to keep pushing forward than let his mind play out the endless list of horrific scenarios. He grabbed the knob and opened the door.

An office. Even a small church needed some place for the leaders to work. Pastors needed to write sermons. What little money they received had to be accounted for. Bake sales had to be planned. And then there were the private conversations — the troubled youth, the cheating spouse, the doubting intellectual. They all needed that one-on-one time with their spiritual leader, and this tiny office had to be the cramped quarters for just such conversations.

Max stepped back into the church proper and noticed Drummond hesitating to enter. "Come on. I want you to check the walls, the floors, and the ceiling — all the places we can't get to. See if Dr. Ernest put her anywhere like that."

"That's not a good idea," Drummond said.

Max shined the flashlight on Drummond to get a better look at his face, but the bright light and white walls washed out the ghost's image. "For crying out loud, get in here so we can be done with this. I don't know what's got you spooked, but I'm not eager to hang around here either."

"This is a church," Drummond said, thrusting his hands wide open. "We should have some respect for the place."

"It's not a church anymore. It's an old, rotting building. That's all."

"Buildings like this, ones used for a holy purpose, they hold on to what they were. They don't forget. Aw, heck, I can't expect you to understand. Trust me, okay? I've had experience with this before."

"That's right. Your mother ..."

Drummond's eyes flared as he soared straight at Max. "How do you know anything about my mother?" he asked, putting his cold hand inches from Max's face.

"I ... kind of ... well, you were lying to us and I realized how little we knew about you —"

"You researched me?"

Sandra whirled on Max. "I told you not to do that."

"Thanks, hon." But Sandra turned away, walking toward the front door.

Drummond kicked at the pew and sailed straight through it. "Of all the low, rotten things you could do. You had no right."

"I'm sorry. I am. I was worried about you and afraid and I made a stupid call." Max tried to speak in a soothing voice even as he saw Drummond getting angrier. He knew he should be most concerned with what he had done but he could only think about Drummond losing control and turning. "I know you must be mad, but please, let's focus on why we're here. When we go back to the office you can yell at me all you want. But not here."

Sandra stood in the doorway. "Max?"

Max turned his head toward her but Drummond whisked in to block his view. "What's the matter, Max ol' boy? Afraid I might snap right here, right now? Maybe you should go research that one."

"Max? Do you see headlights coming closer?"

Both Max and Drummond stopped their argument to look at Sandra. Moving to her side, Max said, "It's pitch black out here. I don't see anything."

Sandra swallowed hard. "I was afraid of that." She nodded to the darkness. "Ghosts are coming."

"Ghosts. Wait, what ghosts? Why?"

Drummond moved to the other side of Sandra. "It must be the witches. Those that haven't been destroyed yet. Nobody else would know or care that we're here. They're coming to stop us."

Max stepped backward, his mind racing to keep up with events. "The ghosts of the witches in the coven. If they're coming that means we're in the right place. A witch has to be buried here somewhere." He turned his trembling body toward Drummond. "It also means Patricia Welling will be with them. Listen to me. I'm terribly sorry for what I did. I don't know how to make that up to you, but right now, I need you to put that aside. I need you to stay calm or you risk turning."

"You're the one that needs to relax. I'm fine. And trust me, I'll find some way for you to make things up. And then some."

Sandra gasped. "They're all here. It looks the whole coven. We're surrounded."

Chapter 16

NOBODY MOVED. Sandra squinted as she looked out the doorway, raising a hand to shield her eyes. Max followed her gaze but saw only darkness. He could imagine it, though, plenty clear. Bright, pale women forming a circle around the church, their faces twisted in pain, their necks slit open and bodies baring the brutal scars of the curse Drummond had participated in casting.

Like a summer shower opening up without warning, Max heard a steady rat-a-tat striking the walls. "What's happening out there?"

Keeping her eyes on the witches, Sandra said, "They're throwing rocks at us."

Since any contact with the corporeal world caused ghosts sharp pain, repeatedly picking up and throwing rocks would not be pleasant for them. It might not be excruciating but it certainly signaled to Max that these witches were more than ticked off.

"Wait a second." Max scrunched his face, puzzled. "Why aren't they coming in here?"

"I noticed, too." Sandra walked back to Max and sat on one of the remaining pews. "It's a good thing. It means that one of the lessons I learned growing up was true — that evil and good are natural forces like the opposite sides of a magnet. They repel each other."

"See that," Drummond said. "That means that this isn't just an old building. It still has its church mojo, and that's what is protecting us."

"He's right. Whatever the history of this place, I have no doubt that when it was built, it served an honest, good sort of people."

Max sat next to Sandra. "This means we have time to find that body, right? They can't get in, so we don't really have to worry about them."

"Until we want to leave."

"It's not like that." Sandra hurried back to the doorway. "Most places in the world hold a mixture of the good and evil, so some turned ghosts can manage to get inside. But this church appears to be filled with a lot of good energy. Enough to hold them back for the moment, until they break through the barrier. That's why they're throwing rocks — rocks handled by evil witches. They're looking for weaknesses, some spot that isn't as holy as the rest."

Max planted his head in his hand. "You mean all they have to do is find the one spot where somebody had an illicit kiss or an evil thought or something and they can break through that?"

"Pretty much."

Without lifting his head, Max stretched out his arm and indicated the office door. "You mean like that pentagram over there?"

Before she could respond, Sandra dropped to the ground, covering her ears and wincing. Banging his hip into the pew, Max rushed to her side. Tears leaked from her eyes, and she clasped her ears ever tighter. She groaned and curled into a fetal position.

Max looked to Drummond for help, but he had fallen to the ground, too. "What's going on?"

Through gritted teeth, Drummond said, "The witches — they're screaming."

The wood floorboards rattled and the walls shook. Puffs of dust exploded from every crevice choking the air. Max coughed as he covered Sandra with his body. She twitched and shook as if having a seizure. Wood creaked and snapped. The shovel fell with a clang. One of the last standing pews toppled over.

The wind rose, howling as it whipped around the building's corners. Through the open doorway, rocks and pebbles, twigs and sticks spewed into the room. Max rolled to his side, placing his back between the doorway and Sandra. One pinprick attack amounted to little, but thousands of tiny strikes added up. He felt his blood soaking his shirt.

Bellowing to be heard, Max said, "How do we make it stop?"

Everything ceased. The floor settled. The walls calmed. The wind silenced. Only the final few pebbles rattled as they found places to rest.

Breathing hard and shaking, Sandra attempted to sit up. Damp with sweat, she put out a hand for Max to help steady her and did nothing more than breathe. Max held her hand tight.

"She okay?" Drummond said as he took the air.

"I don't know. What happened?"

"Just because the witches can't get in here, doesn't mean they can't hurt us. The pentagram, the graffiti, whatever else's been done here wasn't big enough, evil enough, for them to gain entry, but they can certainly cause us trouble."

"That was crazy. It was like a —"

"Like a haunting," Sandra said. "That's what evil ghosts do. Haunted houses, all those dark stories — the ones that are true deal with a ghost that turned."

Max brought his flashlight closer and relaxed a hair upon seeing color return to Sandra's face. "You going to be okay?"

She nodded. "They took me by surprise. That's all."

Max doubted that was all, but he let it be. He helped Sandra to her feet. Once he knew she could stand on her own, he stomped toward the back wall, picking up a broken piece of the pew.

"What are you doing?" Drummond rushed over to Max.

"We've got to find that body. Make sure Dr. Ernest destroyed it. Then we can get out of here. Try, at least." Max lifted the heavy wood, preparing to slam it into the wall.

"You do that, you'll kill us all."

"What now?"

From the doorway, Sandra said, "He's right. If you break open those walls, you'll be desecrating holy ground. You'll be opening the entire building to them. Nothing will hold them back."

Dropping the wood, Max said to Drummond, "Then we need you to go into those walls."

Drummond glanced at the wall. "That might be just as bad."

"Because the dead crawling around in the walls would be another form of desecration? Right?"

"Something like that."

"Well we can't wait around for them to attack again."

Rubbing her temples, sounding exhausted, Sandra said, "Will you two be quiet. Please. I'm trying to think."

A hundred sarcastic comments flooded Max's brain, but he said nothing. Sandra was on edge, too. Probably worse since he, at least, didn't have to listen to the intolerable screeching of a witch coven.

Walking toward Max, her steps more assured, she tapped out her points on her fingers. "First, Dr. Ernest cursed the High Priestess, and second, he buried her here. Why here? Because this is sacred, holy ground. A source of good. The coven's ghosts wouldn't be able to get in here."

"Hold on," Max said, his analytical side overcoming his fear. "How could he possibly bury her here? I mean, she's a source of evil, right? So, if her body were put in here, either her ghost couldn't come in, or the very act of burying her in this building would defile the building making the whole point, well, pointless. Right?"

"You got that right, kiddo," Drummond chimed in.

"But the witches," Sandra continued, "They came here, too. They wouldn't bother troubling us here for nothing. Especially when you consider how painful a lot of their actions are to a ghost."

Drummond snapped his fingers and pointed at Sandra. "The lady's got you there."

Max rolled his eyes. "You're a big help."

"Well, have you two geniuses considered this: The witch coven's here because their High Priestess is here, and since you've figured out that she can't be buried on this holy ground, then she must be buried nearby."

"We already checked around the grounds."

"In the dark with a flashlight. Not the best conditions. But let's say you're right. She's not buried right outside. If it were me burying her, and it almost was me, I'd have put her somewhere that the ghosts who wanted to get to her would mistakenly think she was in the church."

"He's right," Sandra said. "She has to be nearby, so close to the building that the ghosts' own fear of this holy ground would confuse them."

Drummond pursed his lips. "The office."

"Of course," Sandra said.

"Huh?" Max played his flashlight's beam on the office door. "You just got through saying she couldn't be buried here at all."

"She can't be buried on the holy ground. The office is physically attached to this church but it's not the holy ground of the church. The official praying, the gathering of people together and all that happened here, not in the office."

"Okay, let's go."

"You can't, yet."

Max threw his arms in the air. "Why the hell not? You want to hang around for those bitches to make your ears bleed?"

"If we destroy the High Priestess now, we won't get out of here alive."

Drummond nodded. "The second we uncover that body, the coven will know what's going on. The office isn't going to hold them off like the church proper. They'll swarm in on us. We won't stand a chance."

Staring at the office door like a prisoner waiting release, Max sighed. "Then what do you suggest we do? I haven't a clue."

Sandra glanced out the doorway then back to Max. He had seen her brave face many times, but the face he looked upon now went far beyond bravery. He saw grim determination in her. It scared the hell out of him.

"Here's what we're going to do." She crouched before Max and waited for Drummond to join the huddle. "You two go into that office and find the body. I'll go outside and make sure the witches are too busy to notice you."

"Wait. What?" Max looked to Drummond for support but he had the same look as Sandra. "No, no, no. You are not going out there. They practically turned you into mush, and they can't even get in here. They were screaming — that's all. You go out there, and they'll kill you."

"I wasn't expecting their attack. But I am now."

"Wonderful. So you can see the killing blow come. I feel so much better now."

Drummond edged over to the office door. "I'll be here when you're ready."

Sandra took Max's face in her hands. "I know how to resist them. I've been doing it my whole life. If I didn't, I'd never have lived long enough to meet you. So, trust me."

"I do trust you." Her hands were cold against his skin — she wasn't as confident as she acted. "But what I saw —"

"Don't think about them. Think about me. I'm the only one you need to believe. I'm telling you, I can handle them."

Max wanted to argue or reason or even bully her — anything to keep her in the church, safe. Her mouth lifted in a sorrowful smile, and he felt tears leaking from his eyes. How many times had he insisted she believe in him? How many times had she been forced to watch him walk off into dangers she knew he had no way to be prepared for? At least in this case, she had some previous experience. But all his debating aside, he knew he would have to let her go ahead with this plan because they had no other.

He reached out and kissed her. Her soft lips trembled against his, and for a fleeting breath, he thought maybe she would reconsider. But an icy finger traced his heart — she trembled because she knew this might be their last kiss.

When she tried to pull away, he clenched her tighter. He pressed in close against her, as if he could pass right through her. He stroked her hair with one hand and brought her closer with the other. At length, she placed her hands on his chest, and gently, firmly pushed back.

"When you finish with the body, run for the car. I'll be right alongside you."

"Don't you die," he said.

"Don't take too long."

As Sandra headed for the doorway, her hand holding on to Max until the last possible second, her eyes closed. Max watched her body straighten, her focus narrow. She turned all her attention to the witches and her plan. Max scurried across the room to the office door. He placed his hand on the knob and waited for Sandra's signal.

Max's heart dropped with every step she took closer toward the outside. In a moment, he would be in the office and unable to protect her. And he had Drummond to worry about, too. The witch attack had hurt his ghost partner. Max would have to keep an eye on him, consider him a mining canary that would tell him if the witches had hit too hard.

Before stepping outside, Sandra's shoulders rose slowly and fell fast — one last deep breath. And then she was gone. Walked straight out until Max could no longer see her.

Drummond endured the pain it took to poke Max in the shoulder. "Time to move."

"Right," Max muttered. Right, indeed. He had to be sharp now, succeed as fast as possible, make sure Sandra spent as little time out there as he could manage.

He opened the door and started knocking on the walls. At the first dull hit, he turned to Drummond. "Why the hell am I doing it this way? Get in there. This isn't holy ground. Check to see where that witch is."

"You got it." Drummond raised his hand in a mock salute and his face locked in anguish.

From out front, Sandra yelled but Max couldn't tell if it was a yell of someone being defeated or raging against her enemy. Drummond cocked his head and held his lips tight. He looked like he fought against vomiting. Then he shook the whole thing off.

"She's okay," he said. "But let's not dawdle."

"I'm waiting for you. Get in there."

Drummond stuck his head into the wall and pulled it back out fast. "She's in there. Looks like Ernest never made it out here."

Max banged on the wall, hoping to break open a hole big enough to grab the body. Again and again he smashed his fist at the wall, but this old building had been made of wood, not drywall, and he only managed to bloody his knuckles.

"You forgetting something?" Drummond said.

"Damn it," Max said and dashed out of the office. In a flash, he returned with the shovel he had carried from the car. All his fisticuffs with the wall had loosened enough dirt and dust that he could see the seam where two boards met. Using the shovel like a crowbar, he shoved the blade in and pushed on the handle.

Sandra screamed out something, but Max deciphered only a few swears. He snatched a glimpse of Drummond. The ghost's face scrunched tight like he suffered a migraine.

Come on, Max, come on. Neither of them can take much more of this.

Max put all his weight behind the handle and pushed. The wood creaked and the rusting nails whined. He shoved the handle harder until a section of the wall leaned out. Sliding the shovel deeper, Max thought of his wife's pain, and he roared, pressing the handle with all the strength he could find.

The wall gave way, wood splintering and snapping. As the shovel lost hold of anything to grip, Max stumbled forward into the wall. The stench of ancient decay poured out of the new opening.

Max stuck his nose in the crook of his arm, yet the polluted air still managed to seep into his nostrils. With his free hand, he tore down those sections of wood still clinging to the wall. He picked up the flashlight and set it on the office desk, the beam focused on the ceiling to cast dim light everywhere — enough to see the body.

Drummond collapsed across the desk. *Crap.* The wind picked up, its howl growing louder. The floorboards rattled. Though Max couldn't hear the horrid shrieks of the witches, his heart quaked at the thought of Sandra stuck outside, suffering, open to attack.

Only way is through. Max looked in the open wall.

The witch's body appeared like the statue of a woman caught in terrible pain. Her mouth open wide in a vicious scream, while her hands appeared to claw at the wall. A line across her neck marked where Dr. Ernest had slit her throat, and on her chest, the dark lines of symbols carved into her pale skin. Dust and grime covered the corpse, along with rat droppings. But no sign of the little animals gnawing at her.

Max raised the shovel. He widened his legs into a firm stance, in case the witch's eyes snapped open or she tried to take the shovel or she had some other magical ability he never knew. Holding the shovel like a poker, he shoved it at the witch's body. As if made of precariously balanced sand, the entire body crumbled into a pile of dirt on the floor. A long hiss of foul air released from her.

The walls, the floors, the howling wind — all ceased.

Wiping the sweat from his eyes, Max rushed out of the office, up the main aisle of the church proper, and straight out the doorway. Sandra lay on the ground, curled in a ball. He hurried to her side, listening for a breath, hoping to see the rise and fall of her chest. She groaned, and Max had never heard a sound so joyous in his life. She had survived.

Drummond weaved towards them like a drunk. "My head's killing me."

"Where are the witches?" Max asked.

Drummond barely lifted his head. "Gone. With their High Priestess destroyed, there's no point to being here."

Max wondered why they didn't retaliate, but for the moment, he turned all his worry to Sandra. "Put your arms around me, hon." He lifted her up and carried her to the car. It hadn't seemed so far away when they first arrived, but Sandra passed out and her slumbering weight had him breathing heavily by the time they reached the car.

Sliding her into the back seat, he called out, "Drummond? Come on."

"I'm right here." He sat in the passenger seat.

On a normal night, Drummond popping into Max's car like that would have caused a jolt of surprise, but exhaustion overwhelmed such simple reactions. Max merely nodded and got behind the wheel. He put the key in and froze.

"What's wrong?" Drummond asked.

"The witches left us."

"We did get rid of the reason they came."

"But they came to stop us, and they failed. So they float away? They don't want to get even or anything? I thought these were evil ghosts. That seems wrong."

"What are you thinking?"

"Those ghosts came here for a reason and now they've left for a similar reason. We're not done. Leed said he took care of his witches, and we've taken care of Ernest's."

"But there's still mine."

Max turned the ignition and revved the engine. "We've got to get to Patricia before they do. We're going to have to get into the Federal Building."

Chapter 17

BY THE TIME MAX reached the office building, Sandra had recovered enough to stand on her own. With some assistance, she negotiated the stairs, and when they entered the office, she dropped to the couch, panting and perspiring. She offered a feeble smile and gulped down the water Max handed her.

"You want to see a doctor?" he asked.

As she drank, she shook her head. She handed the glass back and patted her sweating forehead. "I think I'll rest here for a little. Then I'll be okay."

"You sure? You don't look so good."

"I'll be fine. It's not the first time I've been attacked by a ghost."

Drummond popped his head through the bookcase. "This was a whole coven of ghosts, doll. You ought to be real careful. Take things slow."

Sandra licked the water from her lips. "That's why I need to rest here. I'll be back to my full strength soon enough."

Something seemed off. Max couldn't figure it out, but he had the sense that all these various strands were not coming together the way they should. And now Sandra was one of those strands. But she had gone a few rounds in an unfair fight, so maybe it made sense that she acted a bit different than he would expect.

Drummond snapped his fingers in front of Max's face. "Wake up. Sun's rising and we've got work to do. Federal Building will be opening up in a few hours. We need a plan."

"Unless the Federal government has invented and installed ghost detectors, I figured we'd walk in there and you'd look around. You don't have a problem checking out the walls of a government building, too, do you?"

"Believe me. Those are far from holy ground."

Max started to chuckle at Drummond's comment but hesitated. "If the building isn't holy ground, then the ghosts of the witch coven can get in there every bit as easily as you."

"You're just getting that now?"

Sandra placed her head on the arm of the couch, swung her legs up, and closed her eyes. "You boys have fun with that. I've got to sleep."

Max dabbed her damp brow with the cuff of his shirt and then stepped into the hall. When Drummond followed, Max walked to the head of the stairs and sat. Whispering harshly, Max said, "You've got to go to the Federal building now. I can't get in until they open, but you know those witches are already there."

"Calm down. They don't know where Patricia is. That was part of the whole point of having Ernest, Leed, and I do our cursing separately."

"Then how did they know where we were?"

"Because Ernest and Leed are dead. The coven probably tracked down their ghosts and forced the information out of them."

"Doesn't that mean they'll come after you, too?"

Drummond scratched his cheek even though he no longer grew stubble. "I'll have to be at my ready. In the meantime, you need to go find Patricia's body."

"You're not coming?"

"If I go with you, the coven ghosts will have an easier time finding us. I'm only invisible to living people. The ghosts will see me standing out."

"I can't go alone. How would I explain to all of law enforcement that I'm banging on their walls looking for a dead body — oh, and I only know about it because of a ghost! They'd lock me up."

A door opened and the old lady stepped into the hall. She peered up at Max's office, her laborious movements painful to watch. Then she turned her head and part of her body towards Max. She scowled, grabbed her newspaper from her doormat, and returned to her apartment.

Drummond tipped his head back. "I think she's warming up to you."

"Well, I'm not warming up to this idea. I won't have the access I need to find Patricia, and if I do manage to find her, there's no way I can do anything about it with all the police around. So either you go with me or we've got to come up with another plan."

"But the witches —"

"I don't see how we can do anything about that, so we can't worry about it," Max said. Drummond had the look of a conman caught in a lie and straining to find a way out. It hit Max right away. "Are you afraid to see her?"

"Don't be foolish. I'm not afraid of her. But I do worry about me."

"You think it might cause you to turn?"

"Don't you?"

Max weighed it all out in his head. "I'm sorry, but I don't see another option. We've got to finish this. Ernest and Leed's witches have been destroyed. If we don't do this now, what was the point? Why did they die? Even worse, what kind of power will this coven of ghosts have?"

"Okay, okay. I know. You don't have to be a pest about it."

Max held back his tongue. He could say nothing that would make a difference. At length, he climbed down the stairs, knowing Drummond would follow close behind.

He decided to walk the whole way. It was only a handful of blocks, but the distance ate up some of the time until the building opened, and more importantly, it gave Drummond a chance to prepare. It also meant Max had time to prepare as well. And he needed it.

When they reached the entrance on the corner of 2nd and Main, a line of people waiting for the place to open had already formed. Some held simple forms that needed filing; some held folders packed with paperwork intended to prove their innocence or the guilt of others. Some joked with each other; some pouted, knowing they would be paying a fine no matter what excuses they gave a judge. Max got on the end of the line, leaned against the cool concrete wall, crossed his arms, and watched cars enter and exit the parking structure across the street.

Drummond scanned up and down the street before sidling next to a cocky-looking young man complaining about jury duty to anybody who would listen. Drummond passed his hand through the man and watched the jerk shiver. Max smirked.

"No witches here, by the way. They might be inside but I don't get the feeling they're around."

Max wanted to answer, but the idea of being hauled off for talking to himself like a crazy person didn't sit well. Thankfully, the doors opened and the line began to move. It went slowly though. A few feet inside the entrance was a security check point similar to an airport — guards, scanners, and walk-through detection equipment.

Drummond bounced around the line. "Come on, come on, come on." He zipped to the head of the line, peeking over the heads of those already inside. "This is ridiculous. Look, I'm going in and see if I can find her. When you get inside, call for me and I'll let you know what I've discovered."

"Wait," Max said, but Drummond slipped through the wall and those in line all stopped to stare at him. "Sorry," he muttered, garnering odd looks.

Security was set up in a long, white hallway with plenty of windows. Once they checked his ID and he passed through the detector, he walked into another hall. This one made him think of every institutional building he had ever walked through — university administrations, hospital wings, and city councils. Utilitarian and boring.

"Max!" Max glanced down and saw Drummond's head sticking out of the floor. "I found her."

Max walked to a quiet corner and pretended to make a call on his cellphone. "That's good to hear. Where are you?"

Drummond rose through the floor until he stood next to Max. "She's down in the basement. Like I said she would be. Near the boiler."

"I don't know how to get there." Max checked around to make sure nobody watched him. "And I don't think it'd be wise to ask anybody."

"Don't bother. She's behind a thick wall of brick. You'll need a sledgehammer to break through."

"Can't you do anything? The last one crumbled from just a touch."

Max glanced up and saw the angry eyes of the ghost. Drummond had used all his inner-strength to face the corpse of Patricia Welling, no way would Max convince him to touch her. Besides, even if he would do so, Max wasn't so sure he wanted Drummond to go back down there. His face had taken on a horrified look — the look of a ghost about to lose control.

"Forget it," Max said. "I shouldn't have asked."

"No, you shouldn't have."

"There's no way we can get to her without being caught." A uniformed policeman strolling by turned his head at the word *caught*. "Let's get out of here," Max said.

Max pocketed his cellphone and headed outside. Drummond followed, swirling around Max like a hawk circling prey. "What the hell are you doing? Leaving? You made me come out here. You made me go find her. And now you want to leave?"

"Calm down," Max whispered through gritted teeth.

"Do you have any clue what I went through? That wasn't easy to do. I had to see her. You understand? I had to see what I did to her. I've spent decades trying to forget about her and you not only make me relive it all, but you forced me to go see her. For what? This isn't right. Not right at all."

As Max stepped onto the sidewalk and headed back to the office, he said, "I'm sorry. But we had to be sure."

"I was plenty sure before. You just wouldn't believe me."

Max halted. "I'm sorry. Get it? I'm sorry. You need to calm down and think through this rationally."

"I don't feel very rational. Not when I've been spun and hung like this."

More odd looks from pedestrians. Shaking it off, Max

stormed away. "Look, I can't change what happened but at least we know she's there and we know the coven hasn't gotten to her yet. All we have to do now is figure out how to clean this up. There's got to be something we can do."

"I got a few suggestions for you, but I don't think you'll like where I put the baseball bat."

Max didn't bother saying more. What was the point when his own anger seemed to fuel Drummond's further? Besides, he had to think. If he couldn't come up with a solution, then Drummond would be right — he would have revisited this horrible event in his life for no reason at all. Worse, though he did not mention it, he thought the witch coven ghosts would have the Federal building surrounded by the end of the day.

"Tell me more about the actual curse," Max said.

"You're suddenly an expert on curses?"

"I'm trying to get more information. The more I know about all this, the easier it'll be to figure things out. Maybe one of us might catch something in what you say, put some more pieces together."

"What we really need is a witch of our own."

Max nearly tripped. "You're right. That's exactly what we need."

"Don't even think about her. Are you kidding? Have you gone soft in the brain?"

"You know any other witches that might be persuaded to help us?"

Drummond frowned. "You destroyed her practice, turned her into an alcoholic, and caused her downfall with Hull. Why would she even think about helping us?"

"She's not part of their coven, for starters."

"And she tortured you. Did you forget that part?"

"What other choice do we have? Unless you'll go face Patricia's corpse all by yourself."

Though he clearly didn't agree, Drummond nodded. "Okay. Dr. Connor's it is."

Chapter 18

AS THEY NEARED THE OFFICE, Max's confidence waned. Bothered by Drummond's acquiescence, he began to second-guess himself. After all, to think Dr. Connor, the Hull's personal witch, would help him out sounded ridiculous. Except that they had helped each other out in the past. Usually through coercion, but help nonetheless. That was the key — he needed some leverage.

Consumed with these thoughts, Max failed to notice Mr. Modesto standing by the stairwell entrance. "Mr. Porter. Once again, it appears that you are failing our employer."

Max put his hands on his hips and sighed. "And how am I doing that?"

Modesto strolled toward Max, his expensive shoes clicking on the sidewalk, arrogance oozing off of his stoic face. "You have shown an appalling lack of regard for our employer and your assignment, but you are mistaken to think you're untouchable."

"I've been trying to find your missing bell, but —"

"Your excuses no longer interest me. I have lost all tolerance for you."

Drummond laughed. "He says that like he ever had any."

"Let me make this clear enough, Mr. Porter. Tomorrow evening, I shall meet you in your office and you will have that handbell. Time has run out. If you fail to show up with that bell, then our employer will be most displeased, and I suggest you and your wife uncover the most rapid exit from Winston-Salem." Modesto's lips part to reveal the tips of his sharp teeth. "Perhaps North Carolina, as well."

Max wanted to act tough, but his face twisted in an effort to hold back a pollen-induced sneeze. Three sneezes later, he said,

"How many times are you going to threaten me a year? It's boring."

"These are not threats. These are guarantees. And of all people, you should know full well how much I relish the moment our employer allows me to fulfill those guarantees. That moment is coming. Fail us with the handbell, and I know there won't be any hesitations left."

"I still have Hull's journal."

"If you tire of my threats, I tire more of your attempt to hold that over us. Some things are simply worth the risks. You wouldn't understand. You don't take real risks. You let others do your dirty work. Drummond or your wife."

"Shut up."

"Without them, what are you really? A boy who can research things. Based on your less than impressive skill regarding the handbell, I question even that much of your ability. You are nothing without your wife's gifts and your ghost's connection to the supernatural world. Nothing."

Max couldn't help it. He shoved Modesto's shoulders hard enough to send the man back a few steps. "You've delivered your message, errand boy. You can go now."

Modesto brushed his shoulders and stepped closer to Max. In a low tone, he said, "Tomorrow evening. Bring the bell here or run for your life." He shoved Max in the chest, and Max fell down onto the sidewalk. "Good day."

As Modesto walked away, Max got back to his feet, coughing and sneezing all the way up. Drummond drifted to his side. "Want me give him a brain-freeze he'll never forget?"

"Forget him." Max headed inside. "Hunting down family trinkets doesn't rate too high on my list of pressing issues. Besides, if we don't fix this coven problem, nothing much will matter since we'll probably be cursed or dead."

"You got a good point."

They walked into the office to find Sandra sitting bolt upright. She turned her head toward them — lips pale and cracked, eyes unblinking, sweat-soaked hair plastered to her head. All thoughts of covens and bells and Hulls and Modesto washed away from Max's mind. He lunged to her side and felt waves of cold air coming off her.

Wrapping a blanket around her shoulders, he said, "What's going on? Are you sick?"

"I'm fine," she said in a voice as dead as her eyes.

"We need to get you to a hospital."

"No. I want to stay." She looked to Drummond, an odd smile crossing her face. "Is this the cold you feel? The cold of the dead?"

Drummond put his hands in his pockets and floated back. "Sweetheart, you need to listen to your husband. Something's wrong here. You should see a doctor."

"They've never helped me before." She laughed — a hard, unusual sound that ended in a drunken snort. "I'd be better off at the church."

Drummond paled. "What the hell?"

Max turned to Drummond. "You ever seen anything like this?"

"Have you?" Drummond asked. "If I had to guess, I'd say those witches did something to her before they left. Cursed her, maybe. But I've never seen a curse like this."

"All the more reason to go visit our old friend."

Sandra perked up. "Oh, where are we going?"

"Not you, hon."

"But I want to come along."

"I'm going to see a doctor. You want to see a doctor?"

She pouted. "No."

"Okay, then. Please stay here and we'll be back soon."

"Make sure Drummond comes back. I've got a lot questions about the afterlife for him."

With that said, Sandra returned to the stark position and expression she had been in when they first entered. Max stared at her, waiting for a small glimmer of Sandra to appear. As he watched her with an ache in his chest worsening every second, he held back his tears.

Kissing her cold cheek, he said, "We're going to help you. Hang on for me, hon. You hear me? Hang on, and I'll stop whatever this is. I love you." He kissed her again before storming down the hall and toward the car.

The last time Max stood in Dr. Connor's office, she had become a drunken hag, crawling on the floor for a nip of whiskey. The last time he talked with her, she had sobered up and regained the limited trust of the Hull family. While she certainly had not returned to her glory days, he now saw that she had risen far closer to that goal than ever before.

On the surface, her office looked like any optometrist's office — an uninspired waiting room with a chest-high reception desk and a red-headed woman in a nurse's uniform sitting behind it. An elderly man with thick glasses and an overbite sat on a couch reading an old issue of Sports Illustrated — swimsuit issue, of course. Over the speakers, radio station 98.7 ("We Play Everything") had Styx urging everyone to sail away into outer-space. Underneath, however, Max knew the real business at hand — witchcraft.

Rapping his knuckles on the desk, Max said, "Hi, there. Will you please tell Dr. Connor that Max Porter is here to see her?"

"Do you have an appointment?" the receptionist asked, tapping on her computer keyboard. "I don't see a Porter here. It is P-O-R-T-E-R, yes?"

"I don't have an appointment."

"Then I'm sorry, but Dr. Connor has a full schedule today."

"I'm sure she does. I'm equally sure that she'll drop everything once you mention my name."

The receptionist faltered. Max felt sorry for her since he had put her in a bind. She clearly wanted to turn him away, perhaps even thought that made the most sense, but there existed this slim chance that she should inform Dr. Connor. But if Dr. Connor wanted nothing to do with Max, then the receptionist will have angered a witch for nothing. But if she sent Max away and Dr. Connor did want to see him, she would also anger that same witch. Any decision she made risked pissing off a powerful witch, and Max knew exactly what it felt like to be on the wrong end of that sentence.

Drummond floated behind the elderly man and took a close look at the Sports Illustrated. "Some days I really wish I was alive. Look at these women."

Doing his best to ignore Drummond, Max leaned toward the receptionist. "Listen, I can make this easier for you. If you don't tell her I'm here, she's going to have an entire coven of cursed witch ghosts to contend with." He peeked over his shoulder. The old man ogling Sports Illustrated raised an eyebrow but whether that was because of what Max said or because of the white, wet number some hottie wore on a beach in Brazil, Max couldn't be sure. Drummond certainly liked the magazine. Turning back to the still-hesitant receptionist, Max added, "I'll make it even easier. If you don't go back, I'm going to barrel my way in there and start calling out for her, causing all kinds of commotion. I think that'll tick her off far more than if you interrupt her."

Scowling, the receptionist stood. "Please have a seat, Mr. Porter. I'll be a moment."

"Thank you." Max sat in a chair opposite the old man and snatched up a copy of Southern Living. He snapped the magazine open and coughed.

Drummond looked up. "Did you want me for something?"

Shaking the magazine, Max coughed again.

"Oh, right. You're afraid the old guy here will think you're nuts talking to me. Well? Just cough once for yes, twice for no."

Cough.

"Fine, fine. I was enjoying the swimwear, that's all. I wasn't going to let you go face Connor all alone. And even if I was, what do you care? You've been one-on-one with her before. You've lived."

Barely, Max thought.

"Are you going to sit there acting like a fool, or is there something you want me to do?"

Cough.

"You want me to check on Sandra?"

had little in it anymore but graffiti and layers of dust. On the left side, a closed door had been painted with a crude pentagram. A handful of pews faced the back wall like tombstones. Stepping in, Max's footfalls filled the emptiness with a hollow sound.

While Sandra moved off to the right, Drummond remained in the doorway. "I'm glad I'm already dead."

"Gee, thanks for the confidence booster," Sandra said.

Max tried hard to ignore the feeling of an unseen weight pressing on him from all sides. He had never been the type to get claustrophobic, but he'd rather that be the explanation than anything else. He leaned the shovel against a pew and approached the door with the pentagram. Supernatural possibilities filled his head.

He put his hand against the door as if he might feel a fire burning on the other side. Of course, he only felt wood — rough and cold. Better to keep pushing forward than let his mind play out the endless list of horrific scenarios. He grabbed the knob and opened the door.

An office. Even a small church needed some place for the leaders to work. Pastors needed to write sermons. What little money they received had to be accounted for. Bake sales had to be planned. And then there were the private conversations — the troubled youth, the cheating spouse, the doubting intellectual. They all needed that one-on-one time with their spiritual leader, and this tiny office had to be the cramped quarters for just such conversations.

Max stepped back into the church proper and noticed Drummond hesitating to enter. "Come on. I want you to check the walls, the floors, and the ceiling — all the places we can't get to. See if Dr. Ernest put her anywhere like that."

"That's not a good idea," Drummond said.

Max shined the flashlight on Drummond to get a better look at his face, but the bright light and white walls washed out the ghost's image. "For crying out loud, get in here so we can be done with this. I don't know what's got you spooked, but I'm not eager to hang around here either."

"This is a church," Drummond said, thrusting his hands wide open. "We should have some respect for the place."

"It's not a church anymore. It's an old, rotting building. That's all."

"Buildings like this, ones used for a holy purpose, they hold on to what they were. They don't forget. Aw, heck, I can't expect you to understand. Trust me, okay? I've had experience with this before."

"That's right. Your mother ..."

Drummond's eyes flared as he soared straight at Max. "How do you know anything about my mother?" he asked, putting his cold hand inches from Max's face.

"I ... kind of ... well, you were lying to us and I realized how little we knew about you —"

"You researched me?"

Sandra whirled on Max. "I told you not to do that."

"Thanks, hon." But Sandra turned away, walking toward the front door.

Drummond kicked at the pew and sailed straight through it. "Of all the low, rotten things you could do. You had no right."

"I'm sorry. I am. I was worried about you and afraid and I made a stupid call." Max tried to speak in a soothing voice even as he saw Drummond getting angrier. He knew he should be most concerned with what he had done but he could only think about Drummond losing control and turning. "I know you must be mad, but please, let's focus on why we're here. When we go back to the office you can yell at me all you want. But not here."

Sandra stood in the doorway. "Max?"

Max turned his head toward her but Drummond whisked in to block his view. "What's the matter, Max ol' boy? Afraid I might snap right here, right now? Maybe you should go research that one."

"Max? Do you see headlights coming closer?"

Both Max and Drummond stopped their argument to look at Sandra. Moving to her side, Max said, "It's pitch black out there. I don't see anything."

Cough, cough.

"You want me to get rid of this old guy? Get the magazine for yourself?"

Cough, cough. The old man sneaked a glance at Max. "Sorry," Max said. "Getting over a cold. Don't worry, I'm not contagious." The old man made a face that said how little he thought of Max's assurances. "I do wish I could see what the doc was up to, though, don't you?"

Drummond nodded. "I get it. You want me to check out what's going on back there."

Cough.

"No need to put attitude in your cough. This ain't the easiest way to communicate." Drummond slid through the wall and in seconds, slid right back. "Receptionist is coming."

Before the door to the back opened, Max had tossed the magazine on the coffee table and stood. The receptionist started as she came through, and the old man looked a bit surprised, too. "Mr. Porter, you may see Dr. Connor in her office. Just go down the hall and —"

"I know where it is," he said with more venom than he intended.

As he walked down the hall, Drummond followed. "You know, we really should come up with a system to talk when you can't really talk. That coughing thing won't work."

In a harsh whisper, Max said, "How many times have I had you do recon while I waited somewhere? It should be standard practice by now."

"We never agreed to anything. And I got distracted."

"Looking at hotties in bathing suits isn't why you're here. For crying out loud, you're a ghost. Go peep on somebody in the shower if you've got to, but when we're working, I expect you —"

"Okay, okay. You're going to draw attention."

Max wanted to argue further, but Drummond was right. Also, they had reached Dr. Connor's office door. Max knocked and entered.

The office was small and cluttered. Dr. Connor sat at a desk drowning in papers, some crinkled and faded yellow, some crisp and smelling of inkjet. Old texts had been piled up in the corners and a row of stuffed birds perched on a cabinet behind Dr. Connor's desk. On the wall to her left, Max saw an eye chart with a huge letter E at the top. On the opposite wall, Max saw a celestial map with the moon's phases marked out along with numerous symbols he did not know (though a few he recognized from the walls of Leed and Dr. Ernest).

A few years younger than Max, Dr. Connor had always been a beautiful woman, but the hard times she had suffered through took a toll. Dark hollows had formed around her eyes, and her mouth no longer smiled brightly. Though she wore a white doctor's coat with a spaghetti-strapped summer dress underneath, her once vibrant sexuality had diminished.

Max tried to hide any guilt from his face. He had caused this woman a lot of harm — but often in the course of protecting himself from her vicious attacks.

As Max stepped in, Drummond followed behind only to smack against the opening of the doorway. "What the hell?" Drummond said.

Max turned around, and Dr. Connor cackled. "You don't think I'd be stupid enough to rebuild this office without some protections?"

Drummond pushed on the barrier several more times until he finally leaned his shoulder against it and pursed his lips. "You let her know I can still watch from here. She does anything to you, and I'll find a way in there."

Max took a seat at the desk. "Drummond says you better be careful. He won't let anything happen to me."

"How adorable," she said, her mouth a stoic line. "Shall we get to talking seriously or are you going to waste more of my time?"

Scrunching his brow in thought, Max glanced back at the doorway. "You put up a barrier against ghosts." His eyes widened. "You already know, don't you?"

"Of course, I know. I wouldn't be this town's top witch, if I didn't know what was going on. You really think a witch like me doesn't keep tabs on every witch hunter in the country? You think all the witches around the world don't talk with each other? We can use the Internet, too, you know."

"Then you know why I'm here."

Dr. Connor lifted her head, leveling a sultry yet sadistic look upon Drummond. "Patricia Welling."

Drummond smashed his palm into the invisible barrier. "I hate this woman. Stop playing games with her. Get what we need and let's go."

"That's right," Max said. "We want to stop these ghosts of the witch coven, and judging by your spell at the doorway, you're afraid of them, too. We know where the last one is, but we can't get to it to destroy it. Now, since our interests are aligned for the moment, why don't you help us out? Tell me how to get rid of the last one, and then you won't be needing to lay down a bunch of wards wherever you go."

Dr. Connor wriggled out of her white coat, letting one of her spaghetti-straps fall off her shoulder, and she licked her lips. "Help never goes just one way. You know that."

"If you're trying to tempt me into cheating on my wife, it's not going to happen."

She pouted. "I don't know why you always resist. I'm young, able, and willing to do all those nasty things a proper wife would never dream of doing. We'd have a great time together."

"For one, I love my wife and actually meant my vows when I gave them. For another, you're a witch, and I don't trust you."

"But you want my help."

"I'm offering to help you out, too, don't forget. My problem appears to be yours."

Fixing her strap, Dr. Connor said, "Don't put your faith in appearances."

Drummond laughed. "She shouldn't be talking, looking like she does."

Dr. Connor opened a low drawer in her desk and pulled out a large book. In any other office, Max would have thought he looked upon an atlas from centuries ago. In Dr. Connor's office, he fought the bile roiling in his gut because he knew that the book's lovely brown hide cover was made of human skin. Having touched one of those books before, he had no desire to ever to do so again.

"In this book," she said, caressing the cover with the tips of her fingers, "is the answer you seek."

Max paused. "I have to say I'm surprised but pleased. Thank you for making this so easy. If you'll tell me what page to look—"

"Bless your heart, aren't you the sweetest thing. I'm not giving you this book, and this won't be easy. What kind of businesswoman would I be if I simply gave everything away?"

"Then what do you want?"

Sliding the book back into the drawer with one hand, Dr. Connor raised her other hand. "Not so fast. You've only just gotten here, and there's so much to discuss. I wonder — how much do you really know about Patricia Welling?"

"Max, get out of there." Drummond pounded his fist against the barrier. "Don't play her games. Come on, now. Leave and we'll find some other way to deal with all this."

"I know enough," Max said. "She's the ghost of a witch, and she's killing off those connected with her coven's curse. We know where she's buried, so all we have to do is destroy her body. Beyond that, the details don't really matter much."

Running her index finger across the other, she tutted. "Naughty, naughty. You shouldn't be lying. Especially to yourself. You know very well that details always matter. For instance, wouldn't you agree that it makes a huge difference, perhaps even an insurmountable difference, if your dear Drummond knew all along that Patricia was a witch?"

"She's lying," Drummond yelled. "Don't believe anything she says."

"What if he had been by that tree with the odd branch on purpose all those years ago? What if he had sought out dear Patricia with the intent of seducing her? And if he did that, why? Why seduce a witch?"

Max glowered at Dr. Connor. "If he did that, then I'm sure he planned to kill her all along."

"Except he hadn't met Matthew Ernest or Joshua Leed yet. That happened after he had begun his relationship with Patricia. I wonder what he wanted from her. After all, he hadn't sought out any old witch of that coven. He targeted her, specifically. Of course, I would, too, if I had been him. I mean, if you want to gain control over a witch's power, you might as well go for the High Priestess."

"What?" Max couldn't help himself. He turned toward Drummond.

"It's not true," Drummond said. "She's lying. I mean maybe Patricia was the High Priestess, I don't know. That's my point. I don't know."

Dr. Connor chuckled. "I see your partner neglected to tell you that little fact. Well then, I suppose you two have plenty to discuss. And I should be getting back to my patients."

"Wait," Max put his hand on her desk. He wanted to grab her wrist but didn't dare. "You still haven't told me what the price for your help will be."

"Oh. That."

"A case of whiskey? Information? What do you want?"

The pleasure that filled her eyes could not be mistaken. She thrilled at the words dangling on her tongue. The longer she waited to speak them, the worse Max felt — this was going to be bad. Really bad.

"You want my help in a very serious matter. There isn't enough whiskey in all of North Carolina to buy this kind of help — and that's a lot of whiskey."

"Then what?"

She placed a glass vial on the table. "Blood."

"Excuse me?"

"Specifically, your wife's blood."

"You leave her out of this."

"I can't do that. Either you give me her blood or we have no deal."

Max jumped to his feet. "You can go to Hell."

As he turned to leave, Dr. Connor tapped the glass with her finger. "There isn't another witch in all of North Carolina that can help you. Not when your time is so limited." She tilted her head. "By the way, before you go, tell me, how many times has Mr. Modesto pressured you to find the Hull's handbell?"

Drummond tried to reach Max, to pull him out of the office, but he couldn't get through the barrier. "She's poison, Max. Leave now. We'll go see Sandra, take her to a doctor. Come on."

Max didn't move. He stood rock-still. "What do you know about the handbell?"

"You really aren't too bright," Dr. Connor said. She lifted the glass vial. "Your wife's blood. I'll tell you everything you need to know to stop the coven, and I'll even throw in the handbell for free."

"I thought you didn't give anything away for free."

"Oh, he has a little bit of brains after all. Get me the blood and you'll get what you need. It's that simple. It's a non-negotiable deal. Bring it to me tonight. I'll be here."

Max took a long stride toward her desk and pointed his finger at her face. "You won't win this. Whatever's going on — I've beaten you before. I will again."

"Hallelujah." She lifted her hands toward the ceiling. In one hand, she held out the vial. "Tell yourself whatever you have to, but get me the blood."

Looking at the vial, Max wondered if he could do it. He believed that Sandra would resist. She understood witches and their spells better than he did — no way would she give up her blood. Yet she knew what they faced with the coven. Perhaps she would take the risk and volunteer.

He reached for the vial but pulled back before he touched it. He hated the thought that had entered his brain, but he couldn't deny it — what if he didn't tell her? In her current state, she might not be able to make such a decision. He could simply lie to her, tell her it's for a medical test, and she might not even remember it in the morning. Shaking off such a moral betrayal, Max glanced back at Drummond. Even if Max were so villainous as to attempt such a thing, Drummond would stop him.

Not that I'm seriously considering it anyway. Having the thought was despicable enough. But no matter how desperate he became, he would never stoop so low.

Perhaps the witch could sense the change within him, perhaps she could read his face better than he thought. Whichever the case, she thrust out her hand and said, "Take the vial, go to your pretty wife, and ask her a personal question. I promise you that's all it will take for you to bring me what I want. One intimate, personal question. After that, if I'm wrong, toss the vial and never bother me again. I'm sure you wouldn't object to that."

"Never seeing you again. That would be wonderful."

"One intimate, personal question. That's all."

Snatching the glass vial from her hand, Max whirled around and left the office. To Drummond, he raised his hand. "Don't say a word."

Chapter 19

RUNNING THE WINDSHIELD wipers to clean off the layer of pollen, Max grumbled in his mind at the inconvenience of city sprawl. He had spent too much time in the last few days stuck in his car. And now, as he headed back to the office, back to Sandra, he could either stew in his own fears or argue with Drummond. Floating above the passenger seat, his ghost partner made the decision easy.

"You got a problem with this?" Max prodded.

"Don't you?"

"I'd rather swipe a bit of my wife's blood than let her die at the hands of a witch coven of ghosts. You got another way out of this? Oh, wait, there's a simple way, isn't there? You could man up and go take care of Patricia's body yourself."

Picking at his lips, Drummond kept his eyes looking out the window. "For the sake of helping Sandra, I'm not taking your bait. And I know you want to help her, too. I only ask that you think through this some more before you do anything you can't undo."

"Sandra'll understand."

"I'm not worried about her in all this. She loves you. And we've all had to make tough choices when dealing with the Hulls. Of course, she'll understand. But giving her blood to Dr. Connor — that's insane. You can't do that."

Max drove on for two minutes without another word. Finally, he said, "I know."

And he did. Beyond his brain and his gut and his love, he knew it straight through to his soul. It reverberated deep inside him like an adrenaline rush that never died. His heart plummeted at the thought of what would happen if he let Dr. Connor have his wife's blood — they both would be slaves to that witch until they died. Perhaps even beyond that.

But at least they would be alive. If he failed to stop the coven, he and Sandra would be lucky if death was the worst result. More likely, they would learn a slew of ancient curses as each witch carved a new one into their skin.

That's why I took the vial.

"Listen," Drummond said, "I know this is a tough situation, but we need to focus on how to proceed. Forget about the dead ends and find something new."

Max wanted to smack Drummond hard on the back of the head, but the act would hardly satisfy considering his hand would go through Drummond and hit the dashboard instead. Besides, as Sandra had often pointed out — with the Hulls, the best way through was barreling straight on. Before he could do that, however, one last matter needed clearing up.

"Connor said Patricia's the High Priestess."

"I heard her," Drummond said.

"And she said that you knew Patricia was a witch long before —"

"I was there. I heard her."

"Well?"

"Well, nothing. Dr. Connor's a witch. Witches lie to fracture a partnership. You ever heard of divide and conquer? That's all she's up to. Telling you lies to make you doubt me and drive a deeper wedge between us."

"She also mentioned the handbell. Knew all about Modesto bugging us for it."

"You do remember that I was right outside the door? I heard everything."

"My point is that if she's so careful with her words, using them in an attempt to splinter us apart, then what does it mean that she mentioned the handbell?"

Drummond rubbed his chin. "It means we better find that damn handbell."

"It sure is sounding like a lot more than a family heirloom. Maybe they really can pull off this spell. But if that were true, then why would they —"

"Go find it, then. That's a smart move. Stop analyzing and go find it."

Max's face pinched as he bit back his anger. "You've got no idea what you're doing."

"About what?"

"You have any clue what I've got to build myself up to do here? With this vial?"

"I thought we were done with that."

"If I don't give Sandra's blood to that bitch, you know—"

"Okay, okay." Drummond kicked at the dashboard, his leg going straight through and his foot sticking out of the car's hood. "I'll do it. I'll take care of Patricia's corpse."

"You will?"

"I can't let anything happen to that doll of yours. I hoped maybe we'd have some way out of this that I wouldn't have to deal with my past, but the moment Matt Ernest died, I had no choice. I'm sorry. I should've told you from the start. Then there'd be no way for Connor to split us apart."

Max sat up, lighter and excited. "You're right. She wants to split us up, so that's what we'll do. We'll go on separate paths, and if she's watching, her arrogance will make her think she's winning. It'll give us a slight advantage when we see her tonight."

"What? You're still going through with the blood thing? There's no need. I'm going to do the job. We don't need Connor and her blood price anymore."

"I guess not. I just thought —"

"You thought you'd fill it with what? Pig's blood? Chicken? She'd see through it. After casting all the spells she's done in the past, I'm sure she knows her blood."

"I suppose. I want to see Sandra. Make sure she's okay."

"Of course. I'll go do what I have to. You check on your wife."

"After you're done, I want you to search for that handbell. Start at Reynolda House. They had the rest of the set on display a long time ago. Perhaps you can find something to help us. If that's a bust, go to a graveyard or to the Other and talk to the ghosts, or use some of those old detective skills of yours. Do whatever you need to do to find that handbell. When we meet Modesto tomorrow night, I've got to have it in hand."

"You can count on me."

"I know I can. Meet me back at the office by ten tonight. I'll look after Sandra and then do research on my end."

"You got it," Drummond said and disappeared.

As Max entered the city, the glass vial in his pocket grew heavier. He had always considered himself a man who could do what needed to be done, make the hard call, face the sacrifice that would save those he loved. But the gulf between what he considered himself and what he knew to be the truth widened in the face of these supernatural threats.

I'm just glad I don't have to deal with it any further.

He parked the car and headed up to Sandra. When he entered, expecting Sandra to be recovering on the couch, he found her pacing around her desk like a trapped panther. Upon seeing him, she rushed over, wrapped her arms around his waist, and kissed him hard on the lips.

"I'm so glad to see you. My mind's going crazy with worry."

"I'm fine," Max said, pulling back but she held tight.

"I know, I know. I love you so much, and with all that's happened, the thought of you out there, facing those dangerous witches — it just got to me."

Finally freeing himself, Max walked to the bookshelf. He pulled out one of Drummond's special books — the one with a flask of whiskey. "I'm here now. And I'm okay. You look a lot better. How do you feel? Besides paranoid for me."

She watched his movements, her eyes darting toward every creak in the building or chirp from a bird outside. "I feel like I had a thick, heavy chain around my throat attached to a big chunk of concrete, and the whole thing dragged me to the bottom of the ocean. And then suddenly, it broke. I was free. At first, I was disoriented. Sat here awhile waiting for you or Drummond or somebody to tell me what was going on. Then it all came back to me in a rush. That's when I started to worry about you. But you're here now. You're okay, right?"

"Absolutely fine."

Sandra's stomach gurgled loudly. "I guess I'm a bit hungry. Actually, now that I'm thinking about it, I'm starving. Let's get something to eat."

"Sure. Where do you want —"

"Fox and Hound. Let's go there."

Max arched an eyebrow. "Isn't that more for college kids?"

"After what I've been through, I could use a taste of youth around me. Come on. It'll be fun."

Thinking of the glass vial, Max said, "We don't really have time for fun right now. In fact, we need to talk about some serious things. Drummond and I met with Dr. Connor, and—"

"Not yet. I need to eat and it won't hurt anything if we go to a place that's a little fun. I promise I won't tell Drummond that you relaxed before dealing with witches, covens, and ghosts. Okay?"

She lowered her chin to her shoulder and gazed up at him with a coy look that often worked on him. He knew it. He knew she did, too. This time would be no different.

"Okay. We'll go eat and take a breather. But then we've got to talk."

"Fox and Hound?"

"If that's where my darling wants to go."

"That's where I want to go." She kissed him, pressing in and opening her mouth slightly — a sensuous kiss, the kind that often led them to more physical activities. When she broke the kiss, Max leaned in for more, but she put her finger across his lips. "Nope. I need food."

The Fox and Hound Pub was located on the edge of the city off Knollwood Avenue. It was part of large strip mall filled with restaurants, clothing stores, a bakery, postal service, and the like. The Pub held a large number of people, had televisions blaring away sporting events, and several pool tables set up on one end. Everything was decked out in wood and brass. The back wall encompassed the bar, and the overall atmosphere exuded youth and vibrancy.

Sandra giggled and twirled when they entered as if by being amongst all these young people had rejuvenated her own youth. Max noticed a fresh sparkle in her eye. Perhaps facing down a coven of ghosts and surviving had given her a new appreciation for living. She certainly seemed happier than he had seen her in a long time.

They ordered their meals and a couple beers. Sandra stretched her arms. "I could sure go for a cigarette."

"Since when do you smoke?"

She laughed — a little too long, too forced. "Since never. But, hon, we only get to live once."

"Cigarettes will make that one time around quite a bit shorter. I doubt you're allowed to smoke in here, anyway."

"That's no fun. I want to have fun. Want to play some pool? I'm not very good, but I do know how to handle a stick." When she saw the shocked reaction on Max's face, she laughed. "I'm going to go freshen up. Be back in two shakes."

Max watched her walk off. He swore she added a bit more sway in her lovely hips but not in her usually sassy manner. This time, she wanted him salivating. Had it really been so long since she acted like this? So long that he was shocked at her behavior? They weren't old by any stretch of the term, but they were far from their college years, too.

Those were the wild times. Meeting up on the weekends — starting the weekend on Thursday — and borrowing a barely-running car from her roommate. Driving up the Michigan coast until they reached the little, northern towns that were too small to warrant a dot on a map. They'd go to the local grocer, stock up, go to the nearest liquor store, stock up, grab a room in a motel, and never leave until Sunday night. The entire weekend would be a two-person orgy of alcohol, sex, laughter, and sleep. Once they removed their clothes, they never dressed until the day they left. Sometimes they'd order a pizza and answer the door in the nude. Sometimes they grew serious, held each other close, and talked of their life in the future.

But that was a decade ago. Another life. Before they suffered through poverty and job loss. Long before Max learned of ghosts and witches, covens and curses, Hulls and Modesto.

Maybe Sandra was right to want to cut loose a bit. Even with all that hung over them, taking what little time they had to clear the mind sounded like a smart move. He also had Drummond working to find the handbell, and before leaving the office, Max had left a note telling Drummond where they went. Should the old detective find anything important, he'll be able to tell them right away. The situation was covered. Besides, there was always the possibility that they would end up dead or cursed after all this, so why not find some time for a little living?

As Sandra sashayed back to the table, Max felt his tensions easing. Running her finger along his shoulders, she bit her lip, leaned in and kissed him again. The electricity from lip to toe and everywhere in between brought back more memories than he knew he had held.

She must have felt it, too, because she caught her breath before melting into his side. "Suddenly, I'm not all that hungry."

"At least, not for food."

"At least."

They gazed into each other's eyes with the innocence and desire of hormone-crazed teens. There was nothing innocent, however, in the way Sandra's hand crept up Max's thigh. She nibbled at his neck, and he could smell the perfume she had dabbed on in the bathroom — a sweet, candy smell.

"Let's go for a walk," she whispered in his ear.

Max tossed more than enough cash to the waitress as they headed outside. Sandra led the way, her hand trailing behind to hold his. Max's heart hammered in his chest, and for the first time in ages, the cause was not fear of impending death.

They turned the corner into the back end of the restaurant. A hill of grass led up the left side, and Max heard the steady rush of cars on Highway 421 from the other side. Three cars were parked next to the building and a filthy dumpster after that.

Sandra took Max behind the dumpster, spun back on him, and planted her mouth against his. Fiery lust ignited along every inch of his body. He pressed against her, feeling every soft curve of hers push back. Her candy aroma mixed with the stench of the dumpster, turning the groping into something both erotic and depraved at the same time.

He brought his hand to her breast, but she shoved it away. "Not until I say so." A devilish grin crossed her lips, and she stepped away from him. She leaned against the wall, arching her body to push out her chest like a vintage pin-up girl, and licked her lips. Max stepped closer, but she put up a warning finger. "Not until I say so."

Max had never seen her take command like this. She had often said that she had to be tough all day long in life, so when it came to sex, she wanted to let go of control. Yet seeing her this way, relishing her life in such a forceful way, thrilled him. He never minded the way things were before, but this sudden change had brought with it a wealth of new sensations to his body.

"Okay," she said. "Take me. Take me hard."

Max moved in, shoving her against the wall as her arms and legs wrapped around him. He kissed and suckled every part of her he could reach, and he heard her moan a guttural animal sound — unlike anything he'd ever heard from her before.

He froze.

Nothing about her behavior had been right. Not just the sex, but the way she threw aside their responsibilities, the way she wanted to be around such a young crowd, even the way she spoke. He had chalked it up to post-life-threatening reaffirmation, only now that sounded false to his ear.

Ask her a personal question.

Why would Dr. Connor have said that unless she knew something and wanted to prove it to Max? She had thought that such a question would change his mind about the vial of blood, so what did that mean about Sandra?

One intimate, personal question.

Sandra reached down between his legs. "Come on, baby. Give me this."

He wanted to sound natural, as if he meant every word, but he heard the cold, monotone delivery that his chilled heart could manage. "You want it like that time in Dallas?"

"Oh, yeah, baby. Just like in Dallas."

The words thundered down upon him, boulders of reality smashing apart the fantasy this woman had built up that he so willingly fell into. He stumbled back a step, afraid to look upon her face, afraid he would lose his will to do what needed doing. And the witch Connor knew all along.

"Honey, don't stop now."

He shook his head slow as the words rose in his throat. "We've never been to Dallas."

Sandra put up her hands in a shrug. "Whoops. Guess you found me out."

"Who are you?"

"This is still your wife's body. You won't be cheating on her."

"Who are you?" he screamed, pulling back his arm and making a fist.

"Sugar, I'm exactly who you think I am."

"Patricia Welling."

She nodded. Max felt as if he had taken a punch. If Patricia possessed Sandra, then what had happened to his wife? Was she still in there or should he be mourning her death? And something bad must have happened to Drummond, otherwise he would have destroyed Patricia's corpse. Had they been set up by Connor?

"Sandra? You in there?"

"She ain't coming out. Now, you come over here and give me a good time. If you don't, I'll go find one of those handsome, young men in the bar. I'm sure they'd love this body."

Max thrust out his left hand, pinning her against the wall. His right hand, still curled in a fist, hung back ready to strike.

Looking in her eyes, he didn't see anyone he recognized, but he saw a tinge of concern — what did she have to fear? Drummond?

She laughed. "You going to hit me? Poor little Sandra's face. Are you a wife-beater?"

Something was wrong here — more wrong than the obvious. Max struggled to find Connor's angle, how it might hurt him, but she had wanted him to ask the questions — she had wanted him to learn Sandra had been possessed. Whatever was going on, these witches were not on the same side. And that meant that he needed the blood of Patricia Welling — no, he needed the blood of his wife, possessed by Patricia Welling.

"Last chance, lover. You can enjoy this body in ways you never have or —"

He punched her. One hard crack to the head.

She went down, rolling on the wet, dirty asphalt into the way of any alley traffic. Max rubbed his fist. Punching a person's skull hurt. And he hadn't knocked her out. In the movies, one punch knocked out a bad guy with ease — apparently it wasn't actually that simple.

She raised up to all fours. "Sorry, hon," he said, walked up to her side and punched her on the back of the head. A muffled cry escaped her lungs as she fell forward. Still, she moved. He had to get her unconscious. That's all he could think to do. Get her unconscious, take her blood, make Connor exorcise this ghost from his wife. But she still moved, still tried to get to her feet. He rolled her over, pulled back his fist again, when her eyes shot open.

"Help! Rape!" she screamed.

Two young men the size of linebackers poked their heads around the corner. "Hey!" one of them called out. Before Max could do anything more, they tackled him and a horrible beating ensued.

Chapter 20

MAX OPENED HIS EYES to see Drummond floating above. His body ached, his mouth felt a size too big, and he tasted blood in his mouth. He tried to sit up but his ribs sent sharp pains into his side.

Drummond slid down next to Max. "Easy there, palooka. You got on the wrong end of a lot of fists. You'll live, but I'm glad I ain't you for the next week."

Max spit blood. His tongue ran along his teeth — thankfully, none missing. "She's got Sandra. Your ghost bitch is in my Sandra."

"I figured that much out."

Trying to stand again, Max groaned and flopped back to the ground. "We've got find her. She could be doing anything with my wife. Or anyone."

"We'll find her. Calm down."

"How the fuck am I supposed to calm down? My wife is possessed by a dead witch. How am I supposed to say that sentence calmly?"

"First, you need to listen. Can you do that? Because I promise you, the last thing on Patricia Welling's mind is bedding down with a man."

"That wasn't how she behaved with me."

"She was toying with you. Screwing with your head. Just like Connor. That's what witches do."

Max hesitated. He wanted to believe Drummond, wanted to know that the woman he loved would not have to spend the rest of her life with memories of strangers. He didn't want to think about it either. Drummond's eyes — so sincere, so convincing.

Holding his jaw tight both from frustration and the bruises

along the bone, Max finally said, "You promise me. You tell me that she won't defile my wife that way."

"She won't. It isn't easy to possess somebody conscious, somebody who will fight to regain control of her body — and you know Sandra's fighting like a cornered tiger. Patricia's going to be using a lot of energy to maintain that possession. And since she went to all that trouble and fight, there's got to be more on her mind than sex."

"You better be right."

"I am. And I'm sorry. I should've been here instead of wasting time following one dead end after another."

Max glowered at Drummond. "You should have finished the job."

"I did. I demolished that corpse."

"Then it wasn't Patricia Welling in the Fed Building."

"It absolutely was. I don't know why it didn't work, but we did what we set out to do."

"Then why the hell —"

"I don't know. But getting angry won't help us. Let's figure this out, find your wife, fix this mess."

Though he managed to stand, it took more effort than he imagined any simple act would require. Yet with each passing minute, he felt his strength returning. The brutes who had battered him caused plenty of bruises but no broken bones. Even his ribs looked to be in the proper place — purple and black all along his side, but nothing where it didn't belong.

"You okay? Can you walk?"

"Give me a minute," Max snapped. "I got my ass kicked in." He took a few tentative steps. "And my ass hurts, too."

The back door to the bar opened, and a heavyset man stepped out carrying two garbage bags. As he threw out the trash, he gave a few cursory glances Max's way.

Once the man went back inside, Max rubbed his jaw. "Help me think this through. What do we know?"

Drummond made a lazy circle as he spoke. "All the witches we know of have been freed from the curse and destroyed. So is there another one? One we missed?"

"Possibly, but why is Patricia Welling still in Sandra? Why didn't she go poof?"

"Maybe because she has a body now."

Max nodded. "She has Sandra's body, so she doesn't need her old one. She must have taken over Sandra back at the church. I should've seen it. I did see it. Sandra was acting weird from the moment we left that church, but I didn't realize — and now she's fighting for her life."

"Focus, Max. Please. I need your help. Sandra needs your help."

With a deep breath that sent spikes of pain straight along his spine, Max nodded. "I'm sorry. I'll be okay. You're right, I've got to focus."

"That's right. Sandra's counting on you."

Max's eyes narrowed. "Connor knew. She had to."

"That's why she wanted you to get the blood. Not so she would have control over Sandra, but so she could control Patricia."

"But why not take care of it herself? If she's so powerful, why get me involved? She hates me."

"Maybe that's why. Hatred can push people to do some dumb things."

Heading back to his car, Max rolled his shoulder. He couldn't afford for his bruised body to stiffen up at a crucial moment. Despite the pain, he needed to stay limber.

The parking lot had emptied, and his car stood a lone vigil, waiting for a driver. "Connor's not dumb. She used me for a purpose. She's waiting for something to happen, maybe, or she didn't want to be seen doing the job or —"

"Modesto." Drummond clapped his hands, startling Max. "The Hulls must not know what she's up to."

"Which is what?"

"I hate to say it, but it looks like there's only one person who has the answers. At least, one who might be willing to talk."

Max nodded gravely. He opened the car door and its whine sounded much like he felt. "If Sandra wasn't in trouble, I'd never agree to this."

"I know. Can you drive?"

"Unless you can, I don't have a choice."

"I'll go on ahead, make sure it's safe."

"Okay. See you back at good ol' Doc Connor's place."

"Promise me one thing."

"What?"

"Don't kill her."

Max raised an eyebrow, then got in the car. He slammed the door shut and started the engine. Drummond hovered for a moment, but when he saw he would get no further answer, he disappeared.

Chapter 21

THE BLUE DIGITAL CLOCK on his dashboard read three a.m. Though his body complained with every motion, he did not feel tired. Too much adrenaline, stress, and fear.

When this is over, I'm going to sleep for days.

As he stepped from the car, the still air smelled of a coming storm. Hot, humid, sticky — soon it would all break under a torrent of rain. But in the morning, the sun would return and pollen would coat the world. By noon, it would be as if nothing had happened.

Not for me.

Max walked a labored stride toward Connor's office. No matter what happened, he knew he would not be the same. Considering the dark thoughts that drifted through his mind, the horrible things he now thought himself willing to do should Dr. Connor prove uncooperative — he never imagined he could think like that.

I haven't done anything, yet.

The word yet echoed in his head.

"There you are." Drummond zipped out of the office, coming straight through a wall, and darted right at Max. "Hurry. She's dying."

Max managed a slow jog, each footfall sending sharp jolts up his leg. Drummond had unlocked the front door, and Max shuffled down the hall toward the back office. The photos on the wall had been knocked askew. A few lay shattered on the floor. Before he entered the back office, Max saw blood streaked on the baseboard.

Connor's office had been ransacked — papers strewn about, book stacks toppled over, wall charts ripped into shreds. A putrid odor rose from a shattered jar containing a pig fetus. Dr.

Connor lay on the floor, her eyes open wide and unblinking, blood pooling beneath her, a wide gash in her forehead. She had strange cuts on her arm like claw marks.

Wrinkling his nose, Max inched forward. "Dr. Connor?"

The witch's eyes rested upon Max. In a weak whisper, she said, "I told you."

"You're alive," he said, pulling out his phone. "I'm calling for help."

"Of course, she's alive," Drummond said. "You think I'd lie about that?"

Connor raised her hand and wagged a finger. "No help. I've reached the end."

Max's thumb hovered over the Send button. He looked to Drummond who answered with a mild shrug. Big help.

Connor lifted her head and coughed blood. "The handbell."

"Where is it? What's it for?"

"Foolish boy. You never listen." She chuckled despite the strain each quiet word cost her. "I warned you what Hull was doing. I warned you."

"You said that they were trying to resurrect Tucker Hull. I listened to you. I did. It's one of the reasons I haven't done any work for the Hulls."

"First, an item from the source — the journal. Second, a powerful charm full of life — Blackbeard's hair. And last, a cursed object that can call upon a soul with all the power of a great witch — the handbell."

"That's really what it's for?"

"Thirteen bells for thirteen witches. And one of them missing."

Drummond drifted in towards Max. "Patricia's bell."

"My mother," Connor went on, "had fallen in love with Hull and knew that if he ever discovered the depth of her feelings, he would destroy her."

"Not a good idea to get emotionally involved with your prime witch," Max said.

"Exactly. She stole the bell to protect herself — she hoped to use its power, if necessary. But she failed and the bell was lost."

"And Hull needs it for his resurrection spell."

Coughing up more blood, Connor nodded.

Drummond bent closer to Max. "Not to be so callous, but if you don't get everything we need from her —"

Max waved the detective off. He knew what needed to be done. "Where's the bell?"

"The bell will draw out Patricia's ghost, leaving your wife an empty vessel for a few seconds. If Modesto can cast the spell at that moment, Tucker Hull can enter your wife's body before her own spirit can reclaim it."

Before she could finish her sentence, Max grabbed her collar and yanked her up. "Then where the hell is the bell?"

Her eyes rolled upward. Max slapped her face hard three times before she focused on him again. "I never found it. That was supposed to be your job."

He dropped her and clutched his head. "We're screwed."

"Don't give up," Drummond said. "Remember, Modesto doesn't know where it is, either. Tucker Hull can't come back without it."

"Great. So, Sandra will just share her body with your old girlfriend forever."

"We'll find the handbell. We'll use it and get Patricia out of there, but we'll do it away from Modesto and his spell. Come on, Max. We're not giving up."

Max glanced down at Connor, her blood pool widening. "You weren't trying to help us. What did you need the blood for? Protection?"

She moved her head up and down slightly, weakly. Inhaling with a wheezing sound, she raised her arm like a marionette on a limp string. She let the breath leave her body and pointed toward her desk. When the last of her breath left her body, her arm flopped to the floor, and she never inhaled again.

"Crap," Max said. Bad enough he failed to get the information he needed from her, but with the way his luck had run, he guessed the FBI would be blaming him for this death, too.

"You okay?" Drummond asked.

"What's it say about me that I'm no longer freaking out over dead bodies?"

"That you're finally starting to understand this world."

Max sighed. "That's dark."

"I'm a ghost. What do you expect?"

Stepping over to Connor's desk, Max said, "She pointed here. Help me look."

Drummond floated around Max as he leafed through her file cabinet. "I see pens, papers, appointment book, some bills."

"I don't need an inventory."

"Well, I can't search like you unless I'm willing to take on the pain of touching things."

"Sandra's life is at stake and you're worried about a little pain?"

"Did you forget what I did in the basement of that crazy art forger? I took on a lot of pain for you both back then. And there was the time —"

"Okay, I'm sorry. We don't need to go into all the times you've suffered for us."

"Then why don't you look at your feet?"

"Huh?"

"On the floor. There's a book at your feet. Must have been knocked off her desk when she was attacked."

Max crouched down and stared at the book. It had that crinkled, leathery covering he hated to see — human skin. With every effort to hide his revulsion, he picked up the book and placed it on Connor's desk. A long feather — maybe an owl, maybe an eagle, probably a vulture — had been used as a bookmark.

Opening the book, Max noticed his fingers shaking. His pulse beat against his neck. As he pushed the cover over, he flinched. He felt like a mouse inspecting cheese on a trap. The bookmark brought him to a page with the words *THE BOOK OF SPELLS* written in a meticulous script.

"I think we've got something," Max said. He snapped the book shut, tucked it under his arm, ignored the involuntary shiver his body made upon contact with the human skin cover, and headed out of the office.

"Where are we going?" Drummond asked.

"My house. We can figure this all out over there."

"But the office is —"

"I'm not sure I want to go back in there just yet."

"Because of Sandra?"

"Why is that a shock? I love my wife and when I last saw her there, she wasn't really my wife. I won't be eating at the Fox and Hound anytime soon either. Besides, if Connor is right, then Hull and Modesto need that bell more than anything. Modesto's been trying to use me to find it, and since I haven't seen him trying to follow me —"

"He's probably staking out the office."

"So we go to my house, take a close look at this book, and see if we can't save Sandra, stop this coven, and prevent Tucker Hull from being resurrected."

"Sounds like a lovely evening."

Chapter 22

AS THEY ZIPPED ALONG the highway, the night's lights danced along Max's face. His stern expression cut through the reds, yellows, and whites leaving only the dark. They had been in dire situations before, but this time, he had no idea if he could ever get his wife back. It wasn't a calculated risk. What he had in mind would be a step into a world he wanted less and less to do with.

Stay strong. Stay focused. Only one thing matters — get Sandra back.

When Max neared his house, Drummond leaned forward, squinting as he looked out the windshield. "Keep driving," he said. "Don't slow down."

"What's wrong?"

"Do it."

Max drove by the house and turned at the end of the street. Drummond waved him onward while watching the road behind them.

"Get back on the highway."

"What's going on? Did you see Modesto?"

Drummond settled back. "Worse. The FBI."

Slapping the steering wheel, Max said, "Damn. Now what?"

"You got a lot of people interested in you. I'd say even if you wanted to, the office is definitely out, now. We could go back to Connor's place."

"And get picked up for her murder?"

"Well, there's that, of course."

Max glanced up at the oversized green signs passing by on the highway. One read — LEXINGTON. "I think I know where to go."

"I'm listening."

"You know what's near Lexington? Thomasville."

Drummond shook his head. "Leed's house? The cops'll have that place taped off."

"That hasn't stopped us before. I doubt anybody's going to be out there tonight. Why would they? It's not a pressing murder for the local cops, and the FBI are involved, so the locals may not even have authority to be out there. We know the FBI are out at my house."

"They might be at both locations."

"You really think the FBI is going to put that much manpower onto this little case?"

"I suppose not."

"Something else bothering you then?"

Drummond shifted uncomfortably. "Leed died there ... in a bad way."

"You afraid his ghost might be hanging around?"

"I'm not afraid of him. But I don't necessarily want to see him either. Especially if he's not quite himself."

"You think he turned?"

"From what you said, he had a pretty violent death. I'd think that might push a guy toward the evil side a lot quicker. Don't you?"

"Well, we don't have many options, and I'm not wasting the night searching for a place to sit down while we work this out. Sandra needs us. It's that simple. If Leed is there, you'll either make friends or you'll suck it up and deal."

Drummond tugged at his bottom lip. "I figured you might say that."

The saying goes *Third times the charm,* but Max felt nothing charming about seeing Leed's house again. Cast in the dim moonlight, the old place had died along with Leed. The porch which had seemed quaint, now looked disheveled. The charisma of the warped wood floors and peeling white paint had turned ugly and dilapidated. Instead of the charming old farmhouse on the hill, Leed's place had taken on the air of a haunted house that children hurried by, afraid they might stir something in the shadows. Worst of all, Max thought they might be right.

Drummond floated into the living room, his eyes roving every corner, every hiding place, every darkened nook. "Looks okay."

Max let the witch's book fall to the floor, leaned his back against the wall, and slid down with an exhausted exhalation. He stared at the furniture but couldn't bring himself to sit on anything in the house. Drummond may not have found anything, but somewhere in the house, Leed's ghost had to be hanging around. He had seen that horrible death. No way did Leed peacefully move on to wherever the moving on go.

While rolling his neck and stretching his arms, Max said, "Let's look at the book and figure this all out. I don't want to spend any more time here than I have to."

Drummond's focus turned toward the kitchen — the place Leed had died. "I think something's in there."

"Help me with the book."

"It's like a miniature ghost that's not all there. Like a little bit of ghost but nothing more. I've never seen that before."

"Ignore it."

Drummond entered the kitchen while Max leafed through the spell book. "It can't be bigger than my hand, and — oh. It's Leed. At least, I think it is. But he's not fully formed. Or ..."

"Do I want to hear the rest of that sentence?"

"Probably not. I think Patricia, when she killed Leed, I think she cut apart his soul. There isn't enough left to make a ghost."

"All the more reason to help me out here. Last thing you want is your old girlfriend to shred your soul to pieces."

But Drummond stayed in the kitchen. Max could hear him cooing to Leed like a little girl taking in an injured bunny. If the whole thing weren't so disturbing, Max would have marveled at this unexpected side of Drummond. But things were disturbing. And they wouldn't get any better on their own.

Max turned page after page, the dried pages crinkling as they moved. A rich, pleasant smell rose from the book, but when he remembered what made the book's cover, he shuddered at what might produce that aroma. From then on, he turned the pages by pinching them with the tips of his forefinger and thumb. He knew he looked prissy and foolish, but nobody was looking — and even Hull couldn't pay him enough to dig his hands into a book made of human beings.

"Poor little Leed," Drummond said from the kitchen. "You're really lost. Don't worry. It's confusing, I know. But I won't abandon you."

The next page Max turned brought him to a section marked *Location Spells*. Though the text had been handwritten, Max's experience deciphering the scripts of people writing from centuries ago made reading this relatively easy.

> *All Location spells are easy to cast, entry level magiks which can be used, as the name would imply, to acquire the location of an object, emotion, or soul. Because of its simplicity, any Location magik can divine if the caster has any basic skill or inner-power. One who fails at this task will never rise amongst those of our Order.*

"We've got something big here," Max called out.

Drummond came back in, his face blank. "Hm? What did you find?"

Max glanced quizzically at the kitchen but decided to let it go. There would be time to ask about Leed later — if they survived. "Well, first, this book isn't a generic spellbook. It's a coven's Grimoire. It's got references to an order and a hierarchy."

"You think it's Patricia's coven?"

"How many covens do you think there are around here? Wait. Don't answer that."

"You're probably right. Why else would Connor point us to this book?"

A disturbing thought struck Max. "Does this mean Connor is part of Patricia's old coven? That it might still be active?"

"Connor and her mother were never the kind of witches to join up with anyone. They worked for hire, and they enjoyed being amongst the most powerful in the area. Covens are formed by witches seeking companions, friendship, access to knowledge, and most of all, they want to strengthen their power through numbers."

"Like a gang."

"And what need does Connor have for joining a gang? My hunch is that she got hold of this Grimoire through one piece of nasty business or another, and the witch ghosts didn't like it too much. That's why they ripped her apart. That's also why she wanted us to take the book."

"So the coven will come after us?"

"They're already after us. But I didn't see any other ghosts at Connor's office. And they obviously didn't find the Grimoire or didn't have time to look or something, because we've got it. Maybe Connor planned to cast some of the spells in it against them. She did want that blood, after all."

"Well, that's the second thing. There's a few location spells in here. I'm thinking we could use one to find the handbell."

Drummond's face dropped. "There's a spell in that book to find the handbell?"

"I think so."

"Then why the hell didn't anybody use it?"

Max read over the spell — its ingredients and procedure. "Maybe it's more dangerous than it looks. Maybe Modesto didn't want Connor knowing what he was up to."

"She already knew. She's been warning you about it for awhile now."

"I don't have an answer. And, frankly, I don't care. Not while my wife is in trouble."

Drummond said nothing more. He simply glanced at the list of ingredients and began searching through the house. Max followed suit, checking out each room of the house carefully. They needed four blue candles, a goblet filled with water, and lotus incense.

As they rummaged through the house, Max noticed that Drummond repeatedly patted his left coat pocket and murmured softly to it. Max had a suspicion about that, especially since all mention of the unformed ghost of Leed had disappeared, but things were creepy enough without adding a new dimension to his understanding of the ghost world. If they made it through all this, if Sandra made it through, he would ask. Sandra knew so much more about it all, and she could explain it in a way that wouldn't disturb him, that might actually make the whole thing logical and benign.

In the dining room, Max located a silver goblet with Roman lettering around the lip. Drummond indicated where several packs of incense had been stashed in the bedroom. And finally, in Leed's office, where Drummond could not enter, Max found two plastic tubs filled with candles — red, black, green, white, and a blue nub.

Max picked up a red candle. "Will any one of these do?"

"Spells are very specific. I don't know why the color matters, but it does. Probably has something to do with whatever's inside them to give them the color."

He glanced at the candle, thought for a second about the deep red color, the blood red color. He shot open his hand, letting the candle bang on the floor. "No candles we can use." Wiping his palm against his shirt, Max stepped out of Leed's office. "We've got to find something. There's no way I'm waiting until morning to pick up blue candles at a store. Who knows what your girlfriend will have done with my wife by then."

"She's not my girlfriend. She's not my anything." Drummond cocked his head toward his coat pocket. "Not a bad idea," he whispered.

"What idea?"

Trying to look casual, Drummond said, "We know one place that's filled with the ingredients a witch would need for spells."

"Really?" Max shook his head as he gathered his things. "I hate that place."

But he knew Drummond was right. Despite the late hour, despite the weariness in his muscles and bones, Max trudged back to his car and headed back towards Winston-Salem, towards Dr. Connor's office. The drive would take an hour — a long time to be stuck worrying for Sandra with nothing active to do — but at least Drummond remained quiet throughout the trip. Any talk with that ghost would have led to the thing in his coat pocket, and Max wanted nothing to do with that at the moment. Not that he feared the little thing might be Leed. More that Max feared it might not be — that Drummond's mounting emotions in this case were pushing him towards insanity and turning him into an evil specter.

At length, they turned onto Westgate Center Drive, passed by Home Depot, and drove into the section of doctor's offices, local accounting firms, and small legal practices. Max had traveled this route more times than he had ever wanted. The quiet darkness of a late night visit to the witch had become too familiar. Except this time, the darkness filled up with flashing lights of red and blue.

Three police cars blocked off the parking lot while detectives walked in and out of Connor's office. A WXII News van sat as close to the action as the police would allow, while a reporter taped her story in front of the bright lights provided by the cameraman.

Before Drummond could say anything, Max said, "I know, I know. Keep driving."

They passed by in time to see a covered body wheeled out the front door. Up ahead, Max turned the car back toward Hanes Mall, figuring they could park on the far side away from this action and plan their next step.

Drummond had a different idea. "Go to Matt Ernest's house."

"What?"

"He's got all sorts of magic-related items there. You know it. There's a good chance he'll have the candles. They're fairly common amongst those who dabble in magic. Considering all the candles Leed had, Ernest would probably have more. And besides —"

"Enough. This isn't a court trial. You don't have to lay out all the evidence. If you think we can get the candles there, then that's what we'll do. But if I get caught and sent to jail, you're doing time with me. I don't know how, but I'll make sure you're there."

"You really want me haunting your prison cell?"

Max thought about it and shuddered. "Shut up."

It took about fifteen minutes to reach Ernest's house. Max parked a few doors beyond to be safe. "Stay here," he told Drummond. He expected a protest, but Drummond waved him on, the detective more interested in talking with his coat pocket than arguing with Max.

Max strolled up to the house as casually as he could manage, taking furtive glances around, seeking any sign of trouble. Nobody watched him. Besides, at such a late hour, anybody still awake was probably drunk.

Or an insomniac happy to watch my every move and report me to the police.

He fought off the avenues of thought that wanted to take him and focused on the job. From Drummond he had learned to act with confidence when doing what one shouldn't be doing. Observers would fill in the most plausible explanations if he behaved as if everything was normal. So, Max didn't hesitate when he reached the house. He walked straight to the back door and pulled off the tape he had recently cut.

Had he time to plan for this break-in, he would have brought along a flashlight. Instead, Max had to pop on his cellphone. The bluish hue cast across the crime scene accentuated the claw marks in the walls and disarray of the rooms. The air smelled damp and dead. Every footstep creaked.

Ignoring all the messages his brain screamed at him, all the instincts to run away from this horrible place, Max pressed straight for Ernest's room — the man's last stand. He stood at the closed doorway to Ernest's room, breathing hard though he had done little more than walk into the house. Courage, bravery — these were acts one took despite the fear raging in one's mind. He wished Drummond were here. Or Sandra. Anybody who could tell him if ghosts occupied the house or if he stood alone in an empty hall.

When Patricia Welling attacked his wife at the church, she had not been alone. Yet Drummond had not mentioned any other ghosts since then — except for whatever Leed had become. But surely, the other coven ghosts had followed them.

"No," he said to the house. "They followed their High Priestess." Wherever Patricia had taken Sandra's body, that was where the other ghosts would be found.

Then I'm alone here.

"Okay, then. Go." Max threw open the door, rushed in, and headed for the closet. The symbols on the walls designed to protect Matt Ernest seemed to slither away in the dim light. He flashed his cellphone around until he saw a stack of boxes. He poured through these as fast as possible, holding his breath most of the time as if to gasp the air in the room would be to inhale evil itself.

On the third box, he struck gold. Well, blue. The candles were square at the base, thin, and as long as his forearm. He grabbed four, stepped away, came back, and took two more — just in case.

Moving fast, he headed down the hall when he heard Ernest's bedroom door slam behind him. Max froze. He tried to sense any change in the air — a drop in temperature, a bright perfume or a foul odor, the general aura of the room. Anything that might hint at a ghost — benign or otherwise. But it was no use. Whatever wiring in his brain allowed him to see and interact with Drummond went no further. He was as blind to other ghosts as any everyday person.

The door banged open and closed again.

Max walked straight toward the back door, not wanting to look behind. As he reached out to open the door, something ice cold tapped across his neck. He whirled around and saw nothing. Fumbling behind him for the doorknob, his eyes darted around the darkness.

Though he could hear the shaking in his breath, he opened his mouth wide and said as firmly as he could manage, "You go tell the High Priestess I'm coming for her. You tell her that if she harms my wife, I'll curse her with the worst things I can find." He swore he could hear confusion and uncertainty in the air. As his hand found the doorknob, he couldn't resist adding a final blow. "Oh, and tell her the spells will come from your own Grimoire."

He opened the door and turned, but before he could exit, the door shut hard enough to crack the panes. An icy touch clamped around his neck. He tried to inhale, but what little air managed to get through chilled his lungs painfully.

Max tried to force the door open. He pulled and kicked at it, but it refused to budge. The darkness in the room grew even darker. Little spots of color danced before him. Max lifted his hand for the doorknob one more time, but his fingers only slapped at it. He couldn't breathe, couldn't feel the air in his lungs, couldn't hear the subtlest wheeze. He fell back, the candles tumbling to the floor, and he had long enough to regret not being able to save Sandra.

"Max?" Drummond's deep voice echoed in the room.

Max saw the detective pop through a wall. Drummond acted fast. Leaping above Max, Drummond engaged in a bizarre fight where his opponent could not be seen — at least by Max.

The grip on his throat loosened, and he coughed and sputtered while Drummond threw punches into the empty air. Drummond ducked, popped back up, and shot a deep uppercut. With his chest puffed, he stared at the corner of the room for a moment before turning to Max.

"You okay?"

Max got back to his feet. "Thanks. Is it a witch?"

"Definitely. Let's get out of here before she wakes up."

Collecting the candles, Max nodded. "Why did you come in, anyway?"

"A car pulled up, parked, but nobody got out. I think the cops are staking out the house. Maybe they found a connection with Connor's murder."

"Or maybe Modesto is playing both sides. The Hulls do have influence with some of the law."

"Doesn't really matter. You've got to sneak out of here

without them seeing you. Crouch down, follow me, and do as I say. It'll be easy."

Even as Max crouched before the back door, he rolled his eyes. Drummond passed through the wall and reappeared outside the house. Here we go. Max opened the back door and slipped out. Keeping low to the ground, he duck-walked around the corner. His thighs burned with the effort, turning his quads into sharp rocks that ground into his bones with every waddling step. But pulling a quad seemed a better risk than getting picked up by the police.

Drummond pointed to a telephone pole. "See the shadow from the streetlight?" A thick black line ran from the base of the telephone pole clear up to where Max squatted. "You can stand and walk in that shadow right up to the pole. Our friend is parked across the street. Stay in that shadow and he won't see you."

When Max stood, his legs screamed in both relief and pain. He wanted to move fast along the shadow, but with his muscles protesting every motion, he had to take small, slow steps. Probably saved his hide. Had he raced over to the pole, he would have most likely slipped out of the shadow's narrow confines. Taking a deliberate pace meant he could place each foot carefully.

Once he reached the telephone pole, Drummond pointed down the street to his car. "This is the hard part. When I tell you, you're going to have make a run for your car. Sprint down there, get in, and drive away."

"But —"

"Trust me. Wait for my signal." Drummond slid into the amber pool of the streetlight. "We'll give you as much time as we can."

"We?"

"Be quiet and wait."

Drummond reached into his coat pocket. When he pulled his hand out, he had it shaped as if he held something, but Max saw nothing. Drummond bent over and whispered to the nothing. Leed?

From the look on Drummond's face, Max discerned that Leed had zipped away. A moment of silence passed. As Max wondered what Leed would do, he heard a car alarm go off several houses up — away from his car. Another alarm went off, this one complete with flashing headlights. Max watched Drummond, waiting for a signal. He rubbed his thighs with his free hand, his other clutching the candles against his body — Sandra's life rested in those candles.

A third alarm went off, the kind that changed tones every few seconds. Whatever Drummond had waited for happened. He clapped his hands and waved Max on. "Come on. Go!"

Max shoved off the telephone pole and rushed for his car. He wanted to sprint, pour every ounce of power into his legs, but his thighs buckled. It took all his will to keep upright.

He snatched a peek over his shoulder and saw a man standing next to a car. The man placed his hands on his hips and looked up the street at the increasing number of car alarms. Though Max only had time to see the man in silhouette, he saw enough — Stevenson, FBI.

That got his legs moving. He half-jogged, half-skipped his way to his car, slipped in the driver's seat and turned the engine over. People had come outside to turn off their alarms only to have the alarms start up again. All that noise and confusion masked Max's engine, and as he drove away, he saw Stevenson in the rearview mirror — standing with his hands on his hips, watching the bizarre car alarms.

By the time Max returned to Leed's house, his adrenaline rush had worn off, dropping his tired body a few notches further toward exhaustive collapse. He stumbled into the house and leaned against the living room wall. As his eyes closed and his breathing slowed, he heard Drummond's deep tones arguing with someone.

"They're not going to understand. Hell, I don't get it either."

With his back, Max pushed off the wall and moved closer toward the hall leading further into the house. Drummond stood near the end of the hall, yelling at his hand which cupped nothing at all — which meant probably the ghost of Leed.

"Shut up already. I appreciate what you did but that doesn't give you any right to meddle here. Patricia Welling is my responsibility. You did your part ... What? ... I'm not still in love with her ... You don't know what you're talking about ... If I had known then ... that doesn't prove I knew anything. And besides, raking over the past won't change where we are now ... Don't tell me to calm down."

Drummond's gray face flushed red for a split second. Max cleared his throat loudly and when Drummond spun toward him, Max nearly fell back from the man's glare.

"What do you want?" Drummond said, his brow turned down sharp, his voice graveled as if he had smoked all night. A haze of darkness lifted off his shoulders.

Max tried to keep his face calm. Inside, every synapse fired off red alert warnings. "Drummond? You in there? Calm down. Stay with me."

"You blame me for this, don't you? For what's happened to Sandra. Everyone blames me."

"I don't blame you for something you did long ago and out of love. And I need your help now. Please, don't turn. Stay the man I know. Come on ... Marshall."

Drummond's face relaxed. He lifted his head and looked around as if unsure how he got to the house. "About time you got here." As he moved into the living room, he placed the object in his hand back into his coat pocket. "Best get this spell done before the sun rises. They tend to be stronger when the stars and moon are visible. At least, that's the lore."

Max gawked as the ghost pointed to the empty space by the living room window.

"That should be a good spot," Drummond said. He raised a quizzical eyebrow to Max. "What?"

"Nothing," Max said and gathered the items needed for the spell along with the Grimoire. He ignored Drummond's odd expression, ignored the pressure mounting in the dusty air, ignored all the warnings blazing in his head. If Drummond turned now, Max didn't see anything he could do to stop it. Only way forward was straight through — do the spell, find the handbell, summon Patricia and his wife, hope he figures out what to do after that.

Max opened the Grimoire to the appropriate page and set the book on the seat of a wooden chair. He then sat on the floor in the spot Drummond had indicated. For his part, Drummond went to the book and guided Max.

"First thing you do is put one candle at each of the four compass points."

Max picked up one candle. "Which way is North?"

Without looking up from the book, Drummond pointed toward the kitchen. Max reoriented himself to face the kitchen and placed the candle in front of his crossed legs. Then he set the other three candles to either side and behind him.

"Next thing you do is fill the goblet with water and set it down in front of you."

Max did as instructed. He went to the kitchen to fill the goblet from the sink, and as the water streamed in, he tried to avoid looking at the wall where he had seen Leed murdered. He thought of all the rage and hatred that gave Patricia Welling the physical and mental strength to destroy that man. "She's not going to like it when I get this bell." The thought brought a grim smile to Max's face.

He returned to Drummond, sat as before, and set the filled goblet in front of him. Drummond leaned closer to the book and read. "Light the incense, then the candles." Max did so. "Now you meditate."

"I what? I don't know how to meditate. I've never even tried to do it before."

"Guess you'll be trying it out now."

"Is there another way? I don't want to screw this up."

"You'll do fine. Listen, in the '70s there were plenty of people coming through my office trying all kinds of stuff. Sex, music, drugs. Lots of drugs. I swear they did so much of the stuff that, even dead, I got a contact high. They also experimented with meditation. I think the Beatles had something to do with that."

"Great. So now you're going to be my guru because you were stuck watching a bunch of stoners pretend to meditate?"

"If you have a better idea, tell me. What's the big deal, anyway? If you don't do it right, the spell won't work. No problem."

"Unless not working means the spell kills me ... or worse."

"This is for your wife, remember?" Drummond said sharply, his eyes narrowing as his anger increased.

Max tried to laugh off the tension. "You're right, you're right. Sorry. I'm really tired and worried and I don't know what to do."

"Of course." Drummond's face relaxed. "I understand. You ready now? Good. All you have to do is focus on the object you want to find. Think about it. Picture it. That's all. Take slow, deep breaths and do your best to picture that handbell. Don't let any other thoughts take you away from that image. You think you can do that?"

"For Sandra, definitely." Max closed his eyes and breathed slow and deep. The incense entered his body, and his muscles loosened up. Sleep threatened to take over his weary body; he even felt his head grow heavy. Focus. He had to stay in control of his thoughts. The handbell — that was the only image he needed to worry about. All other thoughts, all other desires, even sleep, had to go away.

Time loosened. Only the sound of his lungs expanding and expelling filled his ears. Only the handbell filled his mind. He saw it from every angle, practically felt it in his hand.

"Something's happening," Drummond said.

Max opened his eyes but still pictured the handbell in his mind. The candle flames flared, and Max felt something tugging on his skin. No. Not tugging on it — tugging from within it — as if thousands of tiny hooks were in his skin and pulled away from him. It hurt and threatened to break his concentration.

"Max? You okay?"

The handbell. Think only of the handbell.

A force grabbed hold of his chest, pressed in and pulled out simultaneously. Max could feel his life draining away as this force exerted control upon his body. He felt as if this power tossed him around the room though he never moved an inch. Blood shot out his nose, and he coughed up an acidic phlegm.

He strained to keep focus but something smashed his head from the inside. Light-headed, his eyes rolled and he flopped forward.

But as his face fell to the floor, he caught a glimpse inside the goblet. Instead of his reflection, he saw a building — *the* building — *his* building — *his office* building — the place where the handbell would be found.

Chapter 23

UPON WAKING UP, the urgency in Max's stomach forced him to roll over and vomit across the living room floor. His head pounded, his thighs ached, and he had a nasty crick in his neck. Golden sunlight peeked through the windows, each beam a blinding spear through his eyes.

"It's about time," Drummond said, soaring into the room.

Sitting up slowly, feeling his stomach curl again, Max scrunched his brow. "That spell hurt. Besides, the sun's just coming up. I was out for what? A half-hour?"

Drummond flicked his hands toward the window. "The sun is setting, not rising. You've been out for almost twelve hours. I screamed at you, I knocked chairs over, I even passed my hand through you. Nothing worked. We've got to go meet Modesto, and we don't have the handbell. In other words, all our leverage is gone." Drummond leaned toward his coat pocket. "And to top it off, you wretched all over the floor."

"Calm down," Max said, gently rising to his feet.

"How am I supposed to be calm? Everything's falling apart."

"This isn't like you. Relax. Keep control of yourself."

Drummond glowered at Max. Bracing himself, Max turned his head to the side. Instead of an attack, Drummond cocked an ear toward his coat pocket, nodded, and eased back. Right there, Max decided not to fret over the little ghost in Drummond's pocket anymore.

In a less agitated voice, Drummond asked, "Did the spell work at least?"

"The bell is somewhere in our office building."

Drummond brightened. "That's great. That's perfect. It's like a homefield advantage. Let's go."

"Hold on a moment. We need to think this through. It's late now. Getting the bell without a plan won't be of any use to us or Sandra. In fact, that'll be playing right into Modesto's hand. There's a lot about this whole thing that doesn't add up."

"We don't really have time."

"Modesto will wait all night if he has to. He wants that bell badly, and if waiting a while longer than he would prefer means getting it from us, then he'll do it. But why is it in the office building? If Connor's mother stole it, why would she put it there?"

"Hiding it anywhere would be smart. Once Hull discovered it missing, he'd have set Modesto loose to find it. Back then, Modesto was young and eager to please the Hulls — more so than now. He'd have been ruthless in his search."

"So, Connor's mother makes sure the evidence isn't on her or near her or in any way connected to her. But why the office building? Why not rent a storage locker? Or hand it to a trusted friend? Or even bury it in the backyard?"

Drummond snapped out his hand as if smacking Max upside the head. "Do you really not understand? This is a cursed bell with a long history of destruction, a cursed bell that became linked to the ghost of a cursed witch. Not any witch, by the way, but the High Priestess of a coven. And most importantly, this was a bell that the Hulls needed if they ever got it in their heads to resurrect their great-great-grandfather — which is exactly what they want to do. If you stole a bell like that, would you really trust it to a friend? Or leave it unprotected in a storage locker or worse still, bury it in the ground where any kid or dog could dig it up?"

"I guess not. But why the office building? Assuming Connor's mother knew how powerful this bell was, wouldn't she want to hide it somewhere that would protect her from its curse? Some place with a lot of magical mojo. Some place ... oh."

"That's right. You think it's a coincidence that they cursed me in my office? That of all the buildings in Winston-Salem, the one Hull owns entirely on his own is that one? There's power in those walls. Always has been. It's a smart place to hide the bell. Hull would never suspect it to be right under his nose, and Connor's mother must have hoped the building's magic would contain any curse the bell truly had. At the least, all that magic would mask the magic radiating off the bell."

"Why would that happen? The building containing the curse, I mean."

"It wouldn't. It didn't. But one witch can't know everything."

Max shuffled to the kitchen and poured a glass of water. He felt no better physically, but his head had cleared. "This is good. We know the bell is in the building, and we're fairly certain the building's magic won't contain the bell's curse. All we have to do now is figure out how to turn that to our advantage."

"Since the sun is about gone now, you think you can do that figuring on the way back to the city?"

"Yeah. Let's go." Max swiped his keys from the counter and reached for the door. Before he touched it, however, three strong knocks banged away.

"Mr. Porter? It's Agent Stevenson. May I have a word with you?"

Max took enough time to send a stern look Drummond's way. "Please be quiet. Let me focus."

"Always," Drummond said.

Max opened the door to find Stevenson standing in the dimming light, a friendly smile on his face that promised he knew all the answers before he asked the first question. "Mind if I come in?"

"Actually, I'm leaving."

"Actually, this isn't your house." Stevenson walked inside, forcing Max to step back or be plowed over. The FBI agent surveyed the kitchen, glanced into the living room, and wrinkled his nose at the vomit on the floor. "You not feeling well?"

Max rested against the kitchen counter and crossed his arms. "I've had better days."

Stevenson turned his trained eye onto Max. "You look like you've gone a few rounds with a heavyweight. You want me to take you to a hospital?"

"No need. It looks worse than it is."

"Kind of like your situation." Stevenson pulled over a chair and sat. "On the surface, it looks like you murdered Dr. Matthew Ernest, then went after his old assistant, Joshua Leed, then broke into Ernest's home to tamper with the crime scene, and on top of all that, there was a bizarre murder at an optometrist's office which, though quite different from these other murders, does seem connected when one considers all the occult paraphernalia found in the victim's office. Looking at all the bruising on your face, you might even be the subject of an assault investigation that occurred last night at the Fox and Hound Pub. Now, that all looks bad for you, and if I were any other agent, I might've hauled you in already."

"But you know I didn't do those things."

"The only thing I know for certain is that you broke into Leed's house because you're here right now. And I'm fairly certain you were at Ernest's house last night, too. I was there, but whoever broke into that house slipped away."

Drummond perked up, clapped his hands, and opened his mouth. Before he said anything though, he exchanged glances with Max and made a zipper motion across his ghostly lips.

"Am I under arrest?" Max asked, his words sounding more brazen than he felt.

"Not yet." With his index finger, Stevenson tapped a complicated rhythm against his chin and let his eyes rove the kitchen. "It's strange how both this house and Ernest's house had those markings on the walls. Made me think of a cult. Your house, however, doesn't have any markings like that."

"I don't belong to a cult."

"Odd. You don't seem surprised we went through your house." He thought a moment and nodded with a grin. "You came by and saw us, didn't you? That's why you're out here."

Drummond pointed to the wall clock which read 7:30 p.m. Max said, "You seem like a smart guy, probably a good agent, too. But you're not going to figure this all out. I know a lot more of what's going on, and I can't figure it all out."

"Maybe we can help each other. After all, since you know more than I do, and assuming you're innocent of the murders, well then it's only natural you'd want to help the FBI find the real killers and clear your name."

"Do you believe in ghosts?"

"Excuse me?"

"Ghosts. Witches, curses, covens, black magic, and protective wards. Do you believe in any of that?"

"I know that the people involved in all this certainly believed in that kind of thing. But believing in something, no matter how strong the belief, no matter how pure the faith, doesn't make it reality."

"Denying it, even though you can't see it, doesn't make it fantasy."

"You want me to believe in all of this stuff? Believe that the reason Ernest and Leed covered their walls with arcane symbols was because those bits of paint would magically protect them? From what? Ghosts? Except they weren't protected. They ended up dead."

"Leed died outside his protected room. In fact, he died right here in this kitchen."

Stevenson pushed his blazer back enough to reveal his holstered sidearm. "Are you admitting to having killed Joshua Leed?"

"No. Just that I watched him die in here. But I was no closer to him than I am to you."

"Then who killed him? If you're afraid of retribution, the FBI can protect you."

Max knew he should have stopped talking the moment Stevenson had entered, but his mouth had a mind of its own. The pressure and confusion that had been building in him finally released, and if it meant pissing off a federal agent, then so be it. "A ghost killed him."

"A ghost? Really."

"I know you don't believe me, but that's the truth. That's

why you can't help me. This whole thing started with a curse cast decades ago, and now it's come back to haunt us."

"Who is *us*?"

"But you won't open your mind to the possibilities, so I don't see how you can help. I doubt you'd even believe that there's a ghost in this room. He's standing near you, and even if you felt his cold hand pass through you, you wouldn't believe."

Drummond waved his hand across Stevenson's neck. The agent bolted to his feet, whirled around, and stared at the empty room. He spun back, eyeing Max while his hand rested on his firearm.

"Enough games, Mr. Porter. If I can't produce results soon, my superiors are going to insist I arrest you, and I now have at least two charges that I can take you in under — tampering with the Leed crime scene and obstruction. I don't want to do that. I think if I do, you'll shut down, and I'll never learn what happened here. But if you give me no alternative, your sweet wife will have to see you behind bars."

"If you keep wasting my time here, my sweet wife won't live long enough to see me ever again."

"What does that mean? If you know of a threat against your wife, tell me. Let me protect her. For fuck's sake, I'm with the FBI. I have access to some serious power."

Max couldn't help himself. He laughed. "You don't know what power is."

Stepping away, Stevenson tapped his chin again. "Maybe I was wrong. You seem crazy enough to do all these things after all."

"Oh, come on." Max instantly regretted opening his mouth. "Don't take the easy way out. I didn't do any of this. You know it."

"I don't know anything."

"Trust your gut. I'm innocent here."

"Because a ghost did it? Did a ghost kill Dr. Ernest, too? Same one, I suppose?"

"Yes. Exactly."

Stevenson pulled his weapon. "Maxwell Porter, you are

under arrest for the murder of —"

"Wait, wait. I didn't do it. Why would I?"

"That's what you're going to tell me when I take you in."

"But think about it. Why would I kill Dr. Ernest when that's what caused ..." Max's brain started connecting information in a fevered rush. "Oh, no."

Stevenson lowered his weapon. "What's going on? What's wrong?"

"The body. It was undisturbed."

"What body? Who are you talking about?"

Drummond shot forward. "The witch in the church?"

"Ernest never got to that body. She hadn't been touched. It bugged me when we saw it, but I didn't know why."

Stevenson said, "What body? Who was with you when you saw it?"

Drummond turned to Stevenson and raised his hand. "Let me put this guy out for a few hours and we can still try to get that bell. If you're right about this, we've got leverage again."

"Wait. Don't hurt him."

"Hurt who?" Stevenson said, his eyes darting about the room. "Is someone else here?"

"Agent Stevenson," Max said, his voice calm and confident now. "I know who killed Dr. Ernest, and I know why. And I need your help."

Chapter 24

AS MAX PARKED THE CAR outside his office building, the blue-green display of the dashboard clock glowed 9:02. He shut off the engine and sat in the silence, mustering the strength for what he suspected would be the end of this case. He simply hoped it wasn't his end as well.

"How do you want to play this?" Drummond asked from the backseat.

While that old ghost could be infuriating, Max appreciated the way he acted when serious business was at hand. It felt strange putting all his trust in a ghost, but Max had grown accustomed to strange. "I don't think the handbell is anywhere in the actual office. If it was, you would have found it long ago."

"You ain't kidding. I know every rat turd, leaking pipe, and dust bunny surrounding our office."

"So, it has to be somewhere else in the building. I want you to do a sweep of the walls, floors, and ceilings. See if it's hidden behind any of the plaster or floorboards or under the boiler or anything. While you do that, I'm going to the office to do my part."

"It shouldn't take me long. I'll let you know what I find." With that, Drummond disappeared.

Max remained in the car for another three minutes, listening to the rain beat against the roof. "You can do this," he told his rearview mirror reflection. "You have to do this. Not just for Sandra, but for yourself. If this doesn't work out, the FBI will have you in jail before the sun comes up. So get your ass out of the car and get moving."

Thrusting open the door, Max exited and walked straight to the stairwell. His chest puffed up slightly, and he had a swagger to his walk. Somebody yelled from down the street, and Max jolted to safety behind a car. Only when he realized the yelling had nothing to do with him could he stand again. With less bravado, he resumed his walk.

Max entered the stairwell. Though he had been in this same stairwell countless times, a cold and inhospitable sensation covered his skin. Rather than going up to the office, he stepped into the back where a narrow door led to the empty storefront that had once been Deacon Arts. No surprise — the door was still unlocked.

He entered the store, his steps echoing in the wide, empty space. Rain tapped against the large plate-glass window facing the street. A car drove by, its wheels shushing through the growing puddles.

Nothing remained in the former art gallery except for a desk from which Mr. Gold would conduct his crooked business. The desk had been emptied long ago, but Max checked the drawers nonetheless. Not that he expected the handbell to be so easily found, but he had to try. After all, Mr. Gold had worked for the Hulls at one time.

Next, he walked the perimeter of the store, checking for anything unusual, making sure nothing hid in the dark. Nothing turned up. The only real hiding places in the store were in the walls, and Drummond had that covered.

Satisfied, Max left through the back door and headed upstairs to the second floor. On the landing, he stopped to check out the hall before going ahead. There were three doors — two had been boarded over and the third was unmarked. He had never been on this floor before, never had a reason to be, but now he wondered if it had always been like this. He half-expected a serial killer to come busting out the unmarked door, blood dripping from a carving knife.

A loud thud hit the ceiling above — from Max's office. Somebody was up there. Max tore on up the staircase to the third floor, raced down the hall, and stormed through the door.

Sandra/Patricia started at his abrupt arrival, placing her hand on her chest like a proper Southern gal. "My word, you gave me a fright." She chuckled, but her amusement curdled with a malicious tone. "I've been waiting for you all day. That spell you cast really knocked you out. I was beginning to think you might not make it."

Max looked over her — no bruises, no rub burns, nothing to suggest that Patricia had taken his wife's body out for a joyride.

"Relax," she said, sitting on the couch and crossing her legs to show off the fine, unblemished calves. "Do you really think that I would waste my time romping through the young studs of Winston-Salem when there are so many obvious threats to my life right now? That would be stupid. No, I don't screw the town until I know for sure that nobody is going to yank me out of this body."

Now Patricia's earlier words registered with Max. "You knew I cast a spell. You've been following me, watching me, waiting for me to find the bell."

"You *and* Drummond. I'm still in the afterlife. I can see him fine — and he's certainly still a fine looking man."

"So you're here, tearing apart my office, looking for the bell."

"Once I knew where you were headed, I rushed on over here. Frankly, I didn't think I'd get so much of a lead on you."

Max thought of Stevenson bitterly. "We got delayed."

"That's the problem with studious men like you — you're never paying attention to the right things. Always worrying about minor matters while you let the world around you burn."

"Explain that one to me." Max hardly cared what she talked about as long as he kept her talking. Drummond needed enough time to succeed.

Patricia shook her head pitifully. "You really think you're smarter than me. Let me explain to you something far more important. Let me explain why I'm sitting here letting you live. Fairly simple, actually. You are alive right now because you do not possess the handbell."

"Don't be so sure."

"If you had it, you would have used it already. Unless you

like seeing your drab wife embodied by a woman who knows what turns a man on." She licked her lips slowly, leaning forward like Marilyn Monroe, and finished the pose of with a tiny bite on her bottom lip.

"Not interested."

"I doubt that."

"There's only one woman I want, and no matter what you look like, you ain't her."

Patricia shot to her feet, scowling and grinding her teeth. She backhanded Max across the face, snapping his head aside and dropping him to the floor. That woman had serious strength. When he could focus again, he saw that his head missed the sharp corner of the desk by mere inches.

She stood over him like a mighty hunter over a lamed lion. "Do you really think your little body can take much more abuse? Come on, now. It's over. You've lost and simply won't admit it. But you and I both know that you're never going to leave this office unless I allow it, and I'm not letting that happen until you tell me where the bell is."

Blood dribbled into his mouth — a bitter, metallic taste. "Why bother asking? You know I don't have it. And if I knew where it was, I'd have gotten it already."

"Unless it's in here. Unless you walked into this room expecting to take it, but then you found me. So, tell me where it is or I'll start hurting you in ways that will pale even the most perverse thoughts you can imagine."

Max wanted to jump up, surprise Patricia by his action, and pummel her into submission. But to do so meant striking his wife, and no matter how brave his words had been, he still saw Sandra's body when he looked at Patricia.

Patricia bent down and raked her nails across his cheek. "I'm so glad you're resisting. I always have fun torturing fools like you, but this will be even better with your wife trapped inside, forced to watch as her own hands rip you to pieces."

She raised her hand again, her fingers splayed in a claw, and Max clenched his fists, wishing he could fight back. But then Drummond's deep voice called out, "Patricia! Stop it."

Turning with a coy, girlish giggle, she said, "Oh, Marshall, please let me have a little fun."

"I can't let you do this," he said, moving back toward the far corner, forcing Patricia to turn her back on Max. "I can't let you harm good people because you hate me."

"Sweetheart, I don't hate you."

"I helped Ernest and Leed destroy your coven."

"You did what you thought was right. And you were hurt because I hid the truth about myself."

Drummond gazed out the window, and Max swore the ghost's eyes glistened as if he tried to hold back tears. "I knew enough to figure it out. I wasn't hurt because you lied. I understood that. I was hurt because you ... you broke my heart. You let me fall for you when you knew damn well what the outcome would be. But you didn't care enough to worry how it would all hurt me."

Taken aback, Patricia's hand covered her mouth. "I'm so sorry. I had no idea."

"You knew exactly how I felt."

"I meant that I had no idea you could feel so strongly. Honestly, my love, I swear I thought I was just a plaything to you. I wanted more. Always. From the day we met by the tree, I wanted more. I knew it couldn't happen, though. I knew the kind of work you did. How could you ever give that up for a witch? And it hurt you bad, I see that now, but don't think I wasn't hurt, too. I was devastated. I knew all along the ending we headed toward, yet I only wanted to enjoy the small time we had until it all came apart."

"You expect me to believe —"

"Only that my heart was true to you. I fell for you every bit as hard. But look at me now. I have a body — one you can touch. With that handbell, I can become whole. And, Marshall, listen to me — I'm more of a witch than you ever knew. I was very powerful back then, and with the added strength of my coven, I can be more. When I'm whole once again, I can even bring you back."

"What?"

"You can have a body of your own. We can actually be together again. In our hearts and our bodies."

Max watched Drummond carefully, but he couldn't read the ghost's face at all.

Drummond pursed his lips. "You're serious? I could be free from this half-dead existence?"

"And we can be together."

"Together."

She leaned towards him, but this time the motion lacked her seductive leer — this time, she clearly wanted to be closer. "Those days we spent meant everything to me. I've never stopped thinking about our tree and our time there. Never. Not even as I watched the decades pass from beneath the city, as I suffered burning pain that would never stop. Only those memories could cool me, help me endure. All I could dream of was returning to our tree. All I wanted was to be in your arms, feel your lips. If I could turn us back, I'd give up all my power and knowledge in witchcraft — if it meant we could be together."

"I want to believe you. I do."

"Then believe. Because it can still be true. This body and that fool on the floor, they will be our vessels. We can return to the mortal world and live out our lives together. And after I bring you back, I'll never cast another spell. I'll put it all behind us. Don't you want that? To be together again. If you can bring yourself to sacrifice these two, we can have everything we always wanted."

"You think it's fun being the ghost lackey for these two? I've got no problem with getting rid of them. But the problem we do have is that we don't know where the bell is. It's in this building, we know that much, but where?"

"If you'll be with me, if you'll love me, then don't worry. We'll find it."

"Do you know where it is?"

"No, but we'll figure it out."

"Well, where do you think it is? Put yourself in that witches shoes. Where would you hide it? The roof? Basement? Perhaps you knew an old crone witch who would take on the challenge of holding it for you."

Max didn't want to believe it, but it seemed that Drummond had finally turned. He had expected something more flashy, though. At least something involving all that dark mist he had seen previously.

I'm sorry, my friend. I failed you.

Now Max's last ally had become his enemy. The disappointment filling him made it difficult to think beyond the moment, beyond hearing how Drummond and Patricia planned to kill Sandra and himself. All they needed was the bell. In fact, the only thing keeping Max alive was the fact that they hadn't found it yet. Drummond had even resorted to asking Patricia if she had ...

Wait. That doesn't make sense. Drummond had spent the last several minutes going through the building top to bottom. He already knew that the bell wasn't on the roof or in the basement. Or he knew that it was in one of those places and didn't want her going there. He gazed up at Drummond — *did Drummond just wink at me?* And no dark mist. He hadn't turned yet.

"Patricia," Drummond said, "look in my eyes."

"Yes, darling."

"Let me tell you how I see our future."

Drummond launched into a flowery story that sounded like anything but Drummond. This was it. This was Max's chance to get out.

As quietly as he manage, Max rolled to his stomach and from there, up onto all fours. He knew how absurd he looked, but his pride would have to take a backseat to his survival. Like a cowering dog, he scurried out of the office and into the hall. He could still hear Drummond's tale of weddings and children and a small farm away from all the horrors of the world. How long could he keep up his love-tale before Patricia noticed Max's absence?

He needed to find that bell. He paced the hall, thinking over every word Drummond had said since coming into the office.

The answer had to be there or else Drummond would have taken a different tactic. What had he said? He asked Patricia to think about where she would hide the bell — because he wanted Max to think about how Connor's mother would have seen things. But they had already covered that line of thought before. *Wait. What did he say last?* Something about an old witch crone and ... Max lifted his head, his eyes resting on the other door in the hall — the one belonging to the old woman that had always shot him nasty looks when she came out to get her paper.

Though he felt less sure about his conclusions, he also understood that Drummond could only stall so long for him. He had to act or the whole effort had been worthless.

Max crouched in front of the doorknob. Trying to think of what he had in his pockets that he could use to pick the lock, he concluded that even if he had something small enough, he lacked the skill to do it with any speed. He stood and ran his fingers along the top of the molding above the door. No key. He looked around the banister in the hall for a pot or a shoe or anything that one would hide a key in. Nothing.

Except there was a doormat — a coarse, weaved thing, fraying at the edges. Could it really be that easy? Max bent down and lifted the mat. A cockroach scuttled away leaving behind a scuffed, silver key square in the middle.

Max slipped the key into the lock and gently opened the door. Trying to be stealthy, he only opened it wide enough to slide in. He closed the door behind, hoping Patricia had not noticed where he went.

Before his eyes adjusted to the dim interior, he smelled the room — the stale stench of a body unwashed for years. Max tried breathing through his mouth to avoid the odor, but the air tasted awful, too. He could feel it coating his tongue.

Once his eyes adjusted, he noticed that the main living room looked rather bland and unimpressive. An old woman's room, sparsely furnished but each piece held numerous knick-knacks — a coffee table with porcelain figurines, end tables with collector's plates on either side of a long couch, a reading lamp with beaded chains hanging from its neck. The old lady snored peacefully on the couch, one arm draped across her forehead, the other hanging toward the floor and an empty bottle of tequila.

Witches sure loved the hard stuff.

Except this old lady didn't seem like a witch, especially a witch charged with protecting a cursed object. Maybe Drummond had it wrong. But when Max turned to go, his opinion changed. Painted blood-red on the back of the door, Max saw a large pentagram. Beneath it, a series of symbols had been carved into the wood.

Okay. Right place.

A muted screech filtered through the walls. Patricia must have discovered Max's absence. He could hear her yelling as well as Drummond's bass tones thumping a reply. How long would he be able to argue with her before turning? Considering the strong emotions between them, Max didn't think he had much time left.

He figured the old lady wouldn't hide the bell in the front room. Too easy to be spotted by unwanted eyes. The kitchen to his right looked plain and, frankly, untouched. Whatever the old lady ate, it wasn't coming from there. He doubted she ever stepped foot in that room. Which left either the bathroom or her bedroom — both of which were down a dark hall on the left.

The old lady grunted and shifted her body deeper into the couch. With a loud eruption, she passed gas. Other than quelling a juvenile desire to laugh, Max didn't react. Considering the stench in this place, he guessed he would never notice any added odors.

As silently as possible, Max eased down the hall. The closer he came to the bedroom door, the worse the rank odor became. The hall grew darker as if even light wanted nothing to do with this place.

The voices of Drummond and Patricia intensified though Max couldn't make out the actual words. The anger came through clear enough. He hurried to the door, ignoring his internal warnings that urged him to turn around, to get out of that apartment, to run.

"Hold on, Sandra. I'm coming for you," he whispered and opened the door.

He expected to find a room similar to Connor's office or perhaps one filled with protective wards like Dr. Ernest's room. Instead, he discovered a twisted display that belonged in the pages of *Psycho Weekly*. The foul odor that permeated the apartment doubled in the bedroom. Max could barely breathe without throwing up. A bed had been shoved in the corner to his right, the sheets stained with browns, yellows, and reds. Odd-shaped books had been piled next to the bed. Two bookcases leaned against the walls to either side — each one filled with jarred organs, animal fetuses, and various eggs.

Worse — black and white photos covered the walls. A man in hip-waders displaying a half-eaten fish carcass foul with maggots. A girl in her confirmation dress sitting with a book of poetry in her lap and the head of a cat. Children rolling down a hill of corpses. Max couldn't bear to look at any others. He prayed they had been images designed on a computer and not real in any respect.

A wide cabinet sat in the center of the room, out of place and obstructing Max's view of the rest of the room. Slowly, Max entered, walking around the cabinet, trying to prepare for any kind of traps the witch had set, anything that might leap out at him. When he came to the other side, he jumped back, startled by the amazing sight.

The old lady had built a shrine. A circle of salt surrounded the entire thing. Inside, three green candles burned on an altar of wood with a velvet cloth cover, gold pentagrams hanging from the top of the cabinet, and situated on a silk pillow — the thirteenth Bell of the Damned.

Larger than he had imagined, the bell had a small chip in the handle but otherwise matched the photographs exactly. Max inspected around the shrine, attempting to locate any form of security alarm. Then he considered the apartment he was in — witches didn't need security alarms. He reached under the bell and guided the clapper against the side so it would not ring out. Holding it in place with one hand, he lifted the bell with the other. Not a sound. In fact, he had been so quiet, he could still hear the impassioned argument coming from his office.

Max walked around the wide cabinet, took two steps toward the door, and froze. The old lady blocked his way. She stood in the doorway breathing heavy but strong. A growl emitted from her throat, and her head lowered, darkening her eyes, threatening him like a rabid animal.

"I am the protector," she said in a strong but cracked voice, "and you will return the bell or face my wrath."

Had he been a common thief, he might have laughed at the old lady, might even have attempted to bully his way by her, but Max knew witches too well to ignore her threat. Yet as much as he knew he should comply, he could only shrink before her strength and hope that this witch had a heart.

"Please," he said, "I need this bell to save my wife."

"It is cursed, and so will you become if you use it."

"A High Priestess has possessed my wife. The witch, Patricia Welling. I was told that this is the only thing that can save my Sandra. If you know another way, tell me. Otherwise, I must have this."

The old lady thrust out a clawed hand. Max cowered, sure that he would be turned into a toad. When his human form remained, he peeked up at her. She scowled.

"Max Porter, seer of a single ghost, you have been a thorn in the foot of the Hull family since you arrived here. That is the only reason you have remained untouched by me. But should you press forth and remove that bell from this sacred room, I will no longer restrain myself. Put the bell back, and all shall be forgotten. Take one step closer, and you'll learn how powerful an old witch like me can become."

Max clutched the bell closer to his chest. He looked at the hall stretching out behind the old lady. Surely he could barrel her down and make it out through that hall. From there, he'd bust out of the apartment, hurry to his office, ring the bell at Patricia, and pray for the best. Yet even as he considered this plan, the old lady seemed to fill out the doorway even more. It may only have been a trick of his eyes brought on by fear and worry, it may have been an illusion cast by the old witch — either way, he saw his chance to leave diminishing.

He glanced back at the shrine. If he did as she asked, if he returned the bell, would she stay true to her word? Would she let him go and forget his intrusion? And what of Sandra then? A loud crash came from his office. That settled it. If he didn't get in there fast, Drummond would either end up destroyed or turned.

"I'm sorry," he said. "Unless you can help me stop this witch, I don't see any other way."

"Don't think that the bluster you've displayed in the past will aid you today. Turn around. Put the bell back. Forget you ever knew of this place."

Max lowered his body slightly, ready to pounce on the old lady, toss her aside, and race for his office. His heart quickened and sweat broke along his back and neck. He licked his lips and gave one final thought to Sandra.

Before he could launch into action, the old lady's eyes widened. She saw his intentions, and she already had her hand out, prepared to strike with whatever magic she possessed.

"I think you should stop this nonsense," a voice said from the hallway.

Both Max and the old lady peered down the dark hall. Mr. Modesto walked forward. The old lady stepped into the room, allowing him to take the doorway.

"Good evening to you." As always, Modesto wore a smart suit and held his body perfectly straight. "I see, Mr. Porter, that you have acquired the bell after all. Our employer will be pleased."

The old lady squinted an evil gaze at him. "Neither you nor your pathetic employer will ever have this bell. I've pledged my life to protect —"

"Yes, yes. Except, you see, Mr. Porter is the one holding the bell, and quite frankly, you don't have the skill to do anything about it."

"You'll regret those words."

She raised her hands and opened her mouth. A tight, choking came from her throat. Her eyes rolled back and she crumpled to the floor.

Modesto walked in and lifted the bell from Max's stunned hands. Max wanted to fight, but he couldn't imagine how Modesto had defeated this witch with such ease. How could he fight Modesto against that kind of power? It was over. He had failed and now Modesto had the bell. He just couldn't understand what had happened.

As if to answer Max's unspoken questions, Modesto gestured to the hall. A small, thin woman with a deep scar running from her nose to her jaw stood alone. Dressed in a black gown adorned with symbols Max had seen too many times in recent days, the woman lowered her hands and ran a finger along a bone pendant around her neck.

"I'll take care of the others," she said and walked off toward Max's office.

With his free hand, Modesto guided Max back to his feet. "The first rule in fighting with magic," Modesto said, "is to always bring the strongest witch."

Chapter 25

MODESTO HAD NO NEED for a gun. As long as he held that bell, Max didn't see any choice but to go along without a struggle. They left the old lady's apartment and walked back to the office.

Breathing clean air once again revitalized Max's dull senses. His mind leaped from one crisis to another — Sandra and Patricia, making sure Drummond didn't turn, stopping Modesto. All these thoughts made the act of entering the office as a failure that much worse.

The office desks had been shoved against the walls, and two chalk circles with symbols had been drawn on the floor. Drummond pressed against the confines of one circle, and Patricia the other. Neither looked particularly happy. Drummond paced the narrow space like a trapped puma, turning every two steps, fuming and grunting. Patricia, on the other hand, settled cross-legged on the floor, her face a cold burn of controlled rage.

Modesto spread his arms as if presenting his vast treasure to a commoner. "This room, Mr. Porter, is going to be the most valuable room in all mankind. Here, we shall return Tucker Hull to the living so that he may continue his important work. And we owe it all to you."

"Pay me back now by releasing my wife and friend."

Chuckling, though he showed no amusement in his face, Modesto said, "Let's begin the evening with proper introductions. This diminutive yet powerful witch is Kalon. Born to a German family with a long history in the dark arts, Kalon will not only bring Tucker Hull back, but she will serve him better than any witch has before. She makes our former witch look like a peasant, don't you think?"

"Dr. Connor looks like a corpse now."

Modesto ignored the comment. To Kalon, he said, "This annoying man is Mr. Maxwell Porter. He is a pest, and I look forward to the day the Hull family allows me to crush him under my sole. Until then, we must put up with his inability to perform his duties properly."

"Hey, don't soft-sell me. I try hard to be a pain in your ass." Max wished he felt half as a brazen as he sounded, but he had to keep pushing. As long as Modesto appeared to be driving this night, he would be looser with his mouth, and Max needed that stuck-up prick to talk as much as possible.

"You often succeed," Modesto said. "Still, despite your innumerable flaws, we do have to thank you for acquiring all the necessary pieces to this complex spell."

The black-draped witch moved like a graceful ballerina as she drew small chalk circles in front of the large ones that contained Drummond and Patricia. Modesto pointed to the first circle. "Here we have the Hull family journal which you stumbled upon for us." Kalon placed the beaten book into the circle.

"Hardly stumbled," Max said, recalling his first case for the Hulls. He had a ghost stick its hand straight into his skull in order to find that book — an agonizing pain he never wanted to experience again.

Kalon placed a small bowl in the second circle. In the bowl, lay a single hair. Modesto said, "This is, of course, one of the last hairs that belonged to Edward Teach, otherwise known as Blackbeard the Pirate. I believe you found this by accident when you were hired to locate a painting by the granddaughter of a dead art forger."

"You're quite good at revisionist history." Max had been hired by the ghost of a man betrayed by the Hull family which led to a cursed art forger, his mad granddaughter, and their twisted plan involving Blackbeard's ghost.

"And last, we have the handbell which you generously provided this evening. All three key elements, all brought to us by you, and all this time you've thought you were working against us, when in fact, we could not be here without you."

Kalon dashed a white, gritty substance into the bowl containing Blackbeard's hair. With a pestle she produced from a black bag, she ground into the bowl, turning the hair and the white grit into a fine powder. As she worked, Modesto's eyes fired up and he said, "It's begun now. Soon the essence of Tucker Hull locked in his journal will be freed, soon he will rise again."

Max looked at Sandra — her body, but where was the rest of her? She had to be inside there. If he could reach her, get her to fight back. Stupid, Max chided himself. Of course she fought back. In fact, Patricia must have had to work three times as hard to keep hold of that body. No way would Sandra take a backseat. Patricia might be barely holding on.

However, Drummond was the one that looked closest to losing control. That dark mist surrounded him like an aura of night. There would be no help from him at the moment. Max was on his own. He only had his original plan, and that sounded awfully weak to his ears.

Still, a weak plan worked better than no plan. Max pushed aside all his concerns for Sandra and Drummond. He had to focus, now. Clear his thoughts because the next few minutes would be a verbal chess game against an agile and sadistic opponent.

"I'm impressed," Max said. "The way you've orchestrated this whole thing shows a high level of skill at the manipulation of powerful people."

Modesto cocked his head, pleased but cautious. "I don't know what you're referring to."

"Of course you do. It takes a good mind to plan several steps ahead, but this ... this takes a special level of creativity and foresight most people can only dream of acquiring. I may not agree with your goals, but I'm always willing to acknowledge the presence of a great thinker."

Though preening and flush with excitement, Modesto said, "Flattery will do nothing to enhance your position. The fact remains that we have already won this battle."

"That's my point. You've been thinking years in advance of where Drummond and Sandra and I traipsed through. The journal, Blackbeard's hair, the handbell — each case, each element, carefully sent our way so that we would take all the risks in finding them for you, that we would have no recourse but to see you take them from us, that we would not even understand their value, even after we had been warned, until it was too late. Until now."

Kalon dug out an eagle's talon from a pocket in her dress. Gnarled and black with pieces of rotten flesh on the end, the talon clinked against the bowl as Kalon dropped it in. Without pause, she began grinding it into the powder she had made.

"This had to be meticulously planned," Max went on. "I can't think of a better person than you to do such a thing. Not only the long term vision, but thinking of this last piece, the way you manipulated us all is amazing."

Modesto could barely contain himself, yet still he said, "I did no such thing."

"Here's what really impressed me: The fact that you murdered Dr. Ernest and staged it to look like the curse. That was brilliant."

"Excuse me?"

"Oh, don't be coy. When we deciphered Dr. Ernest's notes, we found his witch's corpse in an old church. But here's the thing — the corpse was undisturbed. That bothered me but I couldn't figure it out. After all, the whole reason Joshua Leed came to us was that Dr. Ernest had died at the hands of a coven ghost. Except the body was undisturbed. That can only mean that Dr. Ernest had not touched the corpse at all — after all, nobody else knew where it was to begin with. Especially you."

"You have an intriguing hypothesis going, but I doubt you understand the full ramifications."

"I most certainly do. I wouldn't be praising you, if I didn't. Because you have to look at the whole thing in context, don't you? Here you are with the journal and the hair in hand. All you need to finish your spell is something one of these ghost-witches can do for you. But you have a major problem. Back in the '40s, the coven was cursed and their bodies hidden. You had no clue how to find them. But you did know who was responsible. You couldn't go to Drummond. You cursed that poor man. He'd never help you. Joshua Leed's loyalty to Dr. Ernest meant he'd never betray the man. And, in fact, Dr. Ernest was too, well, earnest to be bribed or coerced."

Kalon added what looked like rat pellets to the concoction. Tension seized Max's muscles. How much time did he have left before she would be ready? He had to hurry. But he had to stay calm, too. Act as if he had all the time he could want.

"So what do you do?" Max said, resisting the urge to walk around the room and tap his chin as he laid this out. "You devised a genius plan. You would have the very people responsible for hiding the bodies uncover them for you by killing Dr. Ernest and leaving hints that only someone knowledgeable in witchcraft, covens, and ghosts would notice. The police would treat this as any old murder, but the person with that special knowledge would see something different in the evidence. Of course, that special person was Joshua Leed. When he hired me, the coven was still intact in the original curse that Drummond, Leed, and Dr. Ernest performed. In fact, it wasn't until Leed contacted me and then went off to destroy the witches he had hidden, only then were the corpses actually disturbed. That's why they were able to attack us at the church, why the corpse in the church was untouched, and why you are standing here with Patricia Welling in my wife's body when that witch should be stuck in the walls of the Federal Building downtown. You created a situation on the gamble that it would result in this outcome. Did I miss anything?"

"Well, I hardly think it was gamble," Modesto said. Max fought to hold back a triumphant smile — he had that uptight bastard hooked. Modesto peered over Kalon's shoulder, nodded, and continued. "I've been studying you for years now. I know you better than you know yourself."

"Maybe so, but you couldn't know how Leed would react."

"A simpleton like that? Honestly, he was the easiest to

predict. Of course, there were several variables I had to stay atop of, but when you're a thinker, a man who understands tactics and strategy, juggling variables and adjusting outcomes is not terribly strenuous. For example, I could not know with any degree of certainty who the High Priestess would choose to possess. She could have picked a stranger off the street. However, I knew the more I pushed you to find that bell, the more you would resist. That would, in turn, push you deeper into the mess that Dr. Ernest had created. It was my calculated risk that a person as attune to the paranormal as your wife would be an easier target for the High Priestess."

"You set us up even more than I realized. But then you actually needed my help to find that bell."

"I'll admit that was the most challenging part of the endeavor. I had others working on it, but you have proven to be the most successful I've ever hired at finding these items."

"With Sandra possessed, that was all that remained. That's why you gave a final deadline." Max made a show of nodding to Modesto's sage wisdom but a thought suddenly caused an authentic frown.

"Something troubling you?" Modesto asked.

"Dr. Connor. There was no way a ghost killed her — not when she put a ward around her office. I saw firsthand how Drummond struggled to get in there and couldn't. Which means that it was another staged event. So, why did you kill her? It couldn't have been because she told us your plan. She warned me of this back when I dealt with the whole Blackbeard thing. There was no point in killing her now."

"For one, she betrayed me. She showed that she could not be trusted, and just because I didn't dispose of her immediately, hardly meant that I forgave her transgression. For another, there was the matter of the bell."

"That's the real answer. If she got hold of that bell, she gained control of this entire situation, and you did not want her to have that kind of control. That's what you feared."

Modesto bristled. "Fear? Me? Do you have any idea what I have endured to reach this point? Can you comprehend the sacrifices I have made for this?"

"I'm sure you have had —"

"You know nothing." Modesto spit the words hard enough to dislodge a lock of his hair. It spilled over his forehead, yet he never fixed it. "A spell as complex as this one, as important as this one, requires more than mere skillful planning. It rests on the sheer will and courage to see it through. That was where Dr. Connor proved lacking. I killed her like I did Dr. Ernest, and you know what I discovered? They both were surprised I could do such a thing. I saw it on their faces. How could that be? I realize I may appear outwardly like a stuffy butler, but surely Dr. Connor knew the ruthless man I am underneath. You're not surprised. Why were they?"

"They've never been on the receiving end before."

"Perhaps."

"And now you will be, too." Max unbuttoned the top three buttons on his shirt. Unable to hold back a little gloating grin of his own, Max revealed a thin, white wire taped to his chest. "The FBI have been listening all along. You've admitted to two homicides, though I'm pretty sure that all your talk of witches, possession, and magic spells will set you up nicely for an insanity defense. And don't try running. They've got us surrounded."

Modesto's reaction troubled Max more than anything so far. There was no fear. No shock. Not even a hesitation. Just a simple raising of the corner of his lips. "If you're relying on the FBI, you have a problem."

Max's throat tightened. "Oh?"

"Kalon finished the prep work on the spell a while ago. I've merely been waiting for the last crucial ingredient."

"There's another object?"

"The journal is an item closest to the soul we wish to bring back. The hair from Blackbeard is filled with the magic's foundation. When a source of extreme power is applied, Tucker Hull's soul will burst into this room. But if he cannot find a body to occupy, then the whole point is moot. Thus, the bell. We force Patricia out of Sandra's body, and before either woman has the chance to regain control, Tucker Hull enters. But we needed that catalyst, and once again you provided."

"I did?"

"Only one thing is powerful enough to jolt a lost soul back to the living — the rage of another lost soul."

Max's eyes shot to Drummond. The ghost was furious.

Modesto's smarmy, sarcastic tone thickened as he spoke. "And here you thought you had goaded me into revealing everything, when what I needed was time to let Drummond realize how trapped he is, to hear how I slaughtered his friend, to let him understand how you've all been my pawns and how worthless he truly is. Now, he's too far gone. There's no returning him. He is the catalyst, and as I believe I hear the stomping of feet downstairs, I know that I've timed this perfectly. Your FBI friends cannot get up here before we cast the spell because, you see, it's already been cast. All that remains is for Kalon to release it all and bring back Tucker Hull!"

Swiping her hand in a wide arc, Kalon broke lines in all five circles. Drummond shot out lightning fast, straight for Modesto, and straight over the journal, the bowl, and the bell.

Chapter 26

HEAT BLASTED FROM THE BOWL, knocking Max and Modesto back several steps. A deep red light strobed and Drummond screamed out. Whatever the spell had done to him, it wasn't enough to contain him. Drummond darted toward Kalon, backhanded her into the bookcase, and turned his dark eyes upon Max. Thick, dark smoke poured off Drummond — some of it flickering like flames, some of it dribbling like fog.

"Marshall, calm down," Max said, trying to coax the ghost back like he had done before. But Drummond huffed like a wild bull, lowered his head, staring straight at Max, waiting to attack.

"Why should you be calm?" Modesto said, and Drummond's head snapped toward the man. "You've been set up, used, and made a fool of. You have every right to be angry, furious, a raging madman, if you so choose." Drummond inched closer to Modesto. "That's right, you annoying piece of garbage. I dare you to strike me."

Max understood that Modesto provoked Drummond to keep him angry, keep him turning, but why was he trying to get Drummond to hit him? Max moved toward the bowl. Drummond hissed at him and pulled back a fist. "I'm not going to hurt you. I want to help you."

"He lies!" Modesto bellowed. "He is the one that brought these objects to me. Without him, I could never have cast this spell that hurts you now. And I am the one to have done it all. You are my puppet. You are weak and worthless. For decades, you've been nothing but a pawn. Even your greatest love was nothing but a witch's whim."

Modesto's words fired Drummond until the ghost opened his mouth and screamed. The air surrounding Modesto turned white with frost, but Modesto only smiled. His words had done more than enrage Drummond, though. They sparked Max's thoughts.

He noticed that Patricia had yet to move, even though her circle had also been broken. She remained seated and serene. Why? Max recalled how he had heard her muffled voice through the walls while he looked for the bell. She had pleaded with Drummond, offered to give up things for him, wanted to be with him. If her pleas had been authentic, if she truly cared about Drummond, what was the point of sitting there doing nothing?

From Max's previous encounters with the High Priestess, he knew she did not handle things calmly. Which meant that this behavior had to be strategic, and since Modesto did all he could to enrage Drummond, Max figured he needed more of that vicious energy than was present. Patricia stayed calm in order to deny Modesto her energy.

She doesn't want Tucker Hull back any more than I do.

Why would she? If Tucker Hull returned, she would have to struggle against his power both financial and magical or become his witch. So, remove the rage and she removes the catalyst.

But she failed to understand how mad Drummond had become. She didn't know him as well as Max — how could she after being stuck in a wall for decades? Max saw that hulking beast that had been his friend and knew Drummond had more than enough energy to fuel Modesto's spell.

An idea popped into Max's head — intuitive, risky, and possibly foolish. Perfect.

With a warrior cry, he dived for the handbell. His eagerness overtook his agility causing his fingers to snap closed too early. Instead of clasping the handle, he bumped it with his knuckles. It slid away from him. Its lip caught on the uneven floorboards, and the bell tipped over, rolling under Max's desk.

Even as he heard Modesto's shout, Max scrabbled across the floor. Like a mouse desperate to find a safe escape, he pressed up against his desk. Unlike a mouse, he could not slip underneath. No time to pull the desk away from the wall and get in the open side. Instead, he stretched his arm under the back lip, feeling around, trying to snatch that bell.

A memory flash in his head from elementary school — standing in front of a wall of boxes with holes cut out, being told to stick his hand inside and identify what he felt, not wanting to but reaching in because teacher demanded it, feeling little bugs crawling over his hands, kids laughing, teacher opening the box. "See that? It's just string hanging from the top," she said, but he dreamed of crawling bugs for weeks.

Max swallowed down the lump climbing up his throat as his hand probed the unseen beneath the desk. The tip of his finger brushed against something. He felt for it again, hoping it wasn't wet, hoping it didn't bite him. Metal. He touched metal. The bell! He tried to get it to roll closer toward him, but his finger seemed to only rub the edge.

He pushed away images of cockroaches discovering his hand. That's when an icy grip wrapped around his ankle and yanked him back. Max screeched both from surprise and from the cold pain numbing his foot.

Floating over him, Drummond gazed down. The ghost's eyes held only madness. Despite the pain Drummond often complained of when touching the corporeal world, he took hold of Max's neck and lifted the man up against the back wall.

Max tried to protest but his freezing throat could not form words. His hearing dropped and returned in waves. When he could hear, everything echoed as if they stood in a massive cavern.

"FBI," a voice called from miles away.

"No, Drummond!" Modesto yelled. "You want me!"

As the sound faded, Max's vision darkened. He had been close to dying before, and that time, a deep sadness overcame his body. This felt similar. He saw the ghost blob that was Leed glowing like a fluorescent rock as he hid amongst the books on the shelf. He saw the spirits of Sandra and Patricia both overlaying Sandra's body like some bad effect from an old 70s horror flick.

With a high-pitched whine, his hearing returned and so did Modesto's incessant yelling. "You idiot! You can't even become a dark spirit correctly! No wonder your mother hated you."

Drummond whirled around, dropping Max onto the desk. As Max struggled for air, he heard Modesto laugh.

"That's right. Your crazy mother wasn't so crazy after all. She locked herself up in that madhouse for one reason only. To get away from you!"

Banging on the door. "FBI! Open the door or we'll —"

The next seconds happened faster than normal yet moved slowly in Max's eye. Drummond launched toward Modesto, snarling as he bared his teeth. Max rolled off the table and wrenched it away from the wall. As Max reached for the bell, he saw Drummond reach for Modesto.

The FBI smashed open the door. Max raised the bell above his head and winced at what might come. Two men wearing bullet-proof vests and carrying assault rifles stormed the office. Modesto, smiling ecstatically, reached into his coat and pulled out a human skull. "Meet Tucker Hull!" he said as Drummond slammed into him. Max rang the bell.

All the sound stilled for an instant.

The explosion that came ripped apart the office. The FBI men were thrust straight out of the room and down the hall. A shockwave pressed Drummond flat against the ceiling and Patricia flew out of Sandra as if punched in the jaw. Modesto fell onto his back, laughing like a drunkard. A hurricane of magic swirled around them all, tearing the desks and books to pieces.

"Sandra!" Max shouted, trying to be heard above the howling winds. He crawled toward her, each inch a struggle. She remained seated in the chalk circle. The gale winds pressing against him never touched her — bright colors of magic shot around the room yet always avoided her. Max called out for her again but she made no response.

Despite the intense winds, Max neared his wife. He tried to call her once more but a cold hand grabbed his head and slammed it into the floor. Blood gushed out of his nose. He rolled on his back, dazed, and the cold force pressed on his chest. But when he opened his eyes, he saw Drummond still stuck on the ceiling.

"Patricia!" Drummond screamed.

The cold lifted and Drummond's head rocked to the side as if slapped hard. Max didn't waste time worrying. He rolled back to his stomach and crawled the final two feet to his wife. He clambered to his knees and held Sandra's shoulders.

"Honey? Look at me. Are you there?" Her eyes looked dead like a coma patient — unresponsive and unaware. "Please, be in there." Tears streamed down Max's face. "Please. You're everything to me. I know life has been rough for us these last few years, but I couldn't do any of it alone. I've always needed you. I know you think you don't give me enough, but you do. If anything, I don't show you enough. Without you, I'm lost. Don't leave me. Please."

The outer wall of the office shattered — brick and glass blasting outward into the street. Max clasped Sandra's hand, but her eyes closed and she slumped forward. The weight on his shoulder grew heavier. Dead weight.

He arched his head back and wailed. Through his teary eyes, he saw the blurred image of Drummond. The ghost's arms surrounded the air in front of him, and his mouth lay open as if pressed in a kiss.

A cold hand touched Max's chin. He braced himself to be struck by Patricia once again. But Patricia was above him kissing Drummond. And the hand, though cold, brought no pain. He looked down and saw Sandra, his Sandra, gazing up at him.

A new pain burst in his chest. One filled with joy. He lowered his mouth and gently touched her lips with his. She grabbed the back of his head and pulled him in tight and hard. The kiss intensified as if they could press into one another and make the world around them disappear. But after a moment, she weakened. He pulled back to make sure she was okay — only exhausted.

"I love you," he said and heard Drummond echo the

sentiment above.

The magic storm subsided. Wood and glass clattered as it found new resting places. Bits of paper drifted to the floor like autumn leaves. Time returned to normal.

The FBI rushed in, waving guns and barking commands. Max tried to raise his arms but the pain in his abused body refused to yield. He settled for collapsing on the floor with Sandra falling on top of him.

An FBI agent grabbed Max and Sandra, sat them up, and yelled words in their faces. A calmer voice said something in the distance, and through bleary eyes, Max saw Agent Stevenson approach.

"It's okay. Just arrest that one," he said. The other agents converged on Modesto.

As they escorted Modesto away in handcuffs, Stevenson turned to Max. "We've got a lot of questions for you."

Max's entire body numbed. "You recorded it all, didn't you?"

"That doesn't mean I understand it."

"Can it wait until tomorrow? We'd really like to rest for a bit."

"Medics are on the way to check you out. Frankly, you both look like you need some time in the hospital."

Max squeezed Sandra's shoulder. "Maybe so. But then we can answer questions at the hospital. Okay? Please? We ain't going anywhere, and you caught the guy who killed everyone. You even have his admission on record — even if the rest of it sounds crazy."

"As long as you go to the hospital, I'm okay with that. Besides," Stevenson said, gesturing to the office, "you got a hell of a cleanup to deal with still."

Max forced a grin which came off more like a pained wince. The EMTs arrived and immediately started to check out Max and Sandra. They flashed a light in his eye and asked him basic questions.

He listened as best he could, answered what he could, but his eyes focused beyond them, to a pile of rubble near the bookcase. It shifted. First a little. Then the debris tumbled away, and Kolan rose up, brushing off the dirt from her black dress.

She stepped away from the pile, graceful and surefooted, and moved to the exit. None of the FBI, none of the EMTs, nobody appeared to notice her. At the doorway, she turned to Max and offered the most malicious grin he had ever witnessed.

"I've got a lot to learn about the world," she said — but her voice was a man's voice. And though he had never heard it before, Max had no doubt in his mind — the voice belonged to Tucker Hull.

Hull walked away, unnoticed by all.

Drummond floated down to the floor, no smoke burning off him, and he watched Hull leave. Then he turned to Max. "Well, that's not good."

Max smiled for real now. Only the Drummond he knew would say that. His friend would be fine.

He heard Stevenson ask a question, but it was too late. He couldn't stay conscious any longer, and with all those important to him safe, he had no reason. Max passed out.

Chapter 27

THE WEEK THAT FOLLOWED dogged Max at every turn. That first night spent in the hospital had been met with police and FBI questions. The drive home involved some reporters following him. And days that were meant to be restful and recuperative filled up with more police on the telephone, visits from the FBI, and ambushes with reporters. Despite it all, Max and Sandra managed to hole up in their house and heal.

One afternoon, Max hopped onto the living room couch, propped his feet on the coffee table, and flicked on the television. Sandra curled her feet under Max's legs and rested her head on a throw pillow. Some mindless reality show blared away with a contestant claiming that she had signed up to win this thing, not to make friends. Max looked to Sandra with a knowing grin, but she barely registered any of it.

She had been quiet since their return. At first, he thought she suffered from amnesia. Not full-blown *I don't know who I am* amnesia, but a localized situation in which she could not recall what had happened to her while Patricia had taken over. But as the week progressed and he mentioned the events that had transpired, he saw it in her eyes — the poor gal knew everything. She had been cognizant of it all, even as she was powerless to do anything about it.

Drummond dropped in from the ceiling. "What's on?" he asked, floating next to the couch.

"Just junk."

"We don't have a case, so might as well watch it."

Drummond had not left them alone since they got home. He meant well, but between his constant chatter to them and his constant chatter to the ghost-blob Leed — which he still kept in his pocket — Drummond made Max consider running back to the hospital. Or perhaps just a library. Anywhere that he knew Drummond would avoid.

Max chided himself for such selfish thoughts. Drummond had been through a lot, too, and in some ways more. After all, Max got his Sandra back. But Patricia — after their kiss and with no vessel to park her cursed spirit, she dissipated like a fog blown away by the hot sun. Max tried to comfort Drummond, assured him that with all the spells cast and completed, her soul must finally have been allowed to rest, but he still caught Drummond with a long, dark gaze and a mournful frown.

One night, Drummond said, "You know, I even feel guilty about my new freedom." The destruction of the office had somehow untethered Drummond — or, at least, widened his range. Max couldn't be sure and Sandra wasn't ready to explain any of it to them. Drummond went on, "At the end, I knew she wanted nothing more than to be with me, and instead, she's been cast away, lost in an eternity of darkness."

"You don't know that. None of us know what happens when we move on."

"That's nice of you to say, but think about it — she was a witch, a High Priestess, and possessing Sandra was the least of her crimes. I love her, but I'm not delusional about her."

Max wondered if he could say the same for himself. He loved Sandra so deeply that he suspected he overlooked and excused her flaws. Isn't that part of being a husband? Accepting the whole person for better or worse?

"I take it back," Drummond said, pointing to the remote control. "This reality crap is really crappy. What else is on?"

Max leaned forward for the remote when a knock came to the front door. He waited. The knock came again.

"Reporters?" Drummond asked.

"Why don't you go peek and find out?" Max snapped and immediately regretted his tone.

"Okay, okay. No need to get snippy." Drummond stuck the top half of his body through the front door, then pulled back in. "It's your FBI pal, Stevenson."

"I thought we were done with all this nonsense." Max

yanked open the door. "What do you want?"

Stevenson's initial smile faltered but he recovered fast. "It's good to see you, too. I'm heading out soon. Everything's wrapping up here, and I wanted to come say good-bye. May I come in?"

They walked into the kitchen. With robotic coldness, Sandra rose from the couch and followed.

Stevenson shifted from foot to foot. "I wanted to thank you both for taking the great risk you did. Most people don't have that kind of bravery, and I don't think we could ever have solved this case without it. In fact, I think Max knows that we probably would have arrested the wrong man."

"You mean me," Max said.

"But, thankfully, that didn't happen. Unfortunately, I have to apologize to you both as well for the failures of our justice system."

Max didn't like the sound of that. "You're not going to arrest me, are you?"

"I don't understand why, especially with a clear admission of guilt on the recording you got for us, but the DA won't prosecute Mr. Modesto. He said that all the witch talk and raising the dead talk and such gives Modesto a valid insanity defense. I said that was fine with me. Insanity requires an admission of guilt, and I'd rather that nutjob spend a sentence in a mental institution than no punishment at all. But the DA wouldn't budge."

"Modesto's free," Max said matter-of-fact. After all, the Hull family always had excellent political connections.

"I'm afraid so. If you want, I can arrange for a patrol car to watch your house for a few nights, just to make sure there's no retaliation."

"Thank you for the offer but no. We know Modesto well. He got what he wanted from all this. He won't bother us now." Max doubted that was all true. In fact, the moment all the attention died down, he expected Modesto to visit with a tasteful gift in hand, an apology for the unpleasantness that had occurred, and a hope that they could focus on the new case his employer wanted to present. All said through gritted teeth that wanted nothing more than to bite Max's heart out. Max looked forward to that day because he wanted to tell off Modesto. Besides, until Sandra said otherwise, they were done — as she had pointed out before, without her, Max only had access to one ghost.

Stevenson awkwardly worked his way back to the door. "Anyway, thank you again. If you change your mind about the patrol car, you have my card. Call me anytime."

Max held the door for the agent. "I'm sure you've heard this before, but I hope I never have to see you again."

Stevenson laughed. "At least, not in this way." He put out his hand. "On behalf of the FBI, thank you."

They shook hands, and Stevenson walked off to his car. He turned back once yet never said anything more. He simply chuckled to himself and returned to his car.

"Never felt too kindly to spooks," Drummond said, "but I'll make an exception for that guy. He could have made things very difficult for you both, but he seems to know when to let it all rest."

Max smiled at Sandra and hugged her. He had done that a lot more lately — every chance he could. "I doubt he would get very far in his career if he started insisting that all of this had actually happened. Better to focus on the concrete things — murder, corruption."

"The return of a centuries dead leader."

"That one he'll probably forget to mention."

Drummond laughed. "It's good for us to be joking around again. Especially at this stuff."

As Sandra nestled against Max's chest, Max said, "If we didn't, I think I'd be the one turning into an evil spirit."

The day dragged on. They watched television for a few hours, nibbled on take-out leftovers from the night before, and slept. Though nobody had mentioned it, Max knew they all were aware that this could not continue for much longer. Soon, they would have to figure out their next steps.

Right before they slogged upstairs for bed, an answer arrived in the form of another knock at their door. Max did not have to say a word. Drummond checked it out.

"It's a young guy. Oh, crap."

"What is it?" Max asked, pulling Sandra closer to his side.

"He's got a manila envelope in his hand, and I can see the name Hull on it."

All the sore muscles and half-healed wounds flared across Max's body as if to warn him away in case his brain failed to do the trick. He wondered if he should have taken Stevenson up on the offer for a security patrol. But if this man was indeed a messenger for the Hull family, he wouldn't leave their doorstep until he delivered that envelope, and any security the police provided would be easily controlled by the Hulls. To underscore Max's thought, the young man knocked harder on the door.

Max walked to the door like a condemned prisoner — slow and unsure. He opened it a crack. "What do you want?"

The young man looked as nervous as Max felt. "Sorry to bother you so late. I've got an envelope to deliver to Maxwell Porter. Is that you?"

Max put out his hand. "You know it's me." He whipped the envelope out of the man's hand. "Get out of here before I call the cops." A worthless threat.

"Sorry, again, sir, but I'm under strict orders to wait for a reply."

Max closed the door. He walked over to the kitchen and dropped the envelope onto the table. Sandra and Drummond joined him.

Drummond whispered to his pocket, agreed, and gestured to the envelope. "We think it's safe to open. So, don't just stare at it. You know that kid won't leave until you answer whatever Hull's asking."

"I wasn't worried it was a bomb or anything," Max said. "But I know that we won't like anything written in there."

Sandra sighed and ripped open the envelope. She pulled out the single sheet of paper and handed it to Max. He hugged her again and kissed her forehead. Then, holding the paper in his right hand and keeping his left wrapped around Sandra's shoulder, Max read to the group:

Dear Mr. and Mrs. Porter and Mr. Drummond,

I trust you are recovering well from your recent troubles and wish you nothing but good health in the future. My own recovery has been strong and rapid, and I assure you that though I've only just returned, I am in full control of all Hull business matters.

After extensive consultation with my most trusted advisor, Mr. Modesto, as well as other knowledgeable individuals, I believe I have a clear understanding of how your small group has fit in with our larger organization. Sadly, I must inform you that the friction of this relationship has become unhealthy for us and, I suspect, for you as well. We can no longer continue along this path with you.

Therefore, I want to thank you for your service and inform you that all ties to the Hull family and the Hull business must be immediately severed. Obviously, this means the office you have ruined and the house we provided are no longer at your disposal. Furthermore, to insure that no false accusations or assumptions are made regarding our relationship by outside sources, all access to Hull-related endeavors will no longer be granted to you. Please understand that the Hull family owns, donates to, or touches upon a considerable number of businesses in North Carolina. Most, actually. We realize this may cause you difficulties in the surrounding area and will require you to move out of state. We apologize for the inconvenience.

Finally, as the returning head of the Hull family, I want you to understand beyond any doubt that you hold no leverage against this family. What you once considered your main threat, the family journal, is no longer an issue. An unfortunate and bizarre fire broke out in the jail cell of the young man in possession of the only copy of the journal. Both he and his copy are nothing more than ash.

A reply to our messenger that you understand and will comply would be greatly appreciated.

Sincerely,

Tucker Hull

Max read over the letter a second time before he could think. He knew a lot of Tucker Hull's history, but to be the recipient of, what amounted to, a threat to get out of town or face the consequences left him with a chill. One had to be fearful of a man like Hull — a man who had no problem putting a threat down on paper, a man who knew more about darkness and its magic than any other Max had come into contact with, a man who had been dead until a week ago.

"I guess this is over," Max said, his shoulders drooping. He put out his hand to Drummond. "I know you can't really shake my hand, but I wish you could. You've been a great and loyal friend. Sandra and I will miss you."

"First of all," Drummond said, folding his arms across his chest, "we don't know how far I can go before I get snapped back. It's very possible that I have no limits to my range now. So, maybe this doesn't have to be good-bye. And second of all, are you really going to pack up and get out just because the Hull family doesn't want you around?"

"I almost lost Sandra to that monstrous family. I'm not going to —"

"By now, you ought to know that if they're pushing you hard to leave, there's a good chance it means you should stay. That they're afraid of you."

"Let them be afraid. I don't care. I'm not —"

The front door swung open. Max and Drummond turned to see Sandra standing in the doorway. She had Tucker Hull's letter in her hand, and in front of the messenger, she crumpled it into a ball. With a flick of her wrist, she tossed the paper ball at the young man.

"Tell Mr. Hull to watch out." Her hard tone sounded even stronger with the scratchiness her unused vocal chords produced. "Tell him that we are not leaving this town."

As she closed the door, Max saw the messenger's cheeks pale. That poor man did not want to face any Hull, let alone Tucker, with that message. More importantly, though, Sandra had spoken.

Max rushed over to her with his arms spread wide. He scooped her up, spun her around, and kissed her hard. "Are you okay? Are you back?"

She playfully smacked Max's chest. "I never left, you fool." Though still cold in her delivery, every new word seemed to replenish Sandra's old self a little more.

Drummond clapped his hands. "There's my sweetheart!"

Before Max could get too excited, Sandra put her hands on her hips and said, "Looks like we don't have a home anymore."

"I'll go get some moving boxes, and we'll start packing up," Max said.

Drummond popped up between them. "Hold on, there. You told that kid to tell Hull that you weren't leaving."

"We're not. But this isn't our house anymore."

Sandra said, "We've got to find someplace new to live in."

"And a new place to run our business."

"And we barely have any money."

Max chuckled. "Sounds like old times."

Sandra giggled. "At least, it's not boring."

"You two are ridiculous." Drummond put out his arms and pointed at himself. "Did you forget who you're friends with? You need a cheap house to live in? I can get that for you. Pick out the house you want and I'll get some of my ghost friends together. We'll haunt that place until they'll give it to you for practically nothing. And don't forget, my friends have plenty of jobs for you guys. We'll be fine. Don't you worry."

Drummond rambled on for a while, but this time Max truly did not mind. In fact, he kind of liked the reassuring sound of his friend's voice. But he would never admit it.

Afterword

Every town on Earth has a fascinating history of murders and mysteries. The older the place, the more bizarre the tales become. Just ask anyone living near a castle in Great Britain. Thankfully, for both of us, Winston-Salem has been around for a long time (at least, long by American standards) and has a rich history of strange happenings.

The Zinzendorf Hotel fire, the DeGraff murder case, the Frank and Lucy Hine case, and the Sarah Tilkey tragedy, are among many of the true stories found in this book. Well, true at their core. I have, of course, embellished upon them by adding in the entirely fictitious cursed Bells of the Damned and their ramifications.

The photo of Patricia Welling in Tanglewood Park is a fiction, though the location is real. The photo of the Zinzendorf Hotel fire is real and can easily be found on the internet. Take a look at it. It's amazing.

Thank you for once more taking the time to join Max, Sandra, Drummond, and myself. I promise, if you keep reading their stories, I'll keep writing them.

About the Author

Stuart Jaffe is the madman behind the *Nathan K* thrillers, *The Max Porter Paranormal Mysteries, the Ridnight Mysteries, the Parallel Society* novels, *The Malja Chronicles, The Bluesman, Founders, Real Magic*, and much more. He trained in martial arts for over a decade until a knee injury ended that practice. Now, he plays lead guitar in a local blues band, *The Bootleggers*, and enjoys life on a small farm in rural North Carolina.

For more information, please visit *www.stuartjaffe.com*

www.ingramcontent.com/pod-product-compliance
Lightning Source LLC
Chambersburg PA
CBHW030519310726
48979CB00010B/1730/J
* 9 7 8 1 7 3 3 7 3 0 8 5 3 *